KOOK

KOOK

Chris Vick

HarperCollins*Publishers*

First published in Great Britain by HarperCollins *Children's Books* in 2016
HarperCollins *Children's Books* is a division of HarperCollins*Publishers* Ltd,
1 London Bridge Street, London, SE1 9GF

The HarperCollins website address is: www.harpercollins.co.uk

1

ISBN: 978-00-0-815832-3

Typeset in Bembo Std by
Palimpsest Book Production Ltd, Falkirk, Stirlingshire

Printed and bound in Great Britain by Clays Ltd, St Ives plc

MIX
Paper from
responsible sources
FSC® C007454

For Sarah and Lamorna

Kook: (*surfer slang*): a learner, a wannabe.

1

JADE GOT ME in trouble from day one.

We moved back to Cornwall one Saturday, early last September. Mum, my kid sister Tegan, and me.

It was a sunny day, with a cool wind. The first day of autumn, or maybe the last of summer.

We drove through the village of Penford, and after a five-minute drive over the moor, bounced our way down a broken track.

When we got there, I saw why the rent was cheap. There were two cottages, storm-beaten old things, with moss on their roofs and rotten wood windows, nestled between the clifftops and the moor. There were stone walls to keep the sheep away, a few brush trees bent into weird shapes by the wind, and not much else.

Half a mile downhill, the land ended in a sharp line at the clifftop.

We were going to live in one cottage. Jade, her dad and their dog already lived in the other. They came over in the afternoon when Mum was arguing with the removal guy about why it wasn't her fault the track had knackered the van's suspension.

Jade's dad introduced them both. Jade hung back and let him do the talking. He said about borrowing a cup of sugar any time and other neighbourly stuff. I didn't pay any attention. I was working hard trying not to stare at Jade.

Her hair was long and black. Her eyes were sea blue-and-green, shining out of a honey brown face. Jade had a glow about her, something no old T-shirt and denim jacket could hide.

She took one look at me with those sea eyes and curled her lips into a half-smile. It put a hook in me.

"How old are you, Sam?" her dad said.

"Sorry, what?" I said.

"How old are you?"

"Fifteen."

"Right. You'll be going to Penwith High with Jade then. You can help each other with homework, hang out and stuff." He was over keen. I think it was awkward for Jade as well as me. I found out later he'd checked me with one look and reckoned I'd be *A Good Influence* on Jade. Different from the type she normally hung out with.

We went into the kitchen to drink tea and eat a cake they'd brought with them, her dad – Bob – and Mum chatting away about Cornwall, me and Jade competing at who-can-say-the-least. She liked Tegan though. Jade gave her bits of cake to feed to the scruffy sheep dog.

When they stood to go, Bob said, "Jade was going to take Tess for a walk. You could go with her... Oh, daft, aren't I? You're unpacking. Another time."

"That's okay," said Mum. "You go, Sam, but not too long. If it's all right with Jade?"

"Okay." Jade and her dog were out of the kitchen before I could say a word.

Jade made a line for the nearby hill, pelting straight up the path like she was on a mission.

"What's the hurry?" I said, catching her up.

"I need to check something." She had a Cornish accent. But soft; husky.

At the top we climbed up on to a large, flat rock and sat down. She pulled a pack of cigarettes out of her pocket and, using me as a wind shelter, lit one.

Beyond the moor was the sea, blue and white and shining. The light of it hit me so hard I had to screw up my eyes. I hadn't seen the Cornish sea in years, not since I was four, after Dad died. I couldn't even *remember* it much. I hadn't expected that just looking at it would make my head spin. It was big as the sky.

"Great view," I said.

"Yeah. Right. Hold this," she said, passing me the cigarette. She pulled a tiny pair of binoculars from her denim jacket, fiddled with the focus and pointed them at the distant sea. Along the coast was a thin headland of cliff knifing into the Atlantic. Jade didn't move an inch. She just stared through the binocs, reaching out a hand for the cigarette once in a while. The dog lay beside her, its black and white head on her lap.

Then, suddenly, she sat upright, tense, like she'd noticed something. All I could make out was a thin line of white water, rolling into the distant cliff.

"What you looking at?" I said.

"Signposts."

"What?"

"That's the spot's name." She sighed, and pocketed the binocs. "I can see the waves there, *that's* why it's called Signposts. Swell's about three foot. Do you surf, Sam?"

"No."

"Shame. I do." She jumped off the rock, leaving me holding the smouldering fag butt. And I thought, *Oh, right, see you then.* But...

"Come on!" she shouted, running down the hill.

"Surfing?" I shouted. But she'd already gone too far to hear me.

2

AS I RAN, I was thinking, *Shit, this is already nothing like London.*
The moors in the sun were nothing like the flats that filled up the sky in Westbourne Park. Running off to the beach was nothing like heading to the dog-turd littered park for a kickaround. And Jade was nothing like... any girl I'd ever met. She wasn't just beautiful. There was something about her. Something raw and naked. Something you wanted to look at – *had* to look at – but felt you shouldn't.

We went past our place and straight to their cottage. They'd built a wooden barn-garage right next to it. It was full of junk: an old washing machine, bikes, crates of books. I clocked the surfboards stacked against the wall, but she walked past them to a ladder leading up to an attic. I was going to follow her, but she said, "No, wait here."

After a minute or two, she climbed back down, carrying a wetsuit and towel.

"What's up there?" I asked. She didn't answer. She stood by the surfboards, eyeing them up before choosing the middle one of the three – a blue beaten-up old thing about half a foot taller than she was, with a V shaped tail.

"Love this fish," she said, stroking its edge. "Flies in anything." She balanced the suit and towel over her shoulder and stuck the board under one arm. Then she took an old bike from where it leant against a fridge.

"You can borrow Dad's bike," she said.

"But I don't surf."

"You said. Come anyway. Don't be a kook."

"What's a kook?"

"It's what you are," she said, getting on the bike.

"Do you want me to carry…" I started. But she was already out of the door, riding the bike with one hand, and holding the board under her arm with the other. The dog followed, jumping and wagging its tail.

"How d'you do that?" I said.

"Practice!" she shouted.

It was making me dizzy. One minute we're eating cake, then we're up a hill, then we're off to the beach. And she was bossy. That annoyed me. But I was dead curious, and yeah, she was that pretty, you wouldn't *not* follow her. I grabbed her dad's bike and pedalled after her.

After ten minutes we took a path off the road and cycled

down a stony trail, with the dog running behind us, stopping where the ruined towers and walls of an old tin mine hung to the cliff edge.

We dumped the bikes. Jade led us past a 'DANGER – KEEP OUT' sign by the mine and down a steep path that ended by a huge granite boulder, right on the cliff edge. She walked up to the large rock, and put the board on top of it, stretching, nudging it over the top with her fingertips. She left it there, balancing. Then, placing her body tight against the rock, and still with the towel and wetsuit over her shoulder, she moved around the rock, till she disappeared. A few seconds later the board disappeared too, pulled over the rock's edge. The dog ran up the cliff and over the boulder.

It was like they'd just vanished.

I stepped up to the cliff edge and looked down. The sight of the sea hit me in the gut. It must have been a thirty-foot drop. She'd shimmied around the rock, casual as anything, along a ledge inches wide. If you slipped, you'd fall. If you were lucky, you'd grab a rock and hold on. Chances were, you'd go over. And die.

"Coming?" said her voice, from behind the rock, teasing me.

"Sure," I said. I knew that without the drop I could do it easy, so why not now? I wasn't going to bottle it in front of this girl.

I pushed my face against the cool stone and edged around the rock. The volume of life was turned up. I could hear every shuffle of my feet, every breath echoing around my head, every beat of my heart. I couldn't see my feet; I just had to trust they were going in the right place.

It only took about ten seconds, but they were long ones.

When I came round, I was panting and she was smiling, with a raised eyebrow and half of her mouth curling, like she was amused.

The path – hidden from the other side of the rock – hugged the cliff, with sheer cliff on one side and a steep drop on the other. It was no more than two feet wide. A tricky climb down. But like with the bike and carrying the board, Jade made it look easy. I guessed she'd done it a hundred times before.

There was no beach when we reached the bottom, just a flat ledge of reef, rock pools and seaweed. Far out to sea, the wind was messing up the ocean, chasing white peaks across the bay. But here the water was still, dark glass. Somewhere between this secret cove and the open sea were two surfers, sat on their boards, still as statues.

"Tell anyone about this place and they'll kill you," said Jade, pointing at them and sounding like she wasn't kidding. Surrounding herself with the towel, she started to change. She had a swimsuit on under her hoody. She must have changed into it when she was in the garage attic.

And there I was again. Staring. I don't think I was dribbling, or had my mouth open or anything. But I might have been, the way she glared at me.

"Oh, sorry," I said, and looked away. "There's no waves." It was flat calm, apart from a gentle lapping at the rock's edge.

"Long wave period. Watch."

After a couple of minutes, like a clockwork doll coming to life, one of the surfers flipped his board round and started paddling towards the shore. At first I couldn't see why, but then, behind him, hard to see against the sea-glare, was a wall of water. It jacked up, rising out of the blue till it formed a feathering edge. The surfer angled his board, paddled a stroke or two, pushed up with his arms and swung his feet beneath him, landing on the board, and in one swoop was riding down and across the wave, gliding in a long line before weaving the board in a series of snake shapes. The wave broke perfectly, carrying the surfer one step ahead of the white mess behind him. Then the other surfer did the same thing on the wave behind. Their whoops echoed around the cliff.

And I got it. Even then, I got it.

It looked like freedom.

Jade appeared at my shoulder, in her wetsuit. "I'm gonna get some of that. Look after Tess," she shouted. She ran to where the rock met the water's edge and launched herself into the sea, landing on the board and paddling powerfully into the dark water.

As the sun sank in the sky, I sat down with the dog at my side and watched.

They made it look easy, carving up and down the faces of

the waves, spinning their bodies and boards round like they were dancing on water.

So yeah, I got it. And this place was part of the buzz I was feeling, this secret cove and the girl and the surfing and the sun falling into the sea. They all added up to something good. Something not-London.

When another surfer arrived it felt wrong, like he'd invaded my own little bit of heaven. Which was crazy. I was the stranger there.

He was about my age, tall and big shouldered, with a lot of scruffy black hair, a scraggy would-be beard and big cow eyes. But there was something intense about those eyes. They were full alert, with a thousand-yard stare, like he was looking through me. He wasn't smiling; his natural look was a sneer. He came over and stood closer to me than he needed to. He looked at Tess like he was puzzled. I think he recognised the dog.

"Your mate's out there?" he said, pointing out to sea.

"No, I'm with this girl…" I said. He looked out to sea, frowning. "I don't mean with…" I stumbled. "She just… brought me here."

"Right. You a surfer?"

"No," I said. He nodded, like I'd said the right answer, and left me alone.

★

Jade returned after an hour or more in the water. And I was thinking that was good, I needed to get back.

10

"Well, that was a score. Did you see me, Sam? Real fun waves," she said, strutting up to me.

She'd been hard edged before; now she was grinning like an idiot and was super friendly, like she'd taken some happy drug.

"Tempted?" she asked.

I shook my head. "Look, I'd better be getting back."

"Wait for me," she said, pleading with her eyes.

That was okay. It was getting late in the afternoon. I'd need to get back and help Mum, but ten minutes more was no big deal. But then two of the surfers came back in, out of the water, and Jade went over to talk to them. I didn't want to hurry her, but I knew it was late, that Mum would be getting wound up. After she'd chatted a bit, Jade came back over to change.

"Rag and Skip are gonna make a fire up top. Let's stay."

"I can't."

"Oh."

I watched the guy still out there, and tried not to look too much at Jade changing, fumbling around with a towel and her clothes. The bits of flesh I saw were the colour of honey, or dark sand. Her body was muscly, but curvy too. I'd seen that when she was in her wetsuit. A body shaped by years in the water. The hook twisted.

The surfer – the one who had asked me who I was – was still out there, further than the others had sat, waiting for the last wave. He got it too, a real freak, bigger than all the other waves that day. Jade and the others stopped what they were doing and watched. This guy was good. All the other surfers had moved with the wave, letting it dictate what they did, but he was in charge of *it*, slicing deep arcs, pulling crazy turns, gouging huge chunks of water out of the wave and sending spray that caught the light in rainbow colours. Halfway along the wave, he pulled one turn too hard, just as the wave was crashing. It punched him into the water, chewing him up in a soup of white water and arms and legs.

"Is he all right?" I asked.

They all laughed. One of the surfers, a stocky guy with curly, long blond hair shouted out, "Cocky bastard!"

Jade was changed now. She came up to me, speaking in a low voice, drying her hair.

"They're sooooo jealous. They can't surf like that." She was still grinning. "Come on. Meet the others, let G know you're okay," she said, throwing her wet towel at me.

"Who?"

"Him, the cocky bastard." She pointed at the surfer getting out of the water. "I spoke to him out there. He's not thrilled I brought you here."

"Why did you?" I threw the towel back at her.

"Just cuz you were there, I suppose." She shrugged.

"What about your dad? Won't he miss you?"

"Nah. He won't care. Anyway, Dad's bike's got lights on, mine hasn't, so you have to wait and…" She paused, looking at me. "Where's your dad, Sam, or is it just you, your mum and sister?"

A lot of people wouldn't have asked. They would have thought it was nosey. Not Jade.

"Yeah. It is. Just us," I said.

We'd come back to Cornwall to make peace with my dad's mum, my grandma, who I hadn't seen in over ten years. Not since Dad died. And now *she* was dying. Of cancer. But I didn't want to explain all that. Not to Jade; not then.

So yeah, it was 'just us' in that small house. And right then I didn't want to be there, unpacking boxes. And Jade was being nice. Really nice. And I thought, *How many chances will I get to make friends?*

We stayed.

3

BACK UP TOP, beyond the rock we'd climbed around, where we'd left the bikes, was the entrance to the old mine. Another 'DANGER – KEEP OUT' sign was stuck on a grille protecting the way in. But they'd cut through the grille then padlocked it back up. Inside they had their own little treasure store: surf kit, piles of driftwood, four-gallon plastic containers full of some brown liquid. Even rugs and a battered old guitar.

One of the gang, a short, wiry kid with sun-blond hair called Skip, made a fire and ran around getting rugs and cushions for us to sit on. Big G – the serious guy with the cow eyes – Jade and me sat where Skip put us. The last of the crew, Rag, brought out two of the demijohn containers. The others were all fit, looked strong, and dressed in jeans and hoodies. Rag was different. He had a gut bulging out from his filthy T-shirt. He wore tartan trousers and finished the look with a Russian fur hat. He looked stupid, but it seemed deliberate.

"My finest batch yet," said Rag, pouring the beer into mugs. "Guests first." He handed me one, and poured a little of his own drink on the ground. They all said, "Libations," and held their mugs to the sky.

"What's that you're doing?" I said.

"Libations. An offering to the sea gods." It was hard to tell if Rag was joking. No one laughed though. Maybe they were just a superstitious lot. I thought it was weird, but I didn't say so. "Now, Sam, tell me. How is it?" said Rag, pointing at my mug of foaming brown liquid, a serious frown on his face.

I drank, and pulled a squirming face. "This is your best?" I said.

"It's all right," said Skip, "you just have to get through the first one. A bit like his songs."

"Aaah, a request?" said Rag.

"No!" they all shouted. But he fetched the guitar from the mine anyway, and banged out a sketchy folk song while we sat around the fire. He could play and sing pretty well, but he spoilt it a bit when he lifted a leg on the final note and farted loudly.

"Sorry about that," he said, grinning.

"Liar! You disgusting pig," said Jade. She got up, and started beating him round the head, while the others fell about laughing.

The dog even barked at him.

We drank. Big G and Rag were smoking roll-ups too, so I

didn't even notice someone had produced a spliff, till it was under my nose. Jade was passing it straight past me to Big G, just assuming I didn't smoke, and that pissed me off, so I grabbed it and took some. I got an itchy tickle in my throat that threatened to turn into spluttering, but I got rid of it with more of the foul beer. I passed it to Big G, who took a few long drags.

They talked about the day's waves and their plans for autumn.

"Thank Christ summer's over," said Big G.

"I thought you surfers liked summer?" I said, trying not to cough. They shook their heads and smiled.

"Autumn's where it's at," Skip explained, sitting bolt upright. "The water's warm. There's no grockles clogging the line up. And we get storms, maybe even a ghost storm."

"What's that?" I said.

"A massive autumn storm…"

"An equinox storm?" I said.

Silence.

"What?" said G.

"Equinox," I explained. "The midpoint between the summer and winter solstices. You get a lot of big storms then, or that's what's believed, as the Earth turns on its axis…" I suddenly wished I'd kept my mouth shut.

"You some kind of geek?" said Big G.

"No," I said, lying. "What's this ghost storm?"

"I'll tell you what it is," said Big G, pointing at me, sounding just as narky as he had on the shore. "It's a bullshit myth they put in books for tourists, a load of shit about a storm that raises ghosts from shipwrecks. What *is* true is that storms come out of the blue. Or a bad storm gets ten times worse for no reason. They're called ghost storms. They're violent. They kick up big waves that catch people off guard…"

"Like the one that creamed you today?" said Rag, taking off his ridiculous hat and letting his long blond hair fall out. They laughed. I joined in, but the look Big G gave me shut me up quickly.

"What about you? What do you do for kicks?" said Big G.

"Bit of footy. Xbox."

This got them shaking their heads. "Don't get it, man," said Big G, stroking his wispy beard.

"You think I should be out surfing, waiting for the ghost storm?" I didn't mean to sound like I was taking the piss, but that's how it came out of my stupid mouth.

Big G picked up a stick and poked the fire. "Last year two miles off the Scillies," he said, "there was this tiny island with this old dude living on it. Nothing there but one fisherman's cottage, a small harbour and a smokery. Ghost storm came out of nowhere. A massive wave swept through, north of the island, ripped open a cargo ship like a sardine can, trashed two fishing boats. Then it hit this little island where this guy lived. All gone. The house, boat, everything. No body found neither…"

"How can water do that?" I said. I was curious. Again, I didn't mean it to come out like it did. I *really* wanted to know

17

about it. I had reasons to *want* to know. Good ones. I knew what water could do. But it sounded like I was having a go.

"You know anything about the power of water?" said Big G.

"No, not really," I said, lying again.

"I'll show you," said Big G. He stood, picked up the near-empty plastic container, and poured the last of the beer into his mug...

Then threw the empty demijohn straight at me.

I caught it, but only just. Drops of beer splashed over my jeans.

"What you do that for?" I said. I looked to Jade, seeing what she'd do, but she smiled, like it was no biggy.

"Easy, right? Nice and light," said Big G, then he picked up the other full one, with both hands and threw it over the flames. I caught that one too, but I fell backwards, with the weight of it. The others froze. No one spoke for a bit. Jade stared at the ground, embarrassed.

"Steady," said Rag, "the kid only asked."

Big G sat back down. "Yeah, sorry, mate," he said. "Just making a point."

He'd done that all right. That was four gallons. It was nothing. Even a small wave was hundreds of times heavier than what I'd just felt. But I didn't like how he'd made his point.

"Maybe we'll get a storm big enough for the Devil's Horns," said Jade, changing the subject. They all got stuck into a long conversation then, about surfing these legendary offshore islands when the big winter storms came. I drank more beer. It seemed every time I was halfway through my mug, Rag would fill it up.

I listened, not really able to join in. But I was fascinated. Not so much by what they said, but by them. They were different from London kids. I'd imagined the Cornish would be right hicks, kind of innocent. But this lot seemed... what? I couldn't say streetwise. But like they'd seen a few things. *Done* a few things. As they were Jade's mates, I guessed they were her age. My age. But they seemed older.

"Do a lot of surfers go to these islands?" I said, trying to join in. Rag disappeared into the mine entrance and came back with a surf mag, which he put in front of me, tapping the picture on the cover.

On the cover was an old black and white photo showing a small island, with a lighthouse on it. And in the corner of the picture, in scrawled writing: 'Devil's Horns, 1927'. Behind the lighthouse, rising out of the sea, was a giant wave. A dark tower of water curling and breaking, topped by a white froth. It was about to hit the island. Maybe even swallow it. In white letters, against the dark black of the wave's face, it read:

WHERE IS THIS?
UK'S BIGGEST WAVE.
UNRIDDEN?

"No one's surfed it," Skip explained. "That's the point. It's like the Holy Grail. There's this old myth about this big wave spot

19

and all the ships that have gone down there. It's calm most of the time, but in the right conditions it goes off. But there are a dozen islands it could be. More. And who wants to go looking when a storm kicks in? It's an old fishermen's legend, you see. No one knows where it is. So no one's surfed it…"

"No one's surfed it and *lived,*" said Big G. "There were two surfers from Porthtowan went missing two years back. Their car was found in Marazion. Some reckoned they'd headed out to the Horns."

"And you're going to surf this place?" I asked.

"Why not?" said Jade. "If we could find it. We'll film it with GoPro cameras, stick it on YouTube. We'll be fucking legends. Every surf mag in the country will want a piece of us!" She was all attitude and bravado, laughing like it was a joke, but kind of believing herself too.

"But you don't even know where it is," I said.

"Detail, Sam! You kook killjoy," she said, grinning.

My skin was tingling from the sun and fresh air, and the beer and smoke were giving me this lazy, glowing feeling. It was cool, but when another spliff did the rounds it all piled up on me quick and I began to get dizzy.

"I'm going," I said, standing, staggering a bit.

"Was it something we said?" said Rag.

"No, just got to get home. I'm in enough shit as it is."

"Might as well make it worth the bollocking, mate," said Rag. But I had to go, and Jade didn't argue.

I cycled in front, watching the ground race towards us in

the cycle light, with Jade following behind. The moon was up, bathing the moors and sea in silver-blue light. There were no cars or streetlights, just this place, with me and Jade whooshing along on our bikes. I can't remember what we said *exactly* – I think she was more wrecked than I was – but I know we held this messed up conversation, her bragging about how she was going to surf the Devil's Horns, and become this famous surfer. Me taking the piss. Then she sang this old Moby song. A slow, haunting tune. Something about being lost in the water, about fighting a tide.

It was like the theme tune of that night. It filled up my head as I raced along, with Jade behind me, the dog following, watching the bike lights eating up the road.

It was pretty perfect, that bike ride to my new home.

Bye, London, I thought. *See you later. Or not.*

*

When I got back, Mum was on her knees in the lounge, pulling out Victorian cups and framed pictures from a box with 'ornaments' written on the side. The place was a mess of boxes and newspaper. And stuff. Lots and lots of stuff. I couldn't see where it was all going to go.

It felt weird. Seeing all the things from our London flat, but in a totally different place.

A different place. A better place? I didn't know. But I was beginning to think it could be.

"Good walk, was it?" Mum said, not looking up, slamming

a vase down on the floor, then crunching up the newspaper it had been wrapped in and throwing it over her shoulder. Her bundled up hair came loose. She blew it out of her face.

"Sorry," I said.

"Where did you go?" She sounded sharp.

"The sea."

She stood up, grinding her jaw. "Do you know what time it is?"

"No."

My head felt like a balloon that needed to take off. Being stoned and drunk had felt good out there, cycling over the moors in the moonlight. But now I was closed in by this maze of boxes, with no escape from Mum's laser stare.

"Did it occur to you I needed help?" she said, with her hands on her hips.

"Yes."

"But you stayed out anyway."

"Yes."

"And why did you do that, Sam? With a whole lorry-load of boxes to unpack... We've got to go and see your grandmother tomorrow, and you're starting at a new school on Monday. Do you even know where all your stuff is? Where your new uniform is?"

"Not really."

"Not really? You either do or you don't. Well perhaps you might... SAM!"

"What?"

"Look at me." She stormed up to me. "What's wrong with your eyes? They're bloodshot." Suddenly I was freaked, like I was totally scared but about to burst out laughing at the same time. The maze of boxes was closing in. I felt really out of it. I was thinking, *I probably look wrecked too.*

"Have you been drinking?" she said, sniffing the air.

"Yes, I had a beer," I said. There was no chance of the silent treatment – this was going to run into a full rant. I got ready to take it on, already planning my escape route and excuses. But then she turned away and sighed, looking over the sea of boxes and newspaper-wrapped ornaments with this odd, empty look. Like she didn't even know what those things were. She looked well and truly knackered.

"Just go to your room, and sort out your stuff. And get Tegan to bed too," she mumbled. "There's cold fish and chips if you want them."

I didn't. I wanted to get away, quick as I could.

Teg's a good kid for a six-year-old. I love her, but she's always been a nightmare at going to bed. And especially, it turned out, when she was in a new house. She eventually got into her pyjamas and stood in front of the chipped bathroom mirror practising jerky dance moves instead of washing, or brushing her teeth.

"Mum's angry with you," she said.

"I know," I said, leaning against the wall.

"Jade's nice. I like her dog. Is she your friend?"

"I dunno. I hope so."

"Is she your girlfriend? Did you kiss her?"

I laughed. "No, Teg. Now brush your teeth."

After a lot of begging, I put her to bed and read her a story. *A* story? *The* story. *The Tiger Who Came to Tea.* The one story she'd loved since she was three; the one story that was sure to get her wrapped up in her quilt, and listening. Sometimes she was asleep before I even got to the end. Not this time.

"Can we look at stars?" she said, as I walked out the door of her room.

"Sure, but not tonight. I haven't unpacked the telescope. Goodnight, Teg."

"But Sam, there's *millions* of them. I can see—"

"Good*night,* Teg."

★

My room was in the attic. Mum or the removal guy had put the boxes marked 'Sam' in there. And there was my telescope in the corner, all bubble-wrapped and Sellotaped, waiting to look at the stars. I didn't start unpacking. I fell on the bed and listened to the distant white noise of the sea. Through the skylight I could see the stars. Even with the moon up, there were more of them in that sky than I'd ever seen.

When I closed my eyes, I could still see the waves, and hear Jade singing.

4

I DIDN'T REMEMBER anything about Grandma. And I only knew what Mum had told me. That she was old and dying of cancer. That she had months left.

Maybe.

She lived in a massive house near a rocky point called Cape Kernow. A house that would be ours one day.

We'd come back, Mum said, so Grandma could get to know her one grandchild and only heir. That was me, Tegan being the result of a fling that had lasted the time it took Mum to get pregnant.

Things were pretty broken between Mum and Grandma, I knew that. They didn't get on. There'd been some fallout after Dad died. Maybe because Mum took us to London. Mum never told me. Now we'd come back to Cornwall to help 'mend' things, though I didn't have a clue as to what it was that needed mending.

I had an idea of some old manor, all dank and dark and smelling of cabbage and cat's piss. I pictured my grandma in a huge bed, with grey hair and greyer skin, fading away, with us at her side, listening to her final, totally wise words.

I was wrong.

The house was big, square and white, with large windows and a front door painted ocean blue. The house's name was painted on the wall in thin black letters. 'Where Two Worlds Meet.'

A short, skinny, tanned woman answered the door. She was dressed in jeans, a smock and headscarf. At first I thought maybe she was the cleaner.

Wrong again.

Grandma had these bright blue eyes that seemed a whole lot younger than she was.

"Oh, Sam," she said, then flung herself at me and held me tighter than anyone ever had.

"Grandma?" I said, hugging her back. Kind of. I felt embarrassed. She was a stranger. She stopped hugging, but got a good hold on my shoulders, like she wasn't going to let me go. Not after all this time.

"My God, if he could see you now."

"Hello, Grandma," I said. It was odd. She was a total stranger, but she had the same eyes and square jaw as my dad. And yeah, I could see how I looked like her too.

"And you must be Tegan," she said. Teg got ready for a big

hug, but all she got was her hair ruffled.

Grandma left Mum till last. "Hello, Jean," she said. They air kissed. Mum had a frozen smile on her.

But Grandma was *really* smiling. She was so happy, she was working hard to stop the tears.

"Are you… okay, Grandma?" I said.

"Never better, Sam. Come in, the kettle is on. There's scones too." She wiped the tears away and led us through a hall to a large lounge on the other side of the house. There were huge leather sofas and chairs, and dark red rugs covering the wooden floor. The walls were white, with bookshelves, a mirror and paintings of the sea.

But what I noticed most was the view. The house was so near the cliff, when you looked out the window you didn't even see rock, or land, just this great big blanket of blue and green.

We sat down, while she went out to get the tea. We didn't talk, we just sat there, taking it all in.

Grandma came back with a tray loaded up with scones and cream, jam and tea. Before she organised it all, she set Tegan up in the biggest chair, by the fireplace, with a set of crayons and a pad pulled out of a WHSmith's bag.

She glanced at Tegan, to make sure she was distracted, then said to me, "I hope you like the house," and gave me this weird loaded look. Then I twigged. She meant, *the house I'm giving you; the house you'll live in when I'm dead*. She was going to die. We were getting the house. Some people dodge around the awkward stuff, the big stuff. Others just get to it. She was one of those. I didn't know what to say to that.

"We'll sort all that out," she said, seeing the look of confusion on my face. "There is so much to plan. But first, tell me all about the move, your new cottage. What you have been up to…"

She talked on and I answered as best as I could. It was nice, but I thought it was weird how everything she said was to me, not Mum. All the time she was staring at me, real keen, and I couldn't help but stare back. Apart from the headscarf, which I guessed was to cover her bald head from the chemo, she didn't look ill. Not even that old.

"So, Sam. You'll make friends here. At your new school. It's hard to go from one place to another, where you're a stranger. But you've done it before; I'm sure you'll cope."

She didn't look at Mum when she said that, but the way she said it… it sounded like a dig.

"He's met a girl," said Tegan, scribbling away with the crayons.

"Excellent," said Grandma. "Is she a looker?"

"Um, yeah, I guess so," I said, "but we're just mates. Not even that. I only just met her."

"Are you going to ask her on a date?"

"I don't think she goes on… dates. She's a surfer."

"Wonderful. A girl *and* a healthy activity."

I thought maybe if Grandma had seen us round the campfire, she might not think it was such a great choice of 'healthy activity'.

"Er, yeah," I said, feeling awkward.

We changed the subject. All the time we talked, Grandma stared at me. A lot.

"You're the spit of him at your age; it's uncanny. It's like the ghost of his teenage self came round for tea and scones."

"Thanks," I said, and spluttered some cream out of my mouth. I couldn't help laughing. Grandma laughed too. Mum didn't.

"Do you remember him much? Do you remember this house?" Grandma asked. I dug into my mind, tried to remember stuff, looking for something. Anything. I felt bad not giving her what she wanted.

"I helped him paint a boat once, like a sailing or maybe a row boat. I remember this dark blue paint and getting it all over my T-shirt. And he used to take me in the sea, paddling. He'd lift me up when a wave came, and say, 'It's only water, Sam,' and…" But there was no "and…". That was pretty much the total of my memories of my drowned, dead father. It didn't upset me going through those memories. It didn't make me happy either. I was kind of removed from them, like they were someone else's memories.

It was different for Mum though. She didn't say anything, but her eyes were wide and worried, darting from me to Grandma, and back again.

Then…

"That smell…" I said it before I even thought it. What was it? Leather, baking, the sea, the coal fire? All of those things together. And I remembered it. The smell of the house, and the heavy tick and tock of the clock in the hallway, with the sounds of sea and wind muffled through the walls. I wasn't just imagining it – I *did* remember being there.

"I only just recognised it," I said. "How weird is that?" I was spooked. In a good way. I was going to go on, but I clocked Mum, her eyes filling up, her hand gripping the side of the chair.

I was trying to find my memories. Maybe Mum didn't want to find hers.

"Your mother and I need to talk," said Grandma. "Have a look around the house. You'll find your dad's room up there." She pointed at the ceiling. "There's a few of his bits and bobs; a few things that didn't get thrown away when you upped and left for London."

Mum clunked her cup on the saucer and glared at a painting on the wall. She was grinding her teeth, stopping herself from saying something.

It was a good time to leave them to it. Me and Teg went upstairs. Teg was chewing her hair. I held her hand.

"This must be weird for you, Tegs. He wasn't even your dad."

"No, but she is my grandma," she said, like she was totally sure it was true. I didn't want to tell her different. We were a tight little team, me, Tegan and Mum, but there were only the three of us, and if the family got to grow, by one, that was cool. Even if it wasn't going to be for long.

"Are we going to live here one day?" she asked. She'd clearly overheard some of what we'd talked about.

"Yeah, maybe."

"But we live in the cottage now."

"Look, it's complicated. I dunno what's going to happen."

"Will we go back to London?"

I couldn't blame her for asking. The situation had to be pretty freaky for her. I just didn't know how to answer. "Reckon she'll see how it goes down here. Mum might not decide till… later. Would you like to live here?" I said. Tegan looked around the hallway, with its big wooden doors and huge window looking over the moor. She nodded.

"Which one would be my room?" she said.

"Any one you want, but you got to bags it." This was a game we played for slices of cake or the best place on the sofa. Now it was for something important. Her eyes lit up like it was Christmas morning. She let go of my hand and ran off to explore.

Either by fluke or some old memory, I went straight to my dad's room. I thought it would be tidy, because the rest of the house was so neat. But it wasn't. It was a mess. The curtains were closed, but thin, letting in a strong light. There were a load of boxes with books in. In the corner was an old record player, and a chunky grey computer from the Stone Age. On the shelves were more books, all of them about the sea. And some old metal instruments, covered with dials and numbers and cogs. I guessed they were navigation instruments.

He had clearly been a total geek. Now I knew where I got

it from. He'd been an oceanographer; a scientist who looked at how currents and gulf streams and storms worked.

I was a geek too. With me it was the stars. With him it had been the sea. There was a whole new world to explore. A world of water.

I wanted to sit down and start going through all the gear, all the books. But the voices downstairs started rising. I couldn't hear what they were saying, but it didn't sound friendly.

"Sam!" It was Mum's voice, shouting up the stairs.

"Just a minute."

Mum was waiting downstairs, with Tegan, already with their coats on. Grandma was by the door, ready to open it.

"We're going. Now," said Mum. There didn't seem much point asking why.

"You can come back though, Sam. Soon," said Grandma. "Did you find anything of interest?"

"Yes. Thanks. Loads," I said.

I hugged her.

5

IF YOU'D CALLED them a gang, they would have laughed. But that's what they were and everyone at Penwith High knew it. The Penford Crew, the Penford surfers. That's what the other kids called them.

They didn't really mix with anyone else, only the older lot in the sixth form over the road. The ones that surfed, that is.

If you'd said they had a leader, they'd have laughed at that too, especially Big G. But if you saw more than two of them together, Big G was there, in the middle, towering over them, looking a good two years older than he was, talking about what the waves were doing.

I didn't know them, but from the little I'd seen, I could tell he was the most sensible. Little Skip was a bag of energy, not knowing where to spin off to next. Rag was a stoner and a joker. Big G was quiet and strong, with a rep for fighting. And Jade? I didn't really know yet. But she seemed like trouble.

I think Big G kind of levelled them out. They looked to him to organise them. So he'd stand, arms folded, eyes staring through his mop of long, dark hair. If he didn't reckon the surf was 'on', one might go, but most didn't. If he said it was good, they *all* found a way. Before school, after school, weekends. Homework, family meals, out-of-school jobs delivering papers or working in cafes – none of it mattered when the waves kicked up. Once they were all off school sick, and turned up the next day suddenly better. Everyone knew where they'd been, but no one could prove it. And even if they could, no bollocking from a teacher or parent could wipe the glow away. For that gang, it was *always* worth it. Surfing came first. It gave them an edge, something different. They even seemed *older* than the others in my year. It was like everyone else was going through school, waiting to start life proper. They'd already started. In some ways, at least.

I would have liked to have been a part of it, after that first day at Tin-mines (all the spots had names – it was part of the surf thing), but if you didn't surf, you weren't in. And even though Skip and Rag were friendly on the first days of term, they pretty much ignored me after that.

I hadn't conned myself into thinking I'd be their mate, but I'd hoped for something different with Jade. Largely because she was the hottest girl I'd ever seen. We got the school bus together; we lived next door. But at the bus stop was the only time she seemed to remember I existed. Apart from when we got difficult homework. Then she became my friend all of a sudden, and didn't even try to hide why. Jade wasn't thick, but to get what you needed to do at home you had to listen in class. And unless it was English or Art, Jade didn't listen. At all. School bored her. The teachers bored her. The other kids bored her. She was friendly with the other girls, but none of them were like best mates. She only really talked to the other surfers. I took my notes in class, half focusing on the class, half watching her dream the day away, with her mind in the sea, knowing that later we'd be on the bus and then she'd wake up to the fact that she'd been at school for the last six hours, and she'd shove a textbook under my nose and say, "What does this mean?" Especially if it was science. My speciality. Which was half good, half bad, as I hated looking like the geek I truly was. But I also liked helping her out.

So I didn't make friends with the surfers, but I wasn't Sammy No-Mates either. I made two friends. Mike and Harry. They *liked* my Xbox, and stargazing through the telescope, and sometimes we kicked a football around. But the truth is, when I played Xbox with them, I was thinking about sitting around the campfire with Jade and her mates. I was thinking about another sunset at Tin-mines. But I didn't surf and Jade never invited me down to the beach again.

The *idea* of surfing crossed my mind, but I couldn't really swim well and we were too hard up to buy things like surfboards and wetsuits. And Mum wouldn't have been keen. Not after

Dad and what happened. So I pushed the idea away. But it nagged at me. Every time I went to sleep, listening to the sea.

★

I'd been there three weeks or so, when, on a sunny Sunday morning, Jade appeared at our front door with her dog, Tess, asking me to go for a walk. She wore trainers, jeans and a hoody, with the same denim jacket she always wore and no make-up. London girls tried a lot harder than that. Jade didn't need to.

"No surf today then?" I said, standing in the doorway, trying to act like I wasn't keen on the whole walk idea. She brushed the hair out of her face and looked away, in the direction of the sea.

"Honestly? Yeah, there is. But I stayed out late last night…"

"How late?"

"About two o'clock late. So Dad kind of grounded me. He's locked my boards away, the twat. If I go off by myself, he'll know I'm borrowing gear and going surfing, but if I'm with you…" She shrugged. *That* was why she was asking me to go for a walk. There were no other options. I could take it or leave it. I didn't like it, but the alternative was homework.

We went to the sea on our bikes, with Tess following. Not Tin-mines this time. We hit the coast path, locked the bikes to an old railing and walked towards Whitesands.

She led me along the cliff and down a steep, rocky path, over the dunes to the deserted beach. We walked where the sand met the dune grass. White-grey granite cliffs stood at one end of the beach with a headland at the other. Inland the honey-coloured moor was spattered with soft purple heather. I'd started to love Cornwall by then, its beauty and its wildness, but I knew better than to go on about it to Jade. She took all that for granted. She didn't know any different.

The sea was a mass of wind-smashed white peaks and dark blue troughs, with the odd shoulder-high wave trying to make a shape in all that anarchy. Jade looked at it. Hungry.

"You know, you're mad to live here and not surf," she said.

"I don't like the water much."

"What? Why?" She frowned like I'd said the most stupid thing possible. I thought we might get into it then; I thought I might tell her about Dad. But then we heard a loud cry. The scared cry of someone in trouble.

At the far end of the beach was a young girl – maybe eleven or twelve – in a wetsuit, standing knee-deep in the shore break. She was shouting and waving at the sea. A surfboard lay on the sand behind her.

"That's Milly," said Jade. "She's far too young to be out by herself. Where's her mum? What the hell is she doing?"

Jade started running. I followed.

The girl was shouting at her dog, a Jack Russell, which was caught in the surf, drifting out, really quickly, like it was being pulled on an invisible rope. Its eyes were wide with panic. Tess started barking like crazy.

"The dog's in a rip," said Jade.

My blood iced. "Um, we should… er…" I said. I sounded weak, feeble. I felt that way too. Jade gave me a look like a whiplash.

"I'll take care of it," she said, starting to strip, chucking her clothes on to the wet sand.

"No! I'll go," I said.

And that was it. Three simple, stupid words. I didn't think about it; I didn't weigh it up. I just didn't want to look as pathetic as I felt right then. So I went. Because drowning's better than looking weak, right?

"I'll come too," said Jade, undoing her laces.

"No!" I said. "It's okay. I can do it." I was acting like Clark Kent, ripping off his clothes to reveal his Superman costume. But there was no Superman underneath. Just my weedy, shaking body. Every inch of my skin screamed at me not to do it, but I watched myself like in some out-of-body trip, kicking off my boots, picking up Milly's sponge surfboard, and running in.

It got deep, quickly. The cold water shocked me, its energy washing round my legs, soaking my clothes. Even the sand turned to liquid under my feet. The shore was only a few feet away, but once my feet lost touch with the sand it might as well have been a thousand miles.

I jumped on the board, dug my hands in the water and paddled. It was frenzied and clumsy, but somehow I moved forward, wobbling side to side, gasping and spluttering as I crashed through the chop, salt water catching in my throat and smacking me in the eyes. I had no idea what I was doing.

I must have been caught in the same rip as the dog, because I went a long way very quickly, but once I was out there, beyond the shore break, I couldn't see the dog. The sea was getting smacked around by the wind and I was rocking madly, trying to stay on the board. It was chaos.

I didn't even see the first wave – the first proper full-of-aggro wave – till it reared up in front of me. I paddled over the top and plunged downwards. A miracle. I was almost relieved, but there was another wave that had been hidden by the first one. It was bigger, but again I made it, just before it broke.

Then the third one came. A solid wall of water. As it pushed me backwards it paused, long enough to let me know what was happening. Then it tore the board from my hands and pummelled me into the sea.

There was no up, no down, no light, no dark. The world was replaced by a tornado of blue fury, and I was in the heart of it, churning over and over like a ragdoll in a washing machine.

It seemed to take forever. When it had finished, my lungs were bursting, and I was filled with sharp, high-pitched panic. A panic that had me by the heart and throat. I pushed and kicked and swam, desperate to get to the surface.

Seconds passed like years.

Eventually I surfaced, but instead of air I breathed foam, a lungful of froth that had me choking and hacking.

The next wave hit me like a truck. No spinning this time,

this one just ground me downwards. Down deep, I opened my eyes. Seeing nothing but bruise-coloured dark, I panicked. Full on. My body gave in to it and I breathed water into my lungs. I heard the next wave roll over me. I swam upwards expecting another wave, half thinking there was no point because this merciless bastard force was going to keep hammering me till I gave up.

But then...

Swimming up, I saw turquoise light. The daylight world of land and air. The world that I'd been torn from was there. Just there. If I could only... get to it.

I surfaced, spasming coughs and gasps.

There was the dog, the Jack Russell, right beside me. Lucky for the dog. I would have gone back and not even have remembered it. Right then I'd have done *anything* to be back on land, but there the dog was, and I clung to it. I kicked my legs and thrashed with one arm and we slowly headed to the shore.

Hands and arms dragged me from the water. They had to get the dog from me. I didn't want to let go. I tried to walk, but the sea had robbed me of strength. I felt like I was liquid. I bent over and puked.

I stayed like that a while, coughing and puking, water pouring out of my nose like a fountain.

Time slowed. I closed my eyes. I listened to the thunder in my ears. Slowly I began to breathe again.

I looked up. There were a few of them surrounding me,

including Big G in his wetsuit, holding the girl's board and grinning with delight. I'd never seen him smile before.

"Nice work," he laughed. Skip was there, hopping about; Rag, a few others. The girl, Milly, was playing with the dog in the sand. Her mum appeared, a blonde woman, in wellies and a scarf. Posh-looking.

"I'm so sorry. I went back to the car to get a flask of tea. I was only gone a moment. Thank you so much. Biscuit owes you his life."

A mock cheer filled the air. *Everyone* was smiling and laughing. Clearly what had happened was No Big Deal.

What?

I focused on standing upright and forcing a smile to my numb face, while streams of snotty water ran from my nose.

Big G and his mates picked up their boards and headed past me.

"You're a hero," said Skip with a nod.

"Rescue me if I get in trouble," said Rag with a wink.

Milly and her mum walked off, making a fuss of the dog.

After they were gone, Jade clapped and whooped. When I didn't react, she put her hand on my shoulder.

"You're okay, right?" she asked.

"I'm fine!" I pushed her hand away and fell down on the sand. I was shaking. Numb. I was freezing too.

"Come on," she said, "let's get you back."

I didn't move at first. I didn't even speak. I had to figure out what had just happened, had to try and put it all in some kind of order in my head. I'd nearly killed myself. Why? For the dog? No. I'd done it to impress Jade. I'd nearly drowned to make myself look good in front of a girl. The only upside was that if I *hadn't* gone, I'd have been sat looking at *Jade* rescue the dog.

It was a pretty messed up situation all round. Half of me was telling myself what a kook I'd been, how I'd been lucky not to drown, how I'd never, ever do anything like that ever again. Ever.

The other half of me was buzzing something stupid.

6

THE ONLY TIME I'd seen her hideaway above the garage was that first day, when she'd taken me to Tin-mines. I hadn't been allowed in. But now I was. She didn't want to have to explain anything to her dad by bringing me to the house.

I shivered as I stripped off my wet clothes. She didn't do me the favour of looking away as I got down to my pants. Every time I leant forward, a fresh stream of snotty water poured out of my nose. I kept coughing up water and couldn't get the salt sting out of my eyes.

There was a makeshift bed there, of rugs and blankets on old crates. Jade made me lie on it.

Apart from the bed, there was an old captain's sea chest and a blue rug. Driftwood shelves had been clumsily nailed on to the white painted walls. She had books, and a pile of tattered surf mags. On the wall, a few torn out and stuck up mag pics of girl surfers.

"Who are they?" I asked.

"Layne Beachley, Lisa Andersen. Old school surfers who carved a space for us girls in the water."

"You going to be like them?"

"Nuh-uh. They're competition surfers. I'm going to be a big wave surfer. Sponsored. The first famous UK female big wave surfer."

"The Devil's Horns?"

"Yeah, when one of those storms come. What did you call it, equinoocibingbong?"

She'd remembered what I'd said that first day, even though it had been weeks.

"Equinox," I said.

"Equi. Nox. Cool word. You know about that shit, huh?" She eyed me up. She wasn't teasing.

"You get bigger storms in autumn. Ever wonder why?"

"Nah. I just want to know when the swells are coming. If I get footage of me surfing the Horns, I'll be made. Sponsorship, free boards and travel, the works." She looked up at the pictures with a glazed far off look in her eyes, then snapped out of it and turned back to me.

"Spliff?" she said. But I shook my head. She didn't ask me about the vodka. She just got a flask, metal cup and a leather tobacco pouch out of the sea chest, then poured me a drink and started rolling herself a cigarette.

"Drink," she ordered. I took it off her with a trembling hand.

"What's wrong with me?" I said, trying to laugh.

"Bit of shock."

"I *did* nearly drown," I said. The vodka burnt my throat. I liked it.

"You got slapped about a bit, but you were close in. I was there, Big G too. I'd have got you if you'd been in trouble."

"If? I nearly drowned," I said again, glaring at her. But she was focusing on rolling her cigarette.

"How long do you think you were down?" she said.

I thought back, to what it had been like under there, to what had happened.

"A minute. Two?"

"No, you kook! Fifteen, twenty seconds. Then you came up, and then you were down another ten. It feels like everything, but it's nothing. It helps if you count when you're down."

"Count what?"

"Count the seconds. If you know what you can do on land, you know you can do it in water. It helps keep the fear off. Ten seconds down there can seem a lot longer than it is. If you surf, you get used to hold-downs." Jade put the roll-up in her mouth and lit it, checking my face to see if I got what she was saying. "You get to like it."

"Like… it…?" I said slowly. I'd liked it afterwards, sure. I'd felt good. But at the time?

"It was scary, right?" she said. "But you came out the other side. Didn't it feel good?" She was calm now, focused.

"I don't know," I said. It was the truth. I didn't know what I'd felt. Scared? Freaked out? Thrilled? Battered? All those things. But mostly just really alive. And I felt good I'd had a go. If she'd had to get in and rescue that dog, Jade would have been disgusted with me. Instead, here we were, talking about my adventure. And I liked her looking at me the way she did, legs crossed, smoking her roll-up, staring coolly, like she couldn't quite make me out.

"Next time hold your breath," she said.

"Next time? You're funny."

"I practise in the bath." She reached out, took the cup off me, drank some vodka, then gave it back. I imagined Jade in the bath. Then tried to shake the idea away before I went red. Or got a boner. "I hold my nose and count, put my head under and see how long I can do. It's not the same, but it helps train for hold-downs. You were brave. Tell Tegan. She'll be dead proud of you."

I had my reasons not to. I had my reasons not to tell Teg or Mum that I'd nearly drowned. Good ones. They'd have freaked.

"…and I didn't know you couldn't swim," she added.

"I can swim!"

"Not really." She squeezed the white cold flesh of my shoulder with her warm fingers. "See. Weak as shit. It was stupid of you to go in. But cool. Maybe you've got potential, even if you are a kook."

Potential for what, I thought.

★

I went home once my clothes were dry. I made excuses about needing to do homework, and went and lay on my bed, watching clouds through the skylight.

Thinking.

My dad had drowned. And I wasn't much of a swimmer. I had plenty reason not to get in the water.

But that kind of pissed me off. You shouldn't always run away from things, should you? Sometimes, the things you are afraid of are the things you need to face up to.

I liked how I'd rescued the dog, and I'd liked lying in the den talking to Jade about it. But I hadn't liked looking weak, like *I'd* almost needed rescuing.

Jade didn't need to face up to anything. She had no fear of the water. She loved it. She loved surfing. She was happy to let it rule her life.

And I liked Jade. I liked her a lot.

I lay there a good hour, just thinking about what had happened.

About Jade. About surfing.

7

I GOT SKIP by himself, at school, by the water fountain.

"All right?" he said, wiping water off his lip, ready to bounce off somewhere.

"Can I ask you something?"

He put his bag on the floor and leant against the wall. "What's up?"

"I want to surf."

"Is that all? Jesus, you looked so serious. But you? Surf?" He shook his head. "You sure that's a good idea after the other day? No offence, dude, but you were a real kook in the water."

"Will you teach me?"

"There's surf schools for that," he said, laughing.

"I don't want to wait till next summer…"

"They do stuff at weekends. You get to wear a yellow rashie, with 'surf school' on it. Might as well be an L-plate. You'll stand out from the ten-year-olds." He picked up his bag and started to walk away.

"Is that how you learnt?" I shouted after him. He turned. Suddenly it wasn't a joke.

"No, I just did it. Got in, kept at it till I rode green waves. Straight up? It's the only way. Even if you get a lesson or two, to start you off, then you got to go at it full on, for a long time."

"Right, but you could help me?"

He came back, and spoke slowly, so I'd understand. "Me? Like I get enough hours in the water and I'm going to waste time teaching a kook. And anyway…"

"There's only one teacher," said a voice from behind me. Big G put a hand on my shoulder.

Shit, I thought, *he must have heard it all.*

"You. Surf. Why?" he glared at me.

"You need to ask, if you love it so much?" I said, giving him back a little of what he dished out. His eyes narrowed.

"I can guess. You won't get anywhere. You're wasting your time," he said. He leant down, took a long drink from the fountain, then walked off.

"I live here. Why shouldn't I surf?" I said to Skip.

"He was talking about Jade. That's what he meant when he said you won't get anywhere."

"Oh. That's… it's… that's not why," I stammered, feeling hot in the face.

"Some have had a go, you know," he said. He rolled his eyes when he saw my shock. "I don't mean *been* there. I mean

49

Rag tried it on with her, and G. Maybe he did more than try… She doesn't seem that interested. Maybe she's into girls. That's what Rag reckons."

I was burning up wanting to ask about *that*. But I didn't.

"I just want to learn to surf," I said, casual as I could.

"Whatever." He picked up his bag, then hesitated. "By the way, how much?"

"What?"

"How much were you going to pay me? To teach you."

"Nothing. I just thought…"

"Shit, you really are a kook," he said, unable to stop himself smirking. "But thanks, you're funny. You've made my day." He smiled, winked and walked off.

*

I tried my luck with Rag. He got the same bus as Jade and me, but was always almost missing it. So I went to the lockers at the end of the day, knowing he'd be pissing about with books and bags. I wanted to get him alone, but he was talking to two girls.

"Rag. Have you got a mo?"

"Shoot."

"It's a bit… Can we talk… *alone*?"

"Oh, right, yeah," he said, nodding, like he already knew what we were going to talk about. "'Scuse us, ladies." He put his beanie over his mop of curly locks, put his arm round my shoulder and walked me out of the building. He looked over his shoulder a couple of times before he whispered in my ear.

"I don't know who told you about me, but they're fucking dead! I can't get expelled. I want names, you hear? Then G will have a word with the loose-tongued bastards. Anyhow, seeing as you're here... Mind-fuck or Mellow Summer's Day?"

"What?" I said. I had no idea what he was talking about.

"The Mellow's better in my humble, but most dudes go for the bang-you-into-a-coma gear. God knows why. Its proper name is Cheese or something, but I call it Mind-fuck, so no one says I didn't warn them."

Then I twigged. He was talking about weed. Rag dealt drugs.

"I don't want any weed." I said.

"Then why are we talking?"

"I want to surf. I was thinking you could help me."

"I ain't got the time, man." He took his arm off me. "Sure you don't want any weed?"

I shook my head. "I know you won't teach me but... some tips?"

He scratched his stubbly chin.

"Sure. Don't do it. It's bastard hard, and distracts you from other stuff you should do. Like live your life." He raised an eyebrow, looking serious, like he was thinking about some deep subject. "On the other hand, it's the best thing you can ever do. Better than girls and spliff and... other stuff I can't think of right now. That's just my opinion. But it's also a fact.

Any surfer will tell you the same, or they're lying. I haven't even got it that bad, but every idiot I know who stuck at it has. Does that help, Sam? How much were you thinking of paying me anyway?"

I tried not to look too hacked off.

"Okay, forget I asked," he said.

"How am I supposed to learn?"

"There's only one teacher."

"What does that even mean, Rag?"

"You'll see. Need a board?"

"Yeah."

"Come round Saturday morning. My bro's got some stuff too shagged to sell to the shops. He'll give it you cheap." He gave me the address, and said I'd find it easy.

8

I WAS DEAD PLEASED Rag was going to help me. But even if he hadn't, I'd have found a way.

I had a lot to prove. To myself. But to Jade too. Even though I had no idea how she'd react. Would she be pleased? Or would she just piss herself laughing? There was no point worrying about it. I'd decided.

Rag lived on a council estate on the moor side of a small village called Lanust. All the houses were dull and granite and square. Rag's house stuck out because of the choice artwork above the garage door. It was a graffiti-style spray job, about four feet high, showing a grown-up, sexy Red Riding Hood. She had a basket full of spray cans instead of apples, and with one in her hand had scrawled a message next to her, in spiky red letters, two feet high:

FEAR MAKES THE
WOLF LOOK BIGGER

A thumping rap tune was blasting out of the window. It took a lot of knocking before the door was answered.

Rag took me to the garage to meet his brother, who was exactly like Rag only older, about eighteen, and perfecting the stoner look even more than Rag, with scraggy, thatched hair, a wispy beard and glazed, bloodshot eyes. There was no sign of any kind of Responsible Adult.

If Aladdin had been a surfer, his cave would have looked something like Rag's brother's garage. At one end was a workshop with a bench, with a half-finished board on it, and a shelf with masks and sanders. The floor was covered with a snowfall of ground white foam. Next to the bench was a line of clean, white, new boards in a rail. In the middle of the garage there were more rails, with more boards. New, old, long, short, wide, thin, white and stainless, yellow with age, smooth and pristine, dinged and knackered. Boards with single fins, boards with three fins, boards with pointed noses and pinpoint tails, longboards with blunt noses, boards with ends shaped like fish tails. At the back there were no rails. It was just a messed up mountain of boards and suits.

All round, Aladdin's surf cave.

Seeing all this made the whole 'me surfing' thing very real, and not just about Jade. I thought riding one of those things might feel good. And going out in the sea and not almost-drowning might feel pretty good too.

"Ned buys and sells, fixes and shapes," Rag explained. "Good to make a crust doing what you love, right?"

"What do you like to ride?" said Rag's brother. "If I don't have it, I can get it."

I reckoned that, dopey as they looked, Rag and his "bro" might just be canny little business heads, and would probably buy or sell anything. If the price was right. And especially if what you were buying or selling was exotic herbs or surf kit.

"He's a virgin," said Rag, slapping me on the back. I waited for the piss-take, but it didn't come. Instead Ned was friendly, but kind of serious.

"Okay." He leant back, eyeing me up and down, measuring me up.

"Weight, age, fitness, how much fat on you, how much muscle, how good at swimming are you, how many press-ups can you do, how flexible are you?"

I gave him the answers, and I didn't lie.

"I'd say foam or pop out usually," said Ned. "Starter boards with soft tops or a factory-made shape, but they don't do you favours in the long run. I got a custom that might be good for you."

"Custom boards are hand crafted, Sam," said Rag, waving his arm around the garage. "Every one is different, made for riders with different weights and abilities and for different types of surfing."

I had to admire the sales rap. I put a nervy hand in my pocket. Seventy quid. My life's savings. Plus a tenner 'borrowed' from Tegan's piggy bank.

"You gonna do this, proper like?" said Rag. I nodded. "Then you need something that's big and stable, but which still goes nice. Know what I'm saying?"

A board had already caught my eye, a long one, sun-red, about eight, maybe nine feet long, pointed and thin, like a rocket, but thick.

"How about that one?" I said.

They smiled like I was a five-year-old asking to drive his dad's new Porsche. Rag ran a finger up the board's rail, with a dreamy look in his eyes. I'd seen Jade do the same thing with a board, the day I met her, and it seemed strange to me.

"This, my friend, is a *gun*. A big wave board. This board is more than ten years old. It gets taken out twice a year, by Ned. If that. Put in a few years, hope you're not busy when the storm hits, maybe you'll get to ride a board like this one. There's a few of these in sheds and garages round here, gathering dust, waiting for the day." He snapped out of his daydream and got back to the business of selling.

"How about Old Faithful?" Rag said to Ned.

"That's what I was already thinking," said Ned. They got busy in the messy heap of boards and suits at the scrappy end of the garage. The board they pulled out was about a foot taller than me, yellow, wide, thick with three fins at the back. It was fatter, older and more battered than any other board in the place. Covered in dents and patches of fibreglass, where it had been dinged, and fixed.

I could feel the sting of being ripped off already, but Ned looked at it like it was a work of art, something he really cared about.

"We used to keep it under the lifeguard hut at Gwynsand. Anyone could use it. It's good for small, good for big, good for learning, with enough rocker to be forgiving, but flat enough to glide. A nice all-rounder. Don't go pulling air though."

It *sounded* good, even though I had no idea what they were saying. But the look of the thing told me the truth. I felt heavy inside. They were going to flog me a board they had no hope of selling to anyone else and take me for every note in my pocket.

All the same, I took it off them, felt the weight of it. It wasn't light but lighter than I'd expected from its size. I looked it over, and generally tried to look like I had a fucking clue.

"How much?" I said.

"Depends. You want a suit too?"

"Maybe."

Rag patted his gut. "Before I graduated to the school of longboard, when I was all slim and lovely, I had this Ripcurl summer suit..." He dug into the mountain again and came out with a greying suit, with loose stitching and a couple of holes in it.

"Try it on."

Now I knew this was a joke, as well as a rip-off. I stripped to my pants and put the suit on. Pulling and panting I squeezed myself into it. It took a while. It fitted, a bit too much, and it stank. If me doing this was anything to do with impressing Jade, I was beginning to feel I might have made a mistake.

"It's a bit tight," I said.

"Needs to be." Ned gave me the board to hold, and they stood back to admire their work.

"He looks ready," said Rag.

"He does."

Again, I wondered what Jade would say. Maybe nothing, if she couldn't get the words out for laughing. I put the board down, picked up my trousers and took out the notes. Rag couldn't see how much was there, but he looked at the green and purple and licked his lips.

"You won't tell Jade, will you? She'll take the piss. I'll tell her myself like... once I'm all right at it. Anyway, how much?" I said, swallowing. Rag pulled his gaze from the cash and looked at me square, serious.

"A hundred and fifty. And that includes the suit."

"Oh, um, well how much just for the board?"

"Well..." He stroked his chin, considering the price... then cracked up. "I'm just messing. You think I'd sell you a suit I pissed in a thousand times?"

Ned put a hand on my shoulder.

"We're giving you this stuff for free, but one day we may ask you a favour. Cool?"

"Cool," I agreed, straight off, without thinking.

"I'll ask you one more time," said Rag. "You're going to do this, Sam, for real?"

"Yes." And I meant it. A grin spread across their faces. They stood back, looking me up and down, admiring what they'd made.

"You're a surfer now, Sam," said Rag. "One less of them…"

"…One more of us," said Ned.

They did a comedy high-five.

9

MUM'S FACE WAS a right picture when I turned up with the board and suit.

There was a row. Course there was. But I was determined.

"It's not safe," she said.

"I'll be careful."

"Your father *drowned* at sea."

"Mum, we *live* by the sea. On the edge of the moor. The edge of *nowhere*. There's nothing else to do…"

Mum chewed her lip.

"Look," I said. "If he'd died in a car crash, would you stop me learning to drive?"

"No."

"But you'd want me to be careful, right? I'll be careful. Safe. I promise."

She gave in eventually, but only after I'd made a *bunch* of promises.

Never alone. I had to be with people who knew what they were doing.

Never when it was big or dangerous.

No going off surfing when I should be doing homework or helping in the house.

I reckon she thought I'd try it for a bit and then lose interest, as soon as I realised I wasn't any good.

I told Mum the night before I started that I was meeting some surfers who were giving me a lesson before school. So that was broken promise number one.

I got up in the dark and sneaked downstairs. I'd laid it all out the night before: board, wetsuit, rash vest, towel, board wax, bananas and a flask of coffee for fuel. The whole thing had to run smooth. I had to be in the water super early, surf for an hour, race home, get changed and get to the bus stop in time. And *then* make it look to Jade like I'd just got up, before asking her if she'd been surfing. Just like every morning.

There was a chance I'd run into her at the beach, and if I did, I'd fess up. But if I could, I'd keep it a secret till I'd at least had a good crack at it. If she was surfing, she'd most likely be on the reefs, so with a bit of luck, she wouldn't see me.

And what would she think if she did? What would she say? It was hard to guess.

All this went through my head as I cycled with the wetsuit half on, up to my waist, and the board under my arm. The bike was old and only had three gears, so I stayed in the middle one as I couldn't change. I was wobbling and rolling like a drunk man, and how I got to the beach without falling off I have no idea. Jade had made it look easy.

I could still see stars in the western sky, but behind the moors the edges of the clouds were burning with light pinks and oranges. I hit the clifftop at Gwynsand, not even thirty minutes after I'd crawled out of bed. I felt like half of me was still there I was so groggy. I couldn't see much of the water, and I couldn't hear any waves. But Rag had given me the forecast, and like he had promised, there were lines of breaking white water bumping over a sand bar on the low tide. I dumped the bike and my bag and walked down to the beach and over the sand to the sea.

There was one surfer already out there, a thin guy on a really long board. Seeing him gave me this sudden wake-up call. I felt stupid, a real pretender, like I'd been in a dream and just come round. What was I doing? Really? But there didn't seem much sense in turning back. That would have felt even dumber.

The sand was cold under my feet, but Rag had said the water would be warmer than the land. He was right, it was. I waded in, lifting the board over the tiny waves till I was chest deep. I climbed on, but even though the board was big, and even though it was calm beyond the shore break, the board rocked and slipped like a horse that didn't want anyone riding it. Once I did get on, the paddling bit wasn't too hard. It was only when I got out to where the surfer was and I tried to sit on it that it went back to being a horse-with-attitude.

I stretched my legs wide and eventually got balance, but if I leant too far forward or back, the board dipped. I leant the other way when it did, but that started the board rocking, or for no reason I started leaning sideways, and I lost balance and fell in. Then I had to go through the hassle of climbing back on and doing the same thing all over again. Lots of times.

The surfer just sat there, with his arms folded, watching. He looked a lot like Jesus but with long, dreadlocked hair and beard. A knackered Jesus, with brown leathery skin and watery eyes. He didn't laugh, but he didn't offer any help either. Eventually I got on and stayed on, and he turned away, and looked out to sea. I did the same, and in silence we watched as the last smudge of dark blue evaporated and night turned to day.

When the waves came I had a go, but they kept running under me before they broke. So I paddled in a bit and waited for one that had already broken. I gripped the end of the board and held on. The slippery horse was suddenly stable and solid, and I got on to one knee, then to my feet and stuck my arms out like a tightrope walker. I rode that wave for all of two seconds before its power fizzled out, and I fell sideways into shallow water.

It was clumsy, awkward, and it lasted a moment. But my skin was on fire and I was grinning like I'd hit the jackpot. I'd stood up. On a surfboard. On a wave. I paddled back out.

It was just a ride on white water. But it was totally unlike anything I'd ever done. Not like riding a bike, not like sledging. Carried along by water. Rushing energy. Filling me up.

The surfer was grinning, ear to pierced ear.

"'Ow was that, dude?" he said in a thick Cornish accent.

"Awesome," I replied.

"Learning?"

"Yeah, that was my first wave. Ever."

"It gets better. Stick with it. Good luck." He leant forward, paddled his board, till he was smoothly riding on a bump of water that wasn't even near breaking, and was gone.

"Awesome," I said, again, to myself. And waited to get another one.

I did too, but I fell off quick, tumbling in the shallows.

Then I got one that was a bit bigger, and lasted a bit longer. And after that I sat further out, waiting for the larger waves. The 'larger' ones being all of knee-to-thigh high. But even so, it was stupidly good fun. I loved it. I got another.

Then another.

And another.

*

For some reason I thought Jade would guess, like she'd smell the sea on me, or know my still-wet hair had been somewhere other than the shower. But she didn't. She dropped her old army bag by the bus stop, leant against it and lit a rolly.

"D'you go surfing this morning?" I asked. It was always a good opener. A way to get Jade talking.

"Nah. Nothing going on. Not worth bothering with."

"Right. Course not…" I couldn't help smiling. She raised

an eyebrow, checking me out with a deep stare that made me feel uncomfortable and good at the same time.

"Something funny?" she said.

"No. No, not really." I sniggered. Stupidly, childishly. In my head I was picturing what her face would be like if I was to say, "Actually the surf was okay. Small, but pretty good." But I didn't; I just laughed.

She reached out a foot and pushed my leg with her boot. "What's the joke then, Sam?"

"No joke. I'm just… happy."

"Expecting a good mark for your physics homework?"

I ran a hand through my hair, feeling the grains of sand still clinging to my scalp.

"No. No, I haven't done it yet. I was going to do it first thing, but… I didn't have time." I cracked up again.

She blew a whoosh of blue smoke at me. Her eyes narrowed. I could almost hear her mind ticking away, trying to figure me out.

"Why you so interested in me surfing anyway, Sam? You always ask."

I shrugged. "Just chatting."

"You still not going to have a go?" she said.

"Maybe, one day."

"Maybe? One day? *Really?* One day might never come, Sam. No point in waiting." She looked away, towards the sea. And I thought, *She's actually keen for me to do it.* For all her acting cool, she was trying to persuade me.

"What's so good about it then?" I said. "Tell me."

"If I told you how good it was, you'd be doing it first chance you got."

"Try."

"Can't. It's one of those things that's hard to put into words, like. You only know by doing it. If you don't go, you won't know. That's what surfers always say. It's true too."

I thought back to that morning. All that getting up and getting cold and knackering myself. All for those few seconds I'd spent standing on a wave, riding and gliding on water.

I had gone; I did know.

"Yeah, that's probably right. Hard to put into words," I said. "Like dancing about architecture."

Jade flicked her dead roll-up away. "What?" she said, frowning like I'd said something in Japanese.

"This old singer Mum likes was once asked to describe his music, and he said talking about it was like trying to dance about architecture."

She took a deep breath, ready to make some piss-take comment. But she paused, thinking.

"Right," she said, nodding. "I get that. But *you'll* never know, will you?"

I grinned a bit more. I couldn't help it.

"It's going to be a great day, isn't it?" I pointed at the blue sky. She stared at me, wary.

"You know, Sam, you're not just a kook. You're also weird."

10

UNLESS THE SEA was flat or totally messed up by wind, I went surfing. Every day, pretty much. Weekends were good. As long as I helped out with Teg, and spent time helping Grandma with shopping, it was cool for me to go. But I did most of my real learning on schooldays.

I had the same routine: wake in the dark, bolt a sandwich I'd made the night before, neck coffee, cycle like mad, surf for an hour, race home, change, get to the bus stop. And then act with Jade like I'd crawled out from under the sheets two minutes before, which was a hard thing to do as I was always buzzing like a bee with the high of it, a high that didn't leak out of my muscles till mid-morning, when I'd almost fall asleep in class.

I got good at it – not surfing, that took time – but the whole routine. Whitesands was my choice surf spot; a half-moon of golden sand, backed by dunes and rocky hills. A cool beach, always, but in the light of dawn, with a mist on it and the sun coming up, it was something special. I was struggling to even remember London.

Whitesands was near enough for me to get to, but far enough that I knew Jade and the others wouldn't go there. There were better spots nearer to where we lived.

Sometimes I'd get there and it wouldn't be breaking, or low tide, so all the waves closed out, smashing straight on to the sand, with no chance of a ride. But I never turned around and went home. I'd sit on the huge, rounded rocks on the edge of the bay, watching the sea change, grey to blue. I'd get a little lost in my mind then, feeling kind of stoned, like round the campfire with Jade and the others, just looking at the sea, waiting for the waves to start breaking. Surf or no surf, I never got tired of the place.

Most times though, it *was* working. Sometimes I'd spend the whole time paddling, being ripped around by vicious currents, or have a whole hour of fun just getting battered. I got held down a few times, but never for long. I tried that Jade trick of counting, but I never got to more than a few seconds before the wave let go and I could come back up. That day, when I'd rescued the dog, it had been worse than it looked. Or maybe I was just getting *used* to it now, and knew what to do. What I'd been afraid of to begin with began to be normal.

Some days I got a total of two rides, other times I lost

count. But whether it went good or bad, I got to understand how waves broke. Waves that were fat and friendly and slow, others that had a nasty, fast edge. Ankle-snappers and shoulder-high white-water mushburgers. And everything in between. Over the days, I spent less time under water, less time paddling and jostling, and more time riding. I mostly rode the white froth of broken waves. But it was surfing, and I was learning.

★

Mum was okay about it at first. Like I said, I reckoned she thought I'd lose interest.

But then, after weeks, it became an almost daily thing. And even with me helping out in the house loads to make up for it, it got to the point where she was going to say *something*.

I came in from school one day to see the table laid. We usually ate tea on our laps in front of the telly.

"It's your favourite," she shouted, from the kitchen. I already knew it was, from the smell. Roast chicken. And that meant crunchy roast potatoes, peas and a dark, steaming gravy. My mouth was already watering.

"Great," I said. I threw myself on the sofa, groaning, putting my feet on Teg's lap. I did this every night, crashed out on the sofa, waiting for dinner like it was my first meal in months. That was how it was from the surfing. I was *always* hungry and *always* tired. I'd scoff dinner, then turn into a surfed-out zombie till I melted into my bed, seeing the waves in my head, mind surfing them all over again. Wondering what it would be like the next day.

When Mum brought tea in, it was a massive effort just to get up off the sofa.

We sat down, and ate in silence for a bit.

"It's not going anywhere," said Mum. "No one's going to steal it."

I paused, with my mouth full.

"Huh?"

"You're wolfing it down, Sam. You'll enjoy it more if you eat it slowly?"

I stared at my plate. Almost empty. Mum and Teg had hardly started theirs.

"Oh, yeah, sorry."

"Make you hungry does it, this surfing?" she said.

"Yeah, loads." I tucked in again. It took me a second or two to realise they were both staring at me, still not eating. I felt a bit awkward. I slowed right down.

"Will you play Lego Star Wars after dinner?" said Tegan. Teg was only six but she was dead good at this Xbox game. She loved me playing it with her too.

"I'm a bit tired to be honest, Tegs."

"Oh," she said, pushing a potato round her plate. Mum glared at me.

I carried on eating. Mum put her knife and fork down.

"You must really love this surfing, if it makes you too tired to spend time with your sister. Sam... you're *always* tired. And when you're not surfing, you're not really… here. Like your head is somewhere else."

"I've been helping out," I said. "Shopping, gardening and that."

"Yeah, but you're in another world. You barely talk to us."

She had a point. I was somewhere else. Mostly thinking about surfing, or Jade. Or Jade *and* surfing. And when I was in the water, I felt like I belonged there. Like everything in between was just waiting, some dream I woke from when I hit the surf.

I wasn't even any good. Yet. But I still lived for it. So much, it needed Mum to point out I was forgetting all about her and Teg.

As I ate, I thought. They were new here too. Mum didn't have any friends here yet. Most of her old friends here had been couples, folk that had been friends of Mum *and* Dad's. It was Dad that had been brought up here. She was from up country. Every face she knew, every place she went, they had to be reminders of him. I hadn't even thought about that.

Shit, I thought. *I love surfing, but I shouldn't let it turn me into a selfish prick.*

I smiled at Teg, looking for forgiveness.

"You used to be fun," said Tegan. "Play Lego. Pleeeease?" She reached out a hand.

"Okay," I said taking it.

"Thanks, Sam," said Mum. "Actually, I'm going to need you to spend more time with each other. Look after each other a bit."

"Oh, um, sure. Why's that then?"

"I need to earn some money. For a while anyway…" her voice trailed away. She meant till Grandma died. Till we inherited the house. And maybe money too. I never asked about that. Didn't seem right. "I'm going to do some pub work," she continued. "Lunches, a few evenings, bits at weekends. You'll need to be home then, Sam. Is that okay?"

"Sure."

She stood, took my plate to go and fill it up again. She smiled.

"It won't interfere with your surfing too much?" she said, gently teasing.

"No," I said. It wouldn't either. *But even so*, I said to myself, *maybe I should go a bit less.*

That's what I told myself.

★

And I did go a bit less. A bit.

But then, one sunny, windless autumn day, when the waves were waist high, I stumbled to my feet just as the wave broke. And didn't fall off. The board cut loose from the white water before it crashed, and I was on the green unbroken part of the wave. The board got this speed in it, like the brakes were suddenly off, and I was gliding along glass, ahead of the white water, feeling the energy of it surge up and into me.

I watched it wall up. I crouched down, got more speed and felt the rush.

I'd liked surfing before, but riding a green wave was a different kind of 'like'. Once I'd got a hit of that, I wanted more. I wanted as much as I could get.

The waves were easy going. Good to catch and not closing out. I got a load of them.

And every time I got a good wave I had the same thought: *What would Jade think? What would Jade say?* I was looking forward to showing her. I imagined I'd paddle up to her at Tin-mines and surprise her, or she'd be paddling out and see me gliding along a wall of water.

That's how I imagined it. But what I planned for and what I got turned out to be two different things.

★

A week or two later, after I'd been a bunch of times and got used to riding green waves, there was a different forecast on the website from what I'd seen before. Three feet at fourteen seconds wave period, with a secondary swell of two feet at sixteen seconds. The guy who did the report on the website was raving about how good a day it was going to be. *There's gonna be some thumping waves,* he'd written. *Autumn's started late, but it's here now.* That seemed odd. Three feet didn't seem that much. And anyway, I'd got used to seeing a good forecast, then turning up and seeing next to nothing.

Still. Winds were light. It'd be an okay size, but not so big I'd get in trouble. It would be a class day, according to the web guy. I reckoned I was ready for a day like that. I knew I was.

I was making progress fast. I even thought maybe better than a learner usually did, but as I was always alone, or out with a couple of surfers who really knew what they were doing, it was hard to tell.

At the beach I saw a couple of surfers heading in. I kept my distance though. I didn't want to bang into them, or them into me, so I walked right down the beach, to get my own space.

I paddled out easily, there were really long gaps between the sets of waves, but when they came through they were bigger than I'd guessed they'd be, bigger than I wanted and way bigger than I'd been out in before.

They were breaking fast too, *really* fast. I was a little nervy, but I still had this itching feeling, this twitchy, bursting energy running through me. The same muscles that had screamed 'enough' when I'd got out of the water the last time were now begging for more.

Rag was right. Surfing was addictive. Day by day, wave by wave, I was becoming a surf junky. So right then I was crapping myself *and* excited as a dog chasing sticks on the beach.

When my wave came, I knew it. I'd been in the water enough times that I could see it was no way going to slip under me or break in front. I was exactly where I needed to be. But when it got close, my stomach flipped. It was rearing up, sucking the water into it.

It was vicious looking, and fast, but peaking, with a shoulder, breaking a way to my right, and there was a good stretch between the breaking point and the unbroken hump of green. A rideable shoulder. So I turned and paddled, and gave it one hundred per cent. I dug my hands into the water. I just went for it. For a second I thought I'd imagined it, thinking, *It should have hit me by now*. Then the water I was in dipped, and I was being sucked backwards, upwards. I put all my strength into getting the board moving, making sure it went a bit to the right, not just straight down, and as soon as the wave's energy took over, thrust my body upwards.

My feet connected with the deck and I pointed the thing down the wave and dropped, turned, raced up the wave, along it, spun the board, digging the fins into the back of the wave and riding straight back into the heart of the thing. It was like a line of energy, and all I needed to do was follow it. It wasn't even me surfing the board. I'd connected with something. Something with more power than my body could ever have. It filled me up. Pure freaking juice.

I didn't plan the carves, twists and turns; they just happened.

Finally it got steep, heaping power on power into an arc of a wall, faster and faster. No need to turn now; I just pointed the board and shot like an arrow, true and fast into the heart of the wave as it jacked up. As it closed, it covered my head. I tried to dive into the wall, to come out the other side. But it ate me. It beat me sideways, churned me over. Walloped me. When I stood, I was in waist-deep water, dizzy and breathless as a kid who's just got off a rollercoaster. I held the board steady and pointed it through two walls, each one pulling me backwards, then stepped forward, threw myself on to the board and paddled like crazy.

I'd ridden a proper wave. Not a lump of white trash, not a two-foot wall, but a proper, over-your-head, make-your-knees-tremble, green, clean wave.

I only had one thing on my mind. More. Now.

Every five minutes or so, another set came in. Curving walls of turquoise crystal. How long would it last? Who knew? When you have a great sesh, you milk the fun out of it till your muscles turn to jelly. After I came off one, I raced out to get another, then sat outside, scanning the horizon, twitching like a landed fish, hungry – no, desperate – for the next one. I surfed long after the juice had been squeezed out of me. But when I *really* had nothing left, I still wasn't done. I caned it till I was stumbling on each wave, falling and floundering every time I tried to get one more.

It was late now, the sun was getting up. I wasn't going to school that day. I'd missed that bus. And I'd have to make up some bullshit for Mum, like a flat tyre on my bike or something. I didn't even worry about it. Detail. I'd sort it out later. I knew it was worth it. Because I'd *never* had it like this. In the weeks I'd been surfing, I'd never even *seen* it like this.

One more, I thought, and kept thinking, after every wave. *Just one more.* Then, when I'd got it, one more again, over and over. There was no 'last wave', no 'done', no 'over'. It went on and on and on, till I was so drained I could barely paddle.

At the end, when I had to finally admit it was time to go,

I sat as far out as I could and just waited for the killer wave to end on, even though I was so knackered I knew I'd struggle to even stand on the thing.

When it came, it was way bigger and meaner than any wave that day. But I wasn't going to let it go. I couldn't tell which way it was breaking, so reckoned I'd go straight and see what happened, then turn. I paddled with all the energy I had left. The board rode up, lurched forward, fast. I was looking down a cliff of water. There was no shoulder, either side. There was only one thing going to happen – getting nailed. I didn't even try to stand. I pushed the board away, put my arms over my head and went down.

It battered me into the water like it was concrete, sending a shock through my body. It got a grip on me and then spun me over, wanting me to know what a sap I'd been for even trying to ride it. It didn't let go till I'd been turned over and over so hard I didn't know which way was up. I tried to swim up, but another one hit before I got near the surface. When I did make the surface, I got a good lungful of air, tried to reach out for the board, but as my fingers brushed against it, I got hit by another wave. This one held me down longer. When it let me go, the wave and the board stayed glued together like they were mates in this Sam-battering routine, dragging me backwards and under.

I began to get scared. Fear rose up in me like sick. I tried counting, holding on. But I couldn't make myself do it. I was too afraid. A small voice in my head was telling me I didn't have enough juice left to cope. The waves were getting stronger and bigger, and I was getting weaker. By the second. And the sea was going at me like it was personal.

I flailed about, swimming, not knowing if I was even going up.

I hit the surface.

"Please! Please!" I shouted. I didn't know who to, and anyway, they weren't listening. I got hit again, went deeper, again. I couldn't seem to stay above the surface for more than a second or two. Half of me didn't accept the sesh had gone from great to pear-shaped in a heartbeat. But the other half of me knew I was beginning to drown.

Bang. Another wave. I hit the bottom. Got rolled along it. But then…

I got to the surface. Pushing my feet downwards, they connected with sand. A whole set had washed me in. I was standing in waist-to-chest-deep water. I almost cried with relief.

There was no way I was going back out so I waded in. Another one got me, knocked me over, but I gave in to it, grateful for every bit further it took me towards the beach.

I had a hold of the board, and half body-boarded in, gripping it, and letting it drag me to the shore.

Right up to two pairs of wetsuited legs.

"Hello, Kook," said Jade. "Shouldn't you be at school?"

I stood up, staggering and reeling. *Just great*, I thought. *Total humiliation.*

Skip was with her. "All right, Sam?" he said. "We been over

at Gwynsand. It was getting big, so we came here. My choice; Jade wanted to stay. Good job we did. You're really keen to kill yourself, aren't you?"

"You saw me?" I said.

"*I* did. Jade didn't. She was way behind me."

"Oh."

Jade's eyes were twinkling, and the side of her mouth was curling into a smile. She looked pleased, but also like she was trying not to laugh.

"Aaaaw, Kook. You're a surfer! Why didn't you say? You could have come with. Loads of times. Might have been safer. Did you learn much today?"

I nodded. The sea had taught me a lesson all right. "There's only one teacher," I said.

"Go on, Skip," said Jade. "I'll catch you up."

Skip hesitated, looking at me and Jade oddly, almost suspiciously.

"Go on!" said Jade. He shrugged, and headed into the water. Jade was frowning; she was curious.

"How come you never said you were learning?" she said.

"Oh. I wanted to get okay at it before I told you."

"I already knew. We all did. Never trust Rag with a secret. Skip saw you surf. He said you did okay out there." She pointed at the waves. "How come you want to surf?"

I looked at the sea, at the sand, anywhere but at her.

"Let's go," I said, picking up my board. Jade put a hand on the rail, and pushed it down.

"No way, Kelly Slater. You just got screwed. That's a serious wave."

"The website said a couple of feet."

"The wave period's super long. It increases the size and power… a lot."

"I've got a lot to learn."

"We'll teach you."

"Really?"

"Sure. You'll only kill yourself otherwise. This Saturday, when it's small. Big G's around too."

She headed out.

I went and sat on the sand. Hard, steady sand, that didn't move around, or try and swallow me up, or hit me. Right then I liked the land a lot more than the sea. My nose burned from the salt water flushed through it, my muscles felt like overcooked spaghetti and my skin was sandpapered by sun. I'd nearly drowned. Again. I'd be in deep shit for bunking school.

And I was just about happier than I'd ever been.

11

I WENT AND TALKED to Grandma. About Jade, about surfing. I needed to talk to *someone*. I couldn't talk to Mum. Not about the danger, leastways.

We had tea and cake in her conservatory, looking out to sea.

"Are you sweet on this girl?" she said. Her hand trembled as she lifted her cup to drink. She looked tired.

"Yeah, I am. I like the surfing too… It's just… I got in a bit of trouble. Almost drowned." I blurted it out. I looked for a reaction, but she was still and calm. She let out a long sigh, and put her tea down.

"Why did you tell me that?" she said. I shrugged. "Are you waiting for me to tell you to be careful? Are you waiting for me to say that's how your father died? That you should stop?"

"I… I don't know," I said. "I can't talk to Mum. She thinks it's a fad that I'll give up. But it's not a fad, and it's…"

"Dangerous."

"Yeah. *Yes*. What would Dad have said?"

She looked out, at the sea.

"He loved the ocean. It had a pull on him like nothing else. Right up to the day he died. I think that angered your mother. She was jealous of it... And if he were here now?" She paused. "He'd understand. He'd want you to love the sea like he did, but he'd want you to be careful too... Sorry, Sam, but you're old enough to make up your own mind."

I thought about my dead, drowned dad. Again, I tried to find memories. But they were vague. Distant.

"Grandma, is it all right if I go and check out his stuff?"

"Of course," she said, and I made my way upstairs.

The room was the same as before, a mess of boxes and piles of equipment. I yanked the curtains back, letting the sun in.

I didn't know where to start. I flicked through books full of numbers and graphs. Stuff I couldn't understand, even though I was good at maths. The equipment was beyond me too.

There was one chest, already open. Inside were papers and charts, messed up like someone had rummaged around in it.

At the bottom of the chest there was a neatly folded piece of paper. I took it out and flattened it on the floor. It was a sea chart. The land part was one big brown blank, but the sea part was full of detail. There were lines and dots and numbers, and on the bottom edge of the chart were scribbled notes. I guessed it was my dad's handwriting. It looked a lot like mine. That spooked me too, just like the smell of the place had.

The writing was above a couple of small dots – tiny, but the same colour as the land, so they had to be little islands. They had lots of rings around them, showing the layout of the seabed.

He'd written:

Trench ends here. 930 isobar. 60mph wind, 90mph gusts.

Then he'd put in a bunch of x's, dotted round the island, and some writing by each of them:

X The Excalibur
PN
X The Hope
BZ
X Star Cross
DH

Something in it struck me. It was like the memories of Dad, with the blue paint, and him holding me in the shore break. Something in it made sense. But I didn't know what.

I took it downstairs and showed it to Grandma.

"I found this. It's got his writing on it," I said. She looked at it, carefully.

"I'm sorry, Sam, I don't know what this is. But take it if you want."

★

I was going surfing with Jade and the others on the Saturday. I went over to Jade's on the Friday night and we hung out in the den. She offered me vodka, like Grandma offered me tea.

"Sorry there's no spliff," she said. "Big G's giving me some of his tomorrow."

"That's okay," I said. I said yes to the drink though.

"I nick it from Dad," she explained. "A bit here or there. He doesn't know."

We couldn't really sit on the makeshift bed without it being awkward, so we squatted on the floor, on cushions, facing each other.

We talked about me, surfing. She wanted to know *everything*: from getting the board off Rag, right to when I'd washed up at her feet. The wind, the waves, what it felt like, how I rode waves, what was difficult, what I found easy. Everything. She seemed impressed, grinning and nodding all the time I was talking.

"Sounds like you done well for a beginner. Sounds like you got hooked too. *That's* why you were grinning, that time at the bus stop. You'd been surfing."

"Did you know then?"

"No, soon after. I figured you'd tell me when you were ready. I also figured you were going out in small conditions. The other day though… shit. I didn't know you'd been out in serious stuff. Respect. You've got some nuts."

"Well, yeah. But I didn't really know what I was getting

into. The forecast said three feet. I didn't know about wave period then. Didn't know what it does or why. Concave refraction, and all that?" I checked her eyes for some recognition. "You know about that, right?"

"Not really. Skip susses out that stuff. Is it good? Where? That's all I need to know."

It was that simple for Jade. She knew waves; she knew what the sea did. But not *why*. Maybe she didn't care. I was different. A geek. I needed to know how things worked, to make sense of them. I knew a bit about the stars. Now I wanted to know about the sea. I also thought it might help me not kill myself. So I'd looked it all up.

"Skip checks the forecasts," I said. "But they're not always accurate, are they? Especially about refraction into the sheltered spots. If you understand, it'll help you get better waves. You're probably surfing okay waves one place when you could be surfing great ones somewhere else."

She sat up dead straight when she heard that.

"Yeah? Prove it."

I took her baccy pouch and hip flask and a magazine and a book and made a rough map on the floor.

"Say this is the land, and the swell's coming from this direction…" I talked a while. About energy moving from wind to water. How the longer and harsher the wind blew, the more fetch it created, and the more likely the chance of decent swell. How it travelled across the ocean, for days, weeks; how it would travel forever if it didn't hit land or opposing wind.

How waves got organised into sets of two, three or even ten. What happened when they hit the coast and why different spots would work well in different swells.

She knew all the spots and had seen them all in different conditions. But she had no idea how a little bit of research could help her get top waves. There were at least two spots, facing north, that I reckoned would fire in a big west or south-west swell, even if the web forecasts reckoned they'd be no more than one to two feet.

"Refraction, you see. Hits the rocky bottom and slows down, but not the wave still travelling in deep water. Hence wrapping around a point."

Jade sat, cross-legged, elbows on knees and hand holding up her chin, staring at me goggle-eyed and silent, and listening in a way I'd never seen her listen to a teacher.

I liked that.

*

Skip couldn't make it the next day.

Jade, Big G and me stood on the shore, in our wetsuits, our clothes in bags on the sand, boards under our arms, watching lines of froth lick our toes. We'd come looking for a wave. And it wasn't there. I was gutted.

"It'll come on the pushing tide," said Big G. But he didn't sound like he believed it.

"All dressed up, no party," said Jade. "Bugger."

"So what do we do now?" I asked.

"Training games," she said. She kept her gaze on the sea, looking serious, but Big G had a smile on his hairy face that got wider by the second.

"Yeah, right, training games," he said, nodding.

"What kind of games?" I asked, but Jade was off, running down the beach, bouncing off the sand.

"What's she...?" I started to ask, but Big G ran off too, following Jade's footprints to the end of the beach, where a thin path snaked through the rocks up to the clifftop.

They leapt up the path, like they had springs in their legs. I followed, panting and stumbling, struggling not to ding my board on the rocks.

They'd run fifty yards to a rocky outcrop, sticking out of the cliff. Their surfboards and bags were stacked in the ferns nearby. I ran along the path, dumped my stuff with theirs and joined them on the rock.

"Take a look," said Jade. I crept up to the edge. The sight of the sea came up and punched me in the gut. There was nothing below, but a long, long drop, into a purple pit of water. Twenty feet? Thirty? Either side of the deep part, below the surface, I could make out rocks, patches of yellow sand and seaweed drifting in the current. Looking at it made me feel dizzy and sick. I pulled back. But firm hands pushed me back to the edge.

"WAAAAOOH!" I shouted.

Jade and Big G had grabbed an arm each and shaken me.

"Sick bastards!" I said, putting a hand on my heart, just to stop it bursting out of my chest. Jade was almost crying, she was laughing so hard.

Big G went over to the bags and started rooting around, looking for something.

"Have a go," said Jade, with a sly smile.

"What... you mean jump?" I looked down again. How far was it? Could I make it? Or would I get smashed on the rocks? "No way. Can't be done."

"Ha!" said Jade. Shaking her hair off her face, she walked back off the rock, turned, then ran straight at the edge. Fast. And jumped off. Right into nothing.

I didn't even try and stop her. She was too quick.

She hung in the air. No more than a second, but the sight of her burned into my head. Her curved black shape in the crystal-blue sky. Her arms out, hair floating in the air. Then time started up again, and she fell like a stone. I went to the edge, almost tripping over, and watched her fall. At the last second, she drew her arms across her chest and slipped into the water. She didn't even make much of a splash. The sea swallowed her.

I watched, waiting for her smug, smiling face to appear, waiting for her to shout at me to jump in after her.

A circle of bubbles floated up where she'd gone in.

"Big G?" I said. He was doing something on his phone. "G, she hasn't come up."

"She's cool," he said, not looking up. Long seconds passed. Tens of seconds. I looked hard, like just staring would make her appear. The circle of bubbles melted away.

Was she hiding, below the rocks where I couldn't see? Was it a wind-up? I got down on hands and knees and leant over as far as I could, so far I felt I was going to puke. I could see right into the gully underneath. No Jade.

"She's not hiding, G. She's not *there*." I kept looking down, then back up at Big G, waiting for him to do something. He just kept playing with his sodding phone. "She hasn't come up!!"

"Okay. Tell me when she does."

"Right. I'm going," I said. I looked for a way to climb down. There wasn't one. It was jump or nothing. Shit. I got ready to leap.

"It's not your turn yet," said Big G.

"Turn?"

"Well?" Jade's voice echoed up the rocks. There she was, right where she'd gone in, treading water. I breathed out. Big G came to the edge.

"One twenty!" he shouted, pointing at the phone.

"That doesn't count. I'm going again." Jade slammed the water with her hand. I looked from Jade to Big G, from Big G to Jade. What was going on?

"Yeah, it does count, you cheating monkey. Go, go!" Big G shooed her. She turned and swam fiercely along the rocks to the beach. Her dark skin, wetsuited body and seal-slick hair all blended together. She was more sea creature than girl.

"Your go," said Big G, slapping me on the back, a sick grin on his face. "Go in straight, or you'll break your back and never walk again. Don't let your arms flap. When you get down deep, grab a thick bit of seaweed, or a rock, and hang on as long as you can. Then swim to the beach, and run back up here. Get it?"

"Er, yeah."

I wanted to do it; I wanted to know what it felt like. And I *didn't* want to bottle it. Not in front of Jade.

But…

"Now?"

Big G rolled his eyes. "Yeah, Kook, now."

I looked into the huge pit of nothing beyond the rock.

When Big G saw me not-jumping he said, "You just watched a *girl* do it. Stop being a pussy. And get a good run-up so you don't smash your brains on the rocks in the shallows. Jump high, jump far. Simple. Go."

Jade was running along the path; she'd be back in a second.

I couldn't feel my legs. My arms were shaking. I took a few steps backwards to get a good run-up, took a last look at Jade to make sure she clocked me going, then ran. *Totally* legged it for the edge, and jumped high as I could.

"Wahoo! Koooooook!!" Jade's shout echoed in the air. I had this plan to hold my body straight, tucking my arms in, but I flapped like a bird, suddenly finding I couldn't fly. There was this moment of just being in the air, not even falling, just floating. I took it all in, the forever of the sky and the blue sea – because I felt, I mean *really* felt, it might be the last thing I ever saw – then the water raced up to hit me in a sickening rush. I tucked my arms in, just as my feet smashed through the surface. I felt like a bomb breaking through ice. My body was pulled apart, like my arms and legs were being torn off me.

Time slowed. My head, heart, body and bones all came together again. I had a second before I'd start floating up. I opened my eyes. Blurs of gold and blue and black danced in front of me. Rocks, sand, seaweed. I turned over, swam down and felt around, till my scrabbling hands found a thick trunk of seaweed.

I was humming with the buzz of it. I'd jumped. I'd got the seaweed. All I had to do was hold on.

Ten seconds. Twenty. Thirty. My hammering heart was growing inside me, filling my chest, my head, my ears. Even my eyes were throbbing with it.

Forty.

Fifty.

I got this tight, squeezed feeling right inside. Deep. My muscles started twitching and dancing, crying for oxygen. But the worse it got, the harder I held on to the seaweed.

It was like being under a wave. The same squeezing in my body. The same helpless panic in my head, like it was talking to me, screaming at me to let go. But this time, *I* was in charge, not the water. This time I had a choice.

Control it, control it, control it, I said to myself, while my body cried back:

Breathe. Escape. Now.

I closed my eyes tight shut.

Control…

Control…

Breathe…

I let go, kicked for the surface and pulled air, huge gasping lungfuls, while shakes ran through me like I was having a fit.

I heard Big G shout, "Fifty three, go!" I started swimming, hard as I could. Everything I saw and felt melted together. The cool water, the sun on my face, the light on the sand. It was a heady, rushing, spinning, dizzy, messed-up feeling, like I was still jumping, still falling, still sinking, still underwater. Like all these things were happening at once.

When I got back to Big G and Jade, I was sweating and panting. I'd done it. I'd given it all I had, and a bit more. I waited for the slap on the back, for Jade's wide-eyed wonder. But she just smiled, like she was amused.

"Oh dear," said Big G, sighing and shaking his head. "Got some work to do, haven't we, Sam?" He gave Jade his phone, and jumped.

"This is nuts," I said, gasping, leaning over, feeling sick. She looked for him in the water, then at the phone, then back at the water, her eyes and her smile calm. She was way more focused than I'd ever seen her in class.

He was down a long time. Longer.

"Come on, you git, come up!" she whispered through pinched lips. Finally, Big G surfaced.

"One ten," she shouted. But I could see the phone over her shoulder – 1:25 was flashing on the screen. I smiled.

"What's next?" I said, still panting.

"You need to do better, Kook. You can hold your breath a long time. Don't fight it when you're down there. Slow your heart down. Don't use up your oxygen. Practise. We'll go again. Five times each."

"What! This is *really* nuts."

"Yeah? Well one day it could save your life."

12

THE SURF DIDN'T come up. We'd skunked, as Big G said. There'd be no surfing that day, no way for me to show Jade that I wasn't that much of a kook any more. Not in the water, leastways.

But we went back to the beach and ran, and did press-ups, and swam and jumped. All of it led by Jade.

Big G was better than her at most of it (and better than me at all of it), but she could outrun him in a short sprint and she could swim better than him too. When they did stuff he was better at, she got really, really determined. I'd never seen anyone strain so much. She made herself look almost ugly, she was pushing herself so hard, and even when Big G was the way-ahead winner, she'd do *anything* not to lose.

She counted him doing press-ups. "Twenty-one, twenty-two, twenty-five, twenty-eight, ninety-four, I mean eighteen…"

He cracked up. "Pack it in!" It was hard for him to do press-ups when he was laughing.

"Ah well, better start again," she said, and kicked one arm from under him so he fell face first into the sand.

It was fun. When we'd finished, we walked back into the dunes where we'd left our stuff. Jade had this kind of tent dress with a hood, made of towel. She called it a 'robey'. She could put it on and fumble about underneath, getting changed, without showing an inch of flesh. It was a one girl changing room. Watching her mess around with bra straps and knickers underneath this tent was weird. Funny, clumsy and sexy, all at the same time. I tried not to look too hard. Or at least not be obvious about it.

When she eventually yanked the robey off, she was in shorts and a T. It was well into October by then, but the summer sun didn't seem to want to finish. Warm days were still pretty normal that autumn.

As she threw the robey on the sand, we heard a whistle. Three guys were walking towards us. They had blond hair and brown skin, wearing the board shorts and hoodies that were like a uniform for a lot of surfers. But they weren't like the Penford crew. They were older, and a whole lot neater. Their clothes had been ironed and they had hair they'd put gel in and taken time over.

The tallest one had short, spiky hair, and perfect teeth.

"Not much of a strip, Jade," he said. She put one hand to her lips like she was about to blow him a kiss, but instead, showed him the finger.

"Screw you, Billy," she said.

They came up to us.

"Thought we'd check it out down here. There's nothing at Porthmeor."

"No surf here either, so you might as well piss off back home," said Jade. She said it in a friendly way, like she was just joking. But she wasn't.

"Oooh, the pretty girl's got 'tude," said Billy. He looked at me, checked out my board and my knackered suit, which was lying on the sand like a dead seal washed up by the tide.

"Who's this?" said Billy to G. But G just stood there with his arms folded, staring at Billy and chewing gum. He didn't seem to have heard what Billy said.

"This is Sam. We're teaching him," said Jade.

"On that thing?" he waved a hand at Old Faithful.

"We all learnt on that thing. Any one of us would piss all over you, even if it was the only board we ever rode." Jade was having a go. And G wasn't stopping her.

"Is that right? Gavin, what do you say?" Billy said to G. Big G just shrugged like talking to Billy was beneath him. This guy was squaring up. If he had been alone, it would have been a very, very stupid thing to do. But there were three of them.

And G, and Jade, and me. My legs went cold. I was afraid. But…

"Leave it out," I said. I don't know where it came from. I just said it.

"What?" said Billy. He took a step towards me. Same as when I'd been surfing, like jumping off the cliff, I pushed the fear down. I didn't step back, even though he was breathing in my face. And I told myself I wasn't going to. My head was doing quick maths. G and two of them, me and Billy, Jade landing a few kicks. We weren't starting anything, but we might be okay if they did. I'd done the cliff, why not this?

"Leave the kid alone," one of his mates said, pulling Billy back. This one was older too, maybe seventeen, good looking, with an easy smile and a far away look in his green eyes. I wondered if I might look like that, if I surfed a few years, had a tan and could afford decent threads.

"Come on," he said, pulling Billy away and pushing him towards the beach. "Sorry. He gets uptight when there's no waves." They walked off, but as they did he turned, smiled and said, "Hey, Jade."

"Hey, Mick." She smiled back at him.

My gut twisted hard, and I felt hot and angry.

"Fancy him, do you?" I hated myself for saying it. I wished I could turn time back just a few seconds. But there it was.

"What's it to you, Kook?"

"Nothing."

"No really, Sam," she said, hands on her hips and her chin in the air, "what's it to you?"

"Nothing."

"Good." Jade's eyes were an ocean most of the time. Cool

and deep. But right then they were blue-green fire. "No surf. Let's go get wrecked. Who's in?"

Big G had stuff to do for his dad.

It was just me and Jade.

13

WE CYCLED BACK to her house, and put the boards and bikes in the garage.

"Got to get weed from the house, wait here," she said, like she was speaking to Tess, or a kid. And straight off, I thought, *What doesn't she want me to see?* Or maybe it was *me* she didn't want to be seen. Either way, I was dead curious.

I left it a few seconds, then went out and stood by the corner of the garage, watching her walk over the pot-holed driveway and up the garden path to the house.

I took a good look at the place. Faded white walls and flaking blue paint, with moss growing on the cracked roof tiles. It was like Rag's house on the estate. But it wasn't on an estate. It was on the moors, in a sea of yellow gorse and green grass. It looked beautiful in the autumn sunlight.

Her dad opened the door. Jade froze on the spot. Bob stood,

leaning against the doorframe, blocking her way.

They started talking. I couldn't hear what they were saying and it all seemed normal at first. But then their voices got loud, quick. Tess ran out of the house, sliding straight up to Jade and rubbing her body against Jade's legs, whimpering. Jade ignored Tess and kept on at her dad, brushing her hair out of her face with one hand and pointing at him with the other. Suddenly, Bob stepped forward and lunged at Jade, trying to grab her arm. Jade was quick, and dodged out of his way. He ended up stumbling down the path. I wondered if he was okay. But as soon as I thought it, I sussed he was drunk. It was the way he was struggling to get upright, swaying and trying to point at her, like she was a moving target.

Not just drunk. Smashed.

He went at Jade again, this time grabbing her arm. But she slipped out of his grip, and headed for the door. Tess went nuts, barking at him.

"Don't walk away from me, you whore!" he shouted. I heard *that* clearly enough. She stopped, and turned to face him. Even at that distance I could see she was all attitude and flashing eyes, ready for whatever was coming.

But what was coming wasn't good. He marched at her, with his arm raised, moving like he was going to hit her.

"No!" I shouted.

Bob turned. Jade melted into the shadows of the doorway, and Bob – weirdly – waved at me with the hand he'd been about to hit Jade with. Like behaving normal was going to make it all okay. I didn't wave back.

Tess was still barking madly at Bob, her hackles raised. He went into the house with Tess following, and shut the door behind him. There was an eerie silence in the air then. Just a whisper of wind, and the far-off cry of a seagull.

I didn't think either of them would welcome me coming over and getting involved, so I just stood there, waiting.

But at the same time, I knew *anything* could be going on behind that door, and that wasn't okay. Their business or not, I wasn't going to just stand there. I ran over. I noticed the door wasn't shut properly. It was open, a fraction. I opened it, but stayed outside. Through the hall, I could just see her dad, in the lounge, in an armchair. He was bent over, with his head in his hands. Crying.

Jade came down the stairs, and straight out the door, followed by Tess. She shut it behind her and walked past without even looking at me. I thought she'd be upset, or maybe angry. But there was nothing in her face, no emotion at all.

"You okay?" I said.

"I told you to stay put."

I followed her to the garage. She climbed up the ladder to the den.

"Are you *all right*?" I said, looking up.

"Stop looking at my arse. And stay there."

"I'm not. He called you a…" I couldn't even say it.

Whore. Just the *idea* of the word was wrong. Poisonous.

"He's just drunk," said her voice from the den. "It is Saturday, after all." She came back down with a tobacco pouch in her hand. "Got weed, got baccy. Best go up the tor, just in case he comes looking." She was weirdly relaxed, like what just happened was no big deal.

"I saw him—"

"You didn't see *anything*, Kook."

She walked out, with Tess at her heel.

★

We sat on the tor, the massive flat rock at the top of the hill, looking out to sea. From up there, on top of the world, the whole sea blended into one great big glass sheet. I watched it, stroking Tess's head, rested on my lap.

Jade skinned up, sighing and breathing deep the whole time, and focusing on the spliff like it was the most important thing in the world.

I wanted to say something to help, though I didn't know what, and I guessed if I did, she'd be off before I'd said more than three words. So I didn't say anything. But I *felt* angry. I didn't show it; I was careful. But I hated her dad. I hated him more than I'd ever hated anyone. I didn't care if he was sitting in a chair, crying, thinking he was sorry.

She lit the spliff and took a deep pull.

"Does he know you smoke?" I said.

"Sure." She blew out a cloud. "He looks for it, so I hide it in the house. Not all my secret stashes are in the den. Too obvious. We play this game. He hides the bottles; I hide the weed. No one looks too hard. Difficult though. Rag's stuff stinks."

She took another hard drag. It was full on, how she was taking it in, getting wrecked as quick as she could.

"Does he drink a lot?" I said, trying to get her talking, thinking it was better than saying, *Does he hit you, Jade?*

She stared at the sky. When she answered, it was in a husky, mellow voice.

"Yeah. He drinks. Since Mum went. It's a year ago. He's into the Scotch a bit. Can't say I blame him."

"Where's your mum now?"

"Truro, last I heard."

"Do you still see her? Does she know… he…"

"Nosy bastard, aren't you, Kook?" she snapped. She was like a wire, and when you touched it, you didn't know if it was going to give you a shock or not.

"Don't mean to be," I said, with a shrug. She held my stare then. Her eyes were hard as ice, and that anger was back for a second, like it was always in her and it just needed to be pulled out by the wrong word or look. But, slowly, that look melted as I stared into her eyes. Pushed under the surface.

"It's okay, Kook," she said, gently, "you're just being nice. That's you. Nice all over." She put her hand on my arm, and squeezed.

After we'd been quiet for a bit, I took a deep breath and blurted it out, before I lost the chance.

"It's not right, Jade… if he gives you aggro like that." I had to say it. I wasn't going to pretend like she wanted.

She took a sharp breath, tensed, sat upright, as if she was going somewhere, then fell back, breathing out. Maybe she was so stoned storming off was just too much effort. She didn't answer for a long time.

"He doesn't, he just…" She sighed. "Look, our family's messed up. You don't know the half of it." She was looking at me like she couldn't figure me out; if talking to me about this was a good thing or not.

"I know what I saw," I said.

"It's my fault. I wind him up. I can handle him. I don't need any help."

"Yeah, you do."

"He goes mental when he's tanked, and I give him a hard time. It's no biggy. He's never, like, really hit me, or anything. Honest." She handed me the spliff and lay down, putting her hands behind her head.

"He's out of order, Jade."

"I *said* I can handle him." And there was that Jade anger back. She sat up. "How long did you do down there?"

"Down where?" I said.

"In the sea. Today."

"About fifty seconds." I was a bit thrown by how she just changed the subject. And how fierce she was.

"Well, that's nothing. And I'll bet it freaked you right out. Well, you gotta get used to it. Not mind it. Like it.

Else you'll never surf it big. You gotta conquer your fear, Kook."

"Fear makes the wolf look bigger, right?"

"Right."

"But fear's a good thing."

"Pussy!"

I cracked up. I couldn't help it. She sounded a bit stupid, with her bring-it-on-I-can-take-it attitude. She cracked up too. She took the spliff off me before carrying on with her mission. "When you get a big wipeout, when you really get held under, it's... the most intense, fucked-up thing that's ever happened to you."

"That's good, is it?"

She smiled. "It is, if you're ready for it. You want to go back there? Deep down. Now. Do some more training."

"What? Back in the water? But it's so nice here." My whole body was melting into the stone and thin moss we were lying on. The tor had stopped being a hard rock and was now, officially, the biggest beanbag in the world. The spliff had crept up and ambushed me. I wasn't going anywhere. I lay down, put my head back and stared at the sky.

The whole world vanished. Jade's dad, my mum, Skip, Billy, school. All that was left was blue sky and Jade's voice.

"If you get a big hold-down on a big wave, or you get held down by one, two, three in a row, you're going to be down longer than a minute. It pushes you deep. Crushes you, makes you know you're nothing. But if you're cool with that, if you're not afraid of it, then you'll be a great surfer, cuz you can take it on, all of it, whatever it throws at you. And you get to be part of it." She sounded really intense.

"Part of what?"

"It, like, the swell? I know I'm wrecked, but… when you surf big, it feels like the energy of the wave, it's inside you, like you're part of it."

"It is. You are."

"You wouldn't know," she said, scoffing.

"That's kinetic energy. No water's moving into shore till the wave breaks; it just goes up and down as the energy passes through it. The thing that's moving to the shore is energy. You have that inside you when you ride a wave. Like the water does."

Silence.

The blue sky was invaded by a giant shadow. Jade's head. Her hair hung down and tickled my cheeks. For one second I thought she was going to kiss me.

"Kine-what? What's that? What do you mean? The water's not moving?"

I'd flicked some kind of switch inside her. Pressed 'on' by accident. I stared up at her hungry eyes.

"Ki-ne-tic. The energy of movement. When you're surfing, you're an object with speed and momentum. The rate of each combined can be calculated as the amount of kinetic energy you have. You absorb it, out of the wave."

She looked at me like I was speaking an alien language.

"Absorb it? Energy? So it's inside me?"

"Uh-huh. Part of you."

"But we're not energy," she said, tapping my head. "How can it be part of me? We're… stuff. Solid stuff."

"You mean matter. Matter and energy are the same thing."

"What? Straight up?" she said.

"Yup. Kind of. Well… energy is actually mass times the speed of light squared. Matter and mass aren't the same, but anything that is matter has mass."

"Well, that's just fascinating," she whispered. But it didn't matter how sarky she tried to sound. She meant it. She *was* fascinated.

"Anyways, Kook, you never answered me."

"Answered what?"

"D'you want to go back there?"

"Where?"

She took the spliff from me and put the burning end in her mouth, then grabbed me by the shoulders and moved her face towards mine, *like* she was going to kiss me, but she started blowing through the spliff instead, so the smoke rushed into my mouth. I inhaled. She blew hard. I sucked it in, till I coughed. I might have had a proper choking fit then, but she put one hand over my mouth and took the joint out of her own mouth with the other.

"Now hold it," she whispered. "Hold it till you're going to pass out."

What?

I wasn't going to do that. I'd hold it in a bit, then push her hand away and cough my guts up.

Ten seconds.

But then I thought… That's what she was expecting. That I'd give in after a minute. Then she'd take a deep drag and do it for two minutes. And it would be like running on the beach. She'd push herself hard enough to almost kill herself, then get that victory look in her eyes.

Twenty seconds.

I decided I wasn't going to let that happen. And I liked her hand on my mouth. And looking into her eyes. Eyes that were checking me out, seeing what I'd do.

Thirty seconds.

Forty.

Fifty.

I wasn't going to give in. She saw it, and she *liked* it.

One minute.

It was starting to hurt now. My body was tensing up, getting tight. Tighter. And I was sinking. The sky and her face were melting.

I wasn't. Going. To. Give. In.

I couldn't count. The numbers weren't…

Working.

The shape of her head, the blue sky, her breath on my face, her hand over my mouth. Not melting now, shaking. Getting…

Lost.

She took her hand off. I blew out, coughed. Gasped. Sat

up. The whole world rushed back into my head. I'd almost passed out.

"Holy shit," I said. I'd been down there all right, but now I was back, going high, right into space. Stoned out of my box.

"One fifteen," said Jade, then took a massive hit off the joint herself and held her nose. I didn't put my hand over her mouth.

I lay back. I didn't even watch her. I knew she'd make my time easy, then add a few seconds on. Just to make a point.

When she was done, she stubbed the spliff out and lay back, next to me.

I turned to face her and she turned to face me. I stared into her sea blue-green eyes, looked at her plump lips and honey skin and the perfect heart shape of her face. And she stared back, not minding me looking at her. Liking it. Maybe it was the weed messing with my mind, but I thought she was just daring me with her eyes and those lips, so I went to kiss her, close enough that our lips brushed. But just as I started to press, she turned away, and stared at the sky.

"Cheeky bastard, as well as a nosy one," she said. But she was grinning. And I was flying like a gull in the sky, burning up inside, hardly breathing. She got hold of my hand and squeezed.

"Feels like the Earth's moving fast," she said, "like you got to hold on, even if you're lying down."

"The Earth *is* moving. It's flying round the sun, through space, right now."

She turned to me, with that hunger-for-facts look back in her eyes again. "How fast?" she said, testing me.

"About eighteen miles a second."

"Shut the front door! No. Way. How do you know all that shit?"

"You know I like physics. Space. Stars. I love all that stuff."

"I must pay more attention in class," she said.

"Yeah, or some attention."

"Eighteen miles a second… We really need to hold on then," she said, all fake serious. We both spluttered. And that was the end of any talk for a bit. We couldn't stop laughing. By the end I was laughing at nothing. Just the sound of her giggling would set me off again. We laughed till my sides ached.

Tess got up and walked off, like she was disgusted.

I was gone. Lost. Deep in the ocean.

★

It took a long time to stop wheezing and calm down. She'd taken us somewhere else. I'd forgotten all about her dad. For a bit. But once the weed wore off a bit, what I'd seen hung between us like this unspoken thing: a nasty, hard-edged bit of reality. We'd gone down deep, but you have to come up for air sooner or later. And there it was. What I'd seen. Bob with his arm raised, about to hit her. And there was no point keeping it a secret, or ignoring it, and she knew it.

"I do things. Surf, stay out. Too much. And he acts like he cares. But he doesn't give a shit, and it winds me up, so I act like a bitch."

"Least you've got a dad," I said. It just came out. I didn't think about saying it; I just *did*. I sat up, looking at the sea. She sat up too. She cocked her head, like a dog that was curious.

"He died, didn't he? Your mum told my dad."

"Yeah."

"Wanna talk about it?"

"Don't mind. I was only four. I never really knew him."

"How'd he die? You don't have to talk about it if you don't want to."

But I think *she* did. It was like the science stuff; she seemed really keen.

"We don't know exactly," I said. "He just disappeared one day." It came out bitter. More than I had expected.

"Well… if he disappeared, he could still be alive?" she said, confused.

"No. It happened at sea, in a storm. He must have drowned."

"Where?" she said.

I looked at the glass sea. It was calm. So calm you couldn't picture it ever being different. Like you couldn't imagine the things it could do.

I pointed at the ocean.

"Out there."

14

I KNEW A FEW things about Dad, but not much about how he'd died. I couldn't ever raise it with Mum without getting her upset. Only, being here, it made me want to know. I don't know why, exactly. I mean, it didn't upset me, him being dead. I'd been so young. But getting to know this place, getting to know the cliffs and beaches and the sea... Suddenly I could picture it: him setting out from the shore. The waves closing over him. It made it all real. Not just a story Mum told me any more.

I wanted to know what had happened.

Mum was a dead end. But I reckoned Grandma would tell me. Later that day, I cycled over to her house.

"Hello, young man," she said, at the door. She looked behind me, checking for Mum and Tegan. "I wasn't expecting you. You should have called." She looked tired, smaller somehow.

A grey shadow lurked beneath her tanned skin. Her eyes were watery and weak where they'd been bright and fierce before. She was wearing a scarf on her head like normal, jeans and an old shirt and sandals.

"Yeah, sorry. Is it okay?" I said.

Her smile chased away the illness, just for a few seconds.

"Of *course* it's okay. Come in."

She took me to the lounge and left me sitting on the giant leather sofa, while she went and made tea.

It struck me again how it was everything our house wasn't. Lots of light and space. Our house was a jungle of crap Mum had bought on eBay. I wondered what this house would look like with all our junk in it. I couldn't picture it.

When she came in with the tea, she sat in her old, worn armchair, asked me the usual stuff about school and friends. I only gave half-arsed answers. She guessed what was on my mind. She got round to talking about Dad before I did.

"So, did you want more of his things?"

"Yeah. I'd like some of his navigational equipment. It's pretty cool. Stuff they had to use before GPS and mobile phones. I like the maps and charts… but I wanted to ask… not so much about his stuff, more about…"

"How he died?"

"How did you guess?"

"It's a question anyone would want to know the answer to. You want to know if there is more to the story than your mother has told you." I liked Grandma, but she couldn't help

113

getting a dig in at Mum, whenever she could. It was subtle, under the surface, but always there. Still, she sat upright, sipping her tea, like she was grateful for it, so maybe being angry at Mum made her feel that bit more alive too. "There's not much I can tell you that you won't already know."

"He disappeared. That's *all* I know. Went out on his boat one day, didn't come back."

She put the tea down, and sat back. She grimaced slightly, and I wondered if she was just tired, or in pain. She looked out of the window, at the sea and blue sky.

"She didn't tell you more than that?" she said.

"No. Nothing. She won't talk about it."

She took a deep breath.

"It was a cold, clear spring day. He came round here for his breakfast. Poached eggs on toast, strong coffee and orange juice. His favourite."

"Why did he come here? Why didn't he have breakfast at home?"

"Two reasons," she said, carefully. "Firstly, he had to get some stuff from upstairs. He stored it here because your mother said there wasn't room in your little house in Penzeal. And... I think they might have been arguing," she added.

"Why?"

"I don't know. But I know she was putting pressure on him to move to London. She said this was a dead-end place to bring you up." The way Grandma said 'she' was like she was spitting out poison. "I think sometimes he went to sea just to get away from her." She stopped then, like she was surprised at what she'd said. "I'm sorry, Sam, it's not for me to tell you these things really."

"No, please. I want to know," I said. And I did. "Mum never talks about it. She folds her arms, tells me the same things, then just says 'I don't know' a lot, and gets upset. So I don't ask. Did he say where he was going that day? What he was doing?"

"He might have been taking readings. He had a contract with the coastguard, doing surveys of some sort. Or he might just have been going out fishing or diving or just sailing. Or looking for wreck locations. He had a lot of theories about that. He reckoned he could take old logbooks and with modern equipment he could find out where they were. He had some idea to find a ship that had gone down, full of treasure. You see, there's hundreds of wrecks out there." She stared out the window, at the flat sea. She looked more than tired. Sad. "It doesn't look like a graveyard, does it? But it is. Just a very pretty one. Your father knew that. You know, the police had a good look through all his stuff, but if he had notebooks, charts, cameras, any clue to his whereabouts, it went down with him." She paused. "They asked a lot of questions. They even thought he might have faked his own disappearance. Sailed off to a new life. People do it all the time, apparently."

"But he didn't do that, did he?" I meant it to sound certain, but it came out like a question.

"Your father loved you more than anything in the whole world. He wouldn't have risked going out in bad weather if he had thought there was a chance of leaving you without a father. But there was bad weather that day; it was just unexpected. A ghost storm."

"You said it was a nice spring day?"

"Yes, the first day of spring in fact. It started out nice enough. Then a squall came; a big one…"

"He died on 20th March. The vernal equinox. First day of spring… of course."

"Yes, a bluster of wind at first, and then rain. Then howling, racing winds. I remember going out and grabbing the washing off the line, it came in so quick…"

Grandma carried on talking, but her words blurred into a stream of noise. There was a lot going through my mind. How could they not know? How could no one know? I remembered the chart I'd taken. I wondered if there was anything else useful up in those chests.

I went up there and riffled through shelves, drawers, chests.

There were more charts. But none that had his writing on them. Nothing that offered up any clues. There was a book about wrecks though, a brown and dusty old thing, with tiny print. I took it home with me, and went straight upstairs to find Dad's chart again.

There was the small set of rocks, coloured brown to indicate they were land rather than some feature on the seabed, and next to them, the scrawls in ink I'd read before:

116

X The Excalibur
PN
X The Hope
BZ
X Star Cross
DH

I took out the book I'd brought back with me. It listed Cornish wrecks. I scanned the lists. And there I found…

Excalibur. I flicked to the page. The section told the story of the wreck, and where it had gone down – by some rock called Pendrogeth's Nose. PN – just like on Dad's map.

My guts flipped.

I flicked back to the list and looked up Star Cross. And there it was. The ship had gone down in 1758.

There had been one survivor. Who'd said the Star Cross had been claimed by the Devil's Horns.

DH.

Dad's chart showed the exact location.

*

You don't always need Mind Fuck weed to mess your head up. Sometimes life can do that all by itself.

I couldn't sleep that night. The same merry-go-round of thoughts kept going round my mind.

I wanted to be with Jade.

I wanted to know about Dad.

I was getting into surfing.

Jade was one major reason I surfed.

Jade and the others wanted to surf the Devil's Horns.

I knew where the Devil's Horns were.

Fear makes the wolf look bigger.

Different things, but *connected*. Sometimes there are things that seem like totally different parts of your life. Then you realise they're connected, but all jumbled up together, not making any sense. Not at two in the morning, leastways.

One thing I did know. I was desperate to tell Jade about the Devil's Horns. I was desperate to tell all of them. But nervous too. If I did, they'd go. And I'd go with them. And how did I feel about *that*? Excited? Afraid? I didn't know.

Through the skylight I could see a dusting of stars and a thin crescent moon. I fell into a half-sleep, dreaming, but not with any pattern or story, just a crazy light show of images and thoughts. The Devil's Horns with the moon and stars in the sky behind the lighthouse. My dad standing on the island. A wolf howling at the moon. Jade's hand over my mouth. Lying down. Spinning. Kissing Jade. Needing to hold on.

15

I WAS BURSTING to see Jade again. Almost boiling over with it. I couldn't wait to see her face when I told her about the Devil's Horns. And then we'd pick up right where we'd left things hanging.

The next day was Sunday. Skip rang early, said there was a wave later in the afternoon, but as there was time to kill, did I fancy coming into town and busking? Just for a laugh.

I did. But I had to smooth it with Mum and Teg first.

"I'll get there soon as I can. I'll come with Jade," I said.

"Great. Everyone's in," said Skip. "Even G, though mooching about town shaking tambourines isn't his thing."

Mum was sat at the table in the lounge-dining room with Teg. They had books, pens and sheets of paper spread out in front of them. Mum's hair was nested messily on her head. She wore an old shirt and tracky bottoms. She was smiling, but frowning too, like the smiling was a bit forced. She looked tired. Teg didn't really do lie-ins, so Mum always had to get up early.

"I'm going surfing later… if that's okay," I said.

"You went yesterday, Sam."

"It was flat; we never got a wave," I gabbled. "But it's on later. Is that okay… and all right if… I go to Penzeal before?"

"Really? I thought you might help your sister with some sums and maybe a bit of drawing. I've got stuff to do, you know, much as I love playing endless games of noughts and crosses." Tegan glared at her. Mum leant over and kissed Teg on the top of her head.

"But you're not working today, are you?" I said, suddenly alarmed at the thought of not seeing Jade and the others. Of not going surfing.

"No. I've got the whole weekend off. I'm trying to do as many weekdays as I can. The idea was for us to spend some time together. Remember?"

"Um, yeah." I felt shit right then. Me being out was chaining Mum to the house, to looking after Teg. I wanted to do my bit. But I wanted to see Jade too. I *really* wanted to see her.

Mum raised an eyebrow. "Friday night you were at Jade's. You were at the beach half the day yesterday, then over at Jade's again. Then you went and saw your grandma. When you got in last night you hardly said a word."

"You like Jade, right? You wanted me to make friends?"

"You got in *two hours* late to school the other morning."

"Flat bike tyre, Mum. I told you. Then there was no bus for ages."

"Really. Two hours. I hear Jade was off the same time. Did she have a flat tyre too?"

Crap.

Mum folded her arms, looked at me steady. She wasn't going to make a big fuss. But she *was* giving me a warning.

"I don't want to hear about any more flat tyres," she said.

"I'll go to town later," I said. I sat down. "Teg, what shall we do?"

"Yay. Star Wars Lego!"

Mum stood. She kissed me on the top of the head just like she had Tegan and went off to make tea.

"Nah," I said. "Drawing, writing, making up a story." I picked up a pen.

"What about?"

"An island. And the monster that lives there. And the kids who go there to kill the monster and steal its treasure."

★

I didn't get to town till early afternoon.

PZ's a quirky little place. All kinds of shops and houses, old and new, smart and rough, all mixed up together. They held a farmer's market, every Sunday, late morning, and it was popular.

Rag and the others had set up on the steps of the old town

hall, slap bang between the car park and the market so they could play to the steady stream of people walking by.

Rag thrashed his knackered guitar and belted out a song, pulling faces, like he felt every word of those love songs. Jade banged the tambourine, dancing a bit and singing, "la, la, la," when she didn't know the words.

Jesus, she looked hot. With her messed-up hair swishing about her face as she moved. No make-up. She wore old jeans, a woolly jumper and dirty trainers. She didn't need anything else. Anything else would have been overkill. Like Rag, she sang like she meant it.

Skip and Big G sat on the steps, G looking bored, sipping Red Bull, but Skip tapping his feet and using his skateboard as a drum, clapping and whistling like Rag and Jade were some hot, unsigned act and he was in the know.

A lot of silver coins and a fair catch of yellow ones were slowly filling up Rag's filthy up-turned cap. And yeah, it might have had *something* to do with how Jade swung her hips. I went to put a twenty-pence piece in the hat myself, just for a laugh.

Rag was near finishing a song when he saw me walking up. He added an extra – new – verse:

> *Here comes young Sam*
> *He's fond of eating ham*
> *And farting and wanking with his left hand*
> *But he don't give a fook*
> *Because he's such a bloody kook!*

He finished the song with a flourish of thrashing guitar.

"Niiiiice, Rag," I said, slow-clapping. "You worked on those lyrics long?"

"This'll surprise you, but I just made them up on the spot," he grinned. They seemed pleased to see me, apart from Jade, who didn't say anything, but went to sit on the steps, with a match in her mouth, looking at the people walking by. Had I done something wrong? It didn't make sense. Rag and Skip kicked off arguing about what the next song should be. Big G took himself off to roll a fag. I went and joined Jade.

"Hi, you," I said.

"Oh, hi, Sam. How's your gran?"

"Good. You'll never guess what I found there. You should come over, meet her and…"

"Nah. I'm not one for family shit. Should be a good wave this afternoon."

She gave me a flash of a smile, then looked back at the crowd.

All the words about the Devil's Horns stuck in my throat.

It wasn't what she'd said; it was how she'd said it. Sounding like a bored checkout girl.

"Yeah," I said, "better than *yesterday*." But when I said 'yesterday' I meant, *Remember that, Jade? Yesterday? The tor?* "I've got something to show you," I said, thinking about the chart.

"Sure, later," she said. Those same eyes that had begged me to kiss her on the tor looked cool and uninterested. She stood up, and went off to join G. She took his rolly off him and took a drag. He said something, she laughed, she said something back, she punched his shoulder. How they talked to each other was warm, friendly and fun. And it pissed me right off.

The truth hit me like a wave. My world had exploded. Hers hadn't. I was different. She was the same.

When they started playing again, I went and sat with Skip and Big G and did a bad job of looking like I was enjoying myself.

There was no point asking her. But why? Why was she like that?

We'd been there about twenty minutes when Billy – the guy from the beach the day before – went by with two girls. Him and his girlfriends were different from our gang. They totally milked the surf look. Zip-up top-brand hoodies, sunnies. Billy was wearing a Billabong baseball cap. He'd put it on backwards, the twat. The girls had long, blonde, silk hair, short skirts and plenty of leg on show.

Billy didn't have Mick with him though, and I was pretty pleased about that. He nodded at Skip and Big G, but pulled a face when he looked at Rag, and stuck his fingers in his ears as he walked by. Which was harsh. Rag was good. Skip stopped drumming on his skateboard, hunched his shoulders and found something on the floor to look at. He didn't want trouble.

Rag changed the tune and thrummed the old guitar harder and sang louder. But Billy and the girls carried on. They didn't see Big G making his fist into a 'wanker' sign, or Jade giving the finger to Billy's back. They walked away.

But then Billy stopped. Just froze, not turning back, but listening. Till Rag had finished his song. He came back, with the girls in tow. He walked straight up to Rag.

"You do requests, Rag?" said Billy, waving a five-pound note in Rag's face.

"Sure," said Rag, eyeing up the fiver. "Something for the lay-deez, praps?"

"Yeah. Just for them." Billy put the note in the hat. Then he reached out and put a hand over the strings on the neck of the guitar, and put a finger to his lips. "Shhh," he said.

He was paying Rag *not* to sing. He walked off to his girlfriends, with a smug smile.

"That's cold, man. Really, really cold," said Rag, shaking his head. He laughed, but it was bitter. Jade stood there, looking at Billy with her hands on her hips. Big G stood up and stared, unblinking, still as a statue. I stayed on the steps, stuck to them like I was glued there.

Skip leapt up, moving to get the fiver out of the hat.

"Tosser, eh?" he said. "I'll give him his money back." But Jade put her foot on the hat before Skip could get to it.

"No," she said. "Rag, play it loud, yeah?"

Rag launched into a punk song. He could make any song sound pretty, but this was ugly on purpose.

Billy turned. He came back to us, still smiling. He leant over the hat, but the fiver was gone. I hadn't even seen anyone take it, but I just knew it was Jade.

There were a lot of us, and he was alone, apart from the

girls. He gave Rag a look that said: *Another day*. For now the joke was on him. And he deserved it.

Jade stared at his back so hard as he walked away, I'm surprised he didn't feel it. She had a look in her eyes. Like she was planning trouble.

I didn't need the day getting any worse. I was thinking we'd go for a surf, and end up at Tin-mines, making a fire, and after a few cans we'd start talking about the Devil's Horns. And I'd tell them what I knew. I'd go home with Jade, maybe even go to the tor, and she'd loosen up, and we'd get back whatever we'd lost since yesterday. And it would all be okay. A chart of the Devil's Horns. I'd be a fucking hero.

But Jade was still looking at Billy, her face a mask of hate. She looked ugly. For her. He was walking off now; all I needed to do was distract her.

"Hey, Jade," I whispered, "why don't we go back up the tor, tonight, just you and me? I've got something to tell you."

She didn't turn to look at me. It was like she hadn't heard what I'd said.

She walked off quickly, following Billy. She went straight up behind him and booted him up the arse. Hard.

He turned.

"What?" he said, mock-laughing. Jade spat on the floor, and fronted up, looking like a guy wanting a fight. She pushed him. He couldn't *do* anything; she was a girl. But he wasn't going to do nothing either. Jade and Billy stared at each other, each looking for the next move. They just stood there. Waiting.

One of the girls tried to drag Billy away, but he shrugged her off.

Big G stood up, sighing. He looked at Rag, with his big soft, cow eyes, and spoke with his big, soft, gentle voice.

"How much is that guitar worth, Rag?"

"Naff all. Why?" G took the guitar off Rag and held it by the neck. He examined it with a long look, then walked up to Jade and Billy.

"I think you broke Rag's guitar," G said to Billy.

Billy held his hands up, palms out, shrugging, doing a laugh like he was about to say, "No biggy, let's sort this out quickly." He didn't get a chance to speak though. He didn't get a chance to do anything.

Big G swung the guitar like a baseball bat, straight at Billy's head.

Billy got an arm up and the guitar smashed on his elbow. The force knocked him to the floor. A sick, broken chord rang out from the guitar.

We ran over.

I felt sorry for Billy, really sorry for him. His eyes were wide with shock. He hadn't expected that. No one had.

"Okay, okay," said Billy, panting, holding a hand up in case G hit him again. His girlfriends picked him up and walked him off, as quickly as they could.

"You're gonna fucking suffer for this," one of them said over her shoulder.

I reckoned Billy had been hurt. Inside and out. If he hadn't got an arm up, we'd be calling an ambulance. G had really tried to brain him.

Fights have rules. This was different. It was *sudden*, full-on violent. I'd never seen anything like it.

We had a crowd around us now. We had more attention than when we were busking.

"Now we got World War Three," said Skip. "What the fuck? What the fuck? What the fuck?" he said, over and over, with his hands on the side of his head. He was almost crying. Rag took the broken guitar off G. He kept looking at the guitar and at G, and back again.

"You broke it, G," he said, like he couldn't believe it.

Big G was calm. Still as a mountain.

And Jade?

"Well, that was intense," she said, smoothly, folding her arms. She looked like a cat that had been given a massive bowl of cream.

I stood on the outside of the gang. I looked at Jade.

And I wondered who she was.

16

I SHOULD HAVE walked away. Right there, right then. I hadn't told Jade or any of them about the Horns yet. And I didn't have to. I could have walked away, before I got too involved.

But Rag's brother Ned rang and offered us a lift to a good spot on the south coast. The timing was perfect. It wouldn't have been smart to hang around in town. Just in case anyone had reported what they'd seen to the police.

"You in?" said Rag.

"Sure," I said, "why not."

I should have walked away.

I went surfing.

★

Ned came to get us in his battered pick-up: a white, ancient wreck, streaked with rust and coughing fumes. Then we drove around everyone's houses, picking up kit.

Ned and his girlfriend, Sue, sat in the cabin, dry and warm, with all of us scrunched up in the open back of the pick-up, with boards and suits and towels. When it started raining, we used the boards as shelter. Compared to the sunshine of the first few weeks in Cornwall, it felt like autumn was coming proper. November was a couple of days away. The sky and water had gone a sudden, serious grey. The wind was harsh. My old summer suit wasn't really right any more, not on a cold day, but they helped me out with a thermal rash vest and boots.

When we hit the coast we got off the road and drove down a track through a muddy field of cabbages to get to the cliff. On one side of the bay was a grim, tall cliff, keeping the wind off, and on the other side a long headland, sloping into the water.

There were at least twenty surfers in the water, some right up against the headland, looking for the bigger waves peeling off the rock there, others tucked in behind the cliff, picking off smaller surf.

There was no beach, no path. Getting in the water meant climbing down over the slippery rocks, carrying boards. I watched where the others put their feet, how they balanced their boards. It took a lot of focusing not to fall over.

At the water's edge there was one long boulder, which they used as a jump-off point. It was only big enough for two surfers at a time, so they took it in turns, waiting for gaps in the sets, then jumping into the grey water and paddling like crazy so the head-high waves wouldn't smack them back on to the rocks.

I thought I'd go with Jade, but she was first in. Then Ned and Sue, then Skip and Rag. It was Big G who stayed back, standing next to me.

"You just started, right?" he said, as we watched Rag and Skip steaming into the water.

"Yeah."

"But you're okay with this?"

"Yeah," I said.

A surfer took a wave right next to the headland, mis-timed it, and got slammed. I watched him getting churned over, the wave carrying him like a piece of driftwood towards the rocks. He came up after a few seconds, a look of wild fear on his face, and paddled out before another big wave came, just making it over the crest. He was fine. Just. Big G had a sick grin on his face, like he was thinking, *Let's see how you handle this.* Without any kind of sign he was about to do it, he threw himself off the rocks, into the water.

I knew better than to wait. I jumped too.

Like G, I got straight on my board and gave it all I had. I even kept up with him. But then, right in front of us, was a wall of water. It came out of nowhere. He took a breath, leant forward on his board, pushed the nose of his board down, into the water, and dived. My board was too big for me to do a

131

duck dive, so I pushed it down as hard as I could, and braced myself. The wave broke, sending an avalanche of white froth down on me. It took me back a few feet but I was soon back at it, using my new muscles to get the board forward, fast as I could. G looked surprised. Maybe surprised I wasn't a bloody stain on the reef.

He followed the guys in our gang, over to the headland. I joined a small huddle of girls and some groms like me in the calmer part of the bay, under the cliff. Sue was there too, on a long board. I'd done so much surfing by myself, it was weird having to keep an eye out all the time, for who was going when a wave came, for who was already on one I wanted to get. There were clearly rules when there were loads of surfers in the water. I just didn't know what they were.

I surfed okay, picking up the smaller late breakers the pack didn't bother with, getting on the shoulder of waves that had already broken, or where a surfer had already come off.

In between rides, I had time to watch the others. I swear, even if you didn't know them, you could tell a lot about them just from how they surfed: Rag, making easy-going swoops on his longer board; Skip, full of energy, tucking in to the power pocket on every ride. And – of course – Jade and G in the heart of it, jostling into waves that weren't always theirs to take, paddling round older surfers and into the take-off point so they could claim it was theirs. And getting away with it. Because they were good. Really good.

G and Jade. Ripping it up, making impossible moves, up,

down, into the air… right into the air… flying, turning, grabbing a rail, crouching, riding back into the juice.

It looked impossible.

I wondered if I'd ever surf like that.

Shit, I was jealous.

They were in the pack, a good fifty metres away. From where I was near the cliff, I could watch them take off and surf almost to where I sat with the other groms. They'd kick off the back of the wave before they got to us, then paddle back out, around and back into the line up. It wasn't like the beach break I was used to surfing. The waves here broke mechanically, in the same spot, peeling down the reef in the same way each time. Like clockwork. It was easy for the surfers to know where they were going to break, and – apart from the get-in point – easy to avoid other surfers, as they could paddle round them. There was none of the relentless paddling through white water you got on a big day on a beach break.

Big G took one wave that had marched out of the ocean from a long way off. When he paddled out quick to get in the right place, no one else bothered to even try. It was moving super fast, but he caught it easy. It had enough power in it to make a long green wall, right across the bay. A skate ramp for him to play on. He rode it in S shapes, up the wave, turning, coming back, then turning again when he hit the breaking part. He was headed straight for me, but then he twisted hard, the fins missing my leg by inches, spraying water in my face.

He landed with his chest on his board – a neat trick – and paddled out.

I felt like a dog had run up and slashed on me. And what he'd done looked deliberate. I paddled after him.

"Hey!" I shouted.

"Yeah?"

"What was that about?"

"Surfing," he said. I was up for asking him what his problem was, but then he pulled up and sat on his board. A green wall was rising up over the reef. It hadn't broken near the headland, so no one was on it. He turned round, and went for it. His way of saying our little chat was over.

I could have paddled over it and let him get on with it. But I was pissed off. I decided *I* was going. I sat up, turned around, dug my hands into the water and went at it. It was nuts: he was a surfer; I wasn't. But I had the bigger board and thought I might just get on it before he did. And if I did, I reckoned it was mine.

I lost sight of him. I paddled, getting into it as the surge picked me up, then I made two big strokes, and the wave took me. I popped up, landed my feet, turned and rode straight into a nice, steep wall of green.

"Hey!" G said, from behind me. I was on the wave. And laughing inside. I'd left him in the foam.

"Hey," he shouted again. But this time, his voice was right behind me.

He'd got the wave too and was shooting straight at me.

I had a second to think, *Oh shit,* before I felt a heavy thud in my back. I was thrown from the board. The world went dark.

I went under, churning over and over. But not just getting battered by water. Big G was right there with me. His knees or foot or elbow went deep in my ribs, my board hit my head and my back hit the bottom of the reef. Hard. It was like being in the usual washing machine, but this time with bricks in it. There was nothing to do but hold on and take the pasting.

After a few seconds, we separated and I came up. The sea and sky were spinning round. I was a little numb, and sore, but I was in one piece and nothing hurt too bad. There was no blood in the water. Big G was already paddling off. I did a quick check on the board. By some miracle it hadn't been dinged. Then I went after him.

Jade was cruising down a wave, heading right at me. She threw herself off it, then got back on her board. I ignored her. I was set on getting after Big G. I paddled and paddled, but I was in slo-mo, going nowhere. It took me a few seconds to suss Jade had a hold on my leash and I was flapping in the water like a fish in a net.

"Let go. Did you see—" I started.

"You dick. What you playing at?"

"What am *I* playing at?"

She shook her head and went after Big G, leaving me catching my breath, and wondering what the fuck had just happened.

It was only when I was back in the little gang with the

other groms and someone said "bad drop in" that I figured I'd done something wrong. There were a lot of embarrassed looks, a few shaking heads.

Surfing alone and surfing in this maze were clearly two different things. I didn't like G much right then, and I still wanted to ask him what his problem was. But for some reason, I'd been in the wrong – not Big G, *me* – and I reckoned I'd look even more stupid if I pushed it further.

"Don't feel bad, man," said Skip paddling over to me. "Let me tell you the rules." He told me about who had rights on any one wave, depending on how it was breaking and where the surfer put themselves. I listened. I *forced* myself to listen.

"Okay, okay, I get it. They didn't say anything about this yesterday when we were training."

"What kind of training?" said Skip.

I told him about Whitesands, about the jumping. His eyes gaped open with horror.

"You did… *what*?"

"It was no biggy; it was fun. Everyone does it, don't they? You've done it, right?"

"*No!* There was a kid from Truro tombstoned it three years back. He smashed his spine. He still can't walk properly. And, if you hold your breath that long you can pass out… and drown."

"Jade and G do it all the time."

He shook his head. "Be careful. They're both mates, I don't want to slag them off, but they'll get you in more shit than

136

you can imagine, trust me. And…" He looked away, noticing something on the shore. "Who's that?" he said, pointing to the rocks, where we'd got in.

A surfer had got out of the water and was standing on the rocks, waving at us. He did a thumbs up.

"Dunno," I said. We did the same, just not to be rude I guess. When he saw our thumbs up, he put his hand to his throat and drew it across like it was a knife. Ice ran through me.

"What's that about?" I said. "Something to do with me?"

Skip shook his head. "Doubt it. It was G you pissed off. No one else. Weird." We kept watching the guy, but he didn't look at us again. He climbed up to the cliff and disappeared.

We surfed another half hour. The tide dropped, leaving the waves closing on to a pebble beach. At least it would be easy to get out, I thought. At the end, our gang were the only ones in the water. After ten minutes of no waves, and under a sky that was getting dark, we made our way in and back to the van.

I was last, with Skip. Ahead of us I could see Ned stamping around. And the others – Jade, Rag, Big G, Sue – all stood around the van in a half-circle, with their heads down.

"Great. Just really great," Ned shouted. They were staring at a very flat tyre.

"You got a spare?" said Skip.

"Yeah, Skip, I got a spare," said Ned, sounding narked, "but I ain't got two!"

137

Someone had slashed both the front tyres, leaving us stranded, a quarter mile from the main road.

Me and Skip looked at each other. We had the same thought. The guy who had drawn his hand across his throat. But neither of us said anything.

"It's because of earlier, isn't it?" said Big G. Skip rolled his eyes. Jade shot him a look. Rag grabbed his bag out of the back of the truck and walked off to get changed.

"What happened?" said Ned. No one answered. "Rag?"

Rag was busy with his towel and bag of clothes. "Not my bad," he said.

"Rag, what happened?" said Ned.

"Ask Big G."

"I'm asking *you*."

Jade stepped in before Ned got to Rag, folding her arms and looking at Ned, pretty much as she'd looked at her dad when he was drunk. Or at Billy. Defiant.

"St Wenna," she said. That was all the explanation Ned needed. He rolled his eyes and threw his hands up to the grey sky.

"Brilliant. Who? How many?"

"They started it," said Jade, suddenly going from defiant to looking innocent as she could, which wasn't much.

"And?" said Ned.

"I finished it," said G. Ned nodded, folded his arms.

"Right. I want details."

They all told him, in bits, talking over each other, bigging up how nasty Billy had been, how Big G had had to do *something,* else it would have turned into a scrap between Jade and Billy. How it had all totally, and without any doubt, *not* been their fault.

When Ned had the full picture, he went and picked up his board, and put it in the back of the truck. "I don't like aggro. I don't want to find out who slashed my tyres and then do the same to their face. I don't want to. But if this kicks off, I may have to." He pointed at each of us in turn. "If you want to avoid that, then you have to sort it out with the St Wenna mob. I don't care how you do it. G, you're the smartest in this gang of lemons. And you kicked it off. So you're in charge. This gets sorted. Understood?"

"Yeah. Understood," said Big G.

Ned and a shivering, very pissed off Sue went into the truck cabin to find a phone and start ringing round Ned's mates for help.

"What we going to do?" said Rag.

"Nice one, G," said Skip.

"It wasn't my fault, man," said G, shaking his head and spitting into the mud.

"I don't think it was anyone's fault," I said.

"You were as much use as you were in the water." G was talking about my drop in.

"I didn't know," I said. "You didn't have to take that wave."

"Twat. Why didn't you just get off it?" G pushed me on the shoulder. A little push. Nothing really, but like everything he did it felt like it was designed to test me. So I pushed him back. Harder.

That surprised him. Especially as he was a good half a foot taller than me, and much wider. He thrust his chest out, lifted his chin. His eyes flashed anger. Then everyone was talking at once. Arguing about my drop in, about what had happened that afternoon, about the tyres. And G was squaring up. Arms at his side, eyes drilling into me. I saw his arm come up, ready to push me again. Just that little bit harder. Then I'd push him. I wanted to. And there'd be a fight. I'd lose. But right then I didn't care.

Jade stepped into the middle of us all.

"Shut up. All of you. Let's just wait for the tyres to get fixed, get changed, calm the fuck down. We'll go to the cafe at Lanust. We can talk there."

"But I gotta get home," Skip complained.

"No one's going home till we have a plan," said G. "Apart from Sam. This isn't his problem. Right, Sam?" He looked right at me.

The others looked at me too, to see how I'd react.

"It's fine," I said. I could feel how hard I was glaring at G, how hard I was breathing. "I'm in."

Sue had thrown all our bags and towels out of the cabin. We picked them up and sulked off to our own spaces to get changed. And to calm down.

17

TWO OF NED'S mates turned up in a bongo van. One of them stayed to help change the tyres, the other gave us a lift to the cafe at Lanust.

The cafe was in a converted church, near the clifftop. It was big. There were lots of wooden tables and a huge black wood burner right in the middle of the place, with a glass front you could watch the fire through. It was the right place for surfers that were cold and starving hungry.

We ordered hot chocolate and bowls of chips.

It was cosy, and it should have been nice, but there was an edge to the group that wasn't going to make talking easy. All round, the day hadn't gone too well. No one even talked about the waves. Everyone was hacked off. Apart from Jade. She sat on the edge of her seat with her elbows on the table, smiling that cat-with-the-cream smile, getting off on the whole drama.

The drinks appeared along with bowls of fat, crispy chips. Without asking anyone how they liked them, Rag and Jade drowned them with vinegar and ketchup and threw a ton of salt on them. I ate and drank quickly, sucking up the heat into my shivering body. The thermal rash vest had helped, but the suit still leaked.

"Okay," said G, "Billy had it coming, and Rag's one of us. I ain't sorry about any of it."

"But you heard what Ned said," said Skip. "Now we have to make like we're sorry. And that's that."

G shrugged. "Sounds weak to me. We don't have anything to be sorry for."

"Right," said Jade. Rag raised his eyebrows, shaking his head. He didn't want aggro. And I was with him. But however it turned out, I'd feel like a *real* kook if I didn't join in or help out.

"Anyone got any ideas?" said Big G.

No one did. After a minute of eating in silence, Big G said, "The St Wenna lot smoke that shit like you, right?" He looked at Rag. "One of us goes up there, next weekend, gives them a big bag, says I was out of order and we don't want any hassle."

"Did you say 'smoke that shit like you'?" said Rag. "Like, all of five minutes ago you couldn't get enough."

"Cutting down. Gets in the way of my surfing. You should give it a rest too. Look at Ned. He ain't exactly an advert." The others laughed but Rag sighed, and pushed the bowl of chips away, like he'd suddenly stopped being hungry.

"Handy right now though, eh? Now you want a bag of it. And say I give them a load of weed. *I* didn't *do* anything. My guitar's screwed and I'm out by… what, quarter or half an ounce?"

"We'll all pitch in," said Big G.

Rag threw two chips at G, to let him know just how bad an idea he thought that was. It wasn't the kind of thing I thought Big G would take, but he didn't get angry; he just picked one of the chips off his jumper, and ate it.

"Anyone got any better ideas? Ones that don't involve us getting our heads kicked in?" He waited. "No? That's sorted then." He picked up two chips from his own bowl, and threw them at Rag.

After a bit more talking about options, we settled into uncomfortable silence. Big G had a lame plan, but the only one we had that would get this sorted, and keep Ned happy. And everyone knew it.

"So who goes?" said Jade. "Rag?"

"If Rag goes, Billy'll be a bastard to him," said G, "and that isn't happening. I'm the one that decked Billy. I'll go."

"Yeah. Sure," said Skip. "You'll say sorry. Billy'll make some smart-arse comment, you'll knock his teeth out and then they'll put you in hospital."

"Skip," said Rag. "It's you or me, mate. Both of us?"

Skip stuttered, panicking. "It could kick off. They might not want to make peace, they might fight, we might…"

"I'll go." Me and Jade said it at exactly the same time.

"I'm a girl; it's less likely to end up nasty," said Jade.

"And they don't know me," I said.

"Fight you for it?" said Jade, winking at me.

"We'll both go," I said.

"You up for this then, Kook?" she said, daring me, like 'this' could mean any kind of mischief.

"Yeah, why not."

Big G glared at me. I don't think he liked the idea, but even he knew it made a horrible kind of sense. Jade couldn't go alone. And if any of the others went, it could go south quickly.

He looked around the table, to see if anyone else was going to say it should be them. Then to see if anyone had a better idea. Then to see if anyone thought it was even a *bad* idea. But Rag and Skip were nodding and smiling at me, more than happy that I'd take the bus to St Wenna instead of them.

Rag had a sneaky look over his shoulder to see if the woman at the counter was watching, then he magicked a half bottle of cheap brandy from his bag and hid it under the table.

"'Scuse me," he shouted to the woman at the counter, putting on a poncey voice, "six more of your very fine hot chocolates, please, Madame."

Everyone sat back, relaxed. This was going to get sorted, and me and Jade would do all the work.

"This'll be fun," said Jade, grinning.

18

IT WAS A WEEK before we got up to St Wenna to see Billy and his mates.

Nights that week I sat at my desk in my attic bedroom, with the dark outside and the wind and rain knocking, like they were trying to get in. Me staring at my school books. Not working.

Why was I getting involved? What was I getting involved *in*?

I asked myself that again and again. I still hadn't told Jade about the chart, about the Horns. Something in me was holding back. Because once she'd seen that chart...

Why *was* I getting involved? *Why?*

Because fear makes the wolf look bigger. Just like it said on the graffiti on Rag and Ned's garage wall.

These thoughts went round my head like a dog chasing its tail and never catching it.

The only other thing I thought about was Jade. Jade in her jeans and T. Jade's skin. Jade's lips. Jade's body... in a wetsuit that showed every curve and muscle, hugging her like a second skin.

It didn't take much to imagine her without a wettie. And I did imagine. A lot.

★

Jade came round Thursday, after tea, with Tess.

"Coming for a walk?" she said, standing at the door. She'd never asked me on a weekday before. I guessed maybe she wanted to talk about the trip we had planned.

"It's getting dark," I said. "Anyway, Mum's working. I'm looking after Tegan."

"She can come too."

Teg appeared, squeezing between me and the door, and heading straight for Tess.

"Yes, Sam. Let's go. Please," said Tegan.

Grey clouds and hard rain had swept through the sky for days. But that evening the sky was clear, with a bright full moon, shining on the moors.

"Yeah, Sam. Please," said Jade, joining in. Lots of girls wouldn't have wanted a tag-along-Teg, but Jade liked my sister.

"Okay," I said. We put on coats and hats and wellies, and headed up the hill, towards the tor.

Tess had a split-open old tennis ball. Tegan threw it for her, but couldn't chuck it far, so they played throw-fetch every few

146

seconds. The thing was covered in dog slobber, but Tegan didn't seem to mind. It didn't look like either of them would get tired of the game any time soon.

Then Jade found a big stick. She threw the ball in the air and, using the stick as a bat, belted the ball for miles. Tess ran off to get it. Teg followed.

"Been stormy, Sam," said Jade. "Proper swell's coming now. Could be a good winter. Your first."

"Yeah," I said. There'd be bigger waves. More hold-downs. More danger. The storms were coming. And God knows what else too. A lot had happened. Quickly. It had all got a bit heavy. All because Jade couldn't stop herself booting Billy up the arse.

The trip to St Wenna. The chart. They sat in my thoughts all the time. More dogs with tails. And how Jade had been on the tor. How she'd been in town. How she changed, quicker than the weather.

Could I trust her? Did I even know her? I thought maybe I'd just come straight out and ask her what was going on between us. Something? Nothing? Maybe tell her about the Horns.

But then Teg reappeared, with Tess, panting. The moment was gone.

"Can we have a dog?" said Teg.

"Ask Mum," I said. Teg took the ball out of Tess's mouth and ran off giggling, with Tess following, trying to get it off her. Jade stared at them, studying them like she did waves.

"What's it like? Having a sister?" she said.

"Pain in the arse."

"Don't believe you. I see the mums with their brats in Aldi. She's not like them; she's cool."

"I guess so. Dunno how it would be if it was just me and Mum. Not very peaceful. You reckon your family's messed up? Me and Teg are from two different dads. Mine's dead. Teg never sees hers. Mum's stressed all the time. If she didn't need Grandma's money, we wouldn't even be here…"

Jade jolted at that. She glared at me. She spoke in almost a whisper.

"And how is it, Sam? Being here." She was a bit accusing, like maybe I was saying I was forced to be here, like I was just making do.

"It's the best thing that ever happened to me," I said, looking straight at her. She smiled at that. She shone with how much she smiled.

"Good," she said, looking away.

Teg and Tess came back, panting even harder.

"Jade, can I come for a walk with you and Sam and Tess again?"

"Sure. Any time you like," said Jade. Then she turned to me. "You're lucky, Sam. Really."

★

When Saturday came, it was a massive relief to finally get on the bus to St Wenna. I had a bag of Rag's finest, heavily wrapped up and stuffed down my underpants. It felt like a nasty weight to carry. A possible criminal record. I couldn't wait to be rid of it. But apart from that, I was looking forward to the trip. Me, Jade, surfing (we had our boards and wetties with us, plus boots and hoods). It'd be a good day once we'd done the business.

The road ran along the coast. The moors weren't spattered with colour any more. Now there was nothing but dull brown and green, carved into squares by the old stone walls, and on the other side, the sea, the same flat grey as the sky.

The bus was empty, apart from an old woman and kid up the front. Me and Jade landed our bags and boards on the back seat. I stared out the window, looking forward to getting rid of the weed. She sat on the other side painting shapes on the steamed-up window with her finger.

"Why'd you come?" she said after a while. "You didn't have to."

"Something to do," I said.

"Naaaaah. Don't believe you. Was it cuz of me?" She stopped finger painting and turned to look at me.

I couldn't say yes. I didn't *want* to say yes. But saying no would have been a lie. So I didn't say anything.

"Why?" she said, pressing me.

I folded my arms, kept my eyes on the sea.

"You weren't afraid of this, were you?" she said. "Rag was. Skip too. You went for it."

"I would have felt lame if I hadn't." I shrugged, to let her know it was the only answer I was giving.

"Okay, Kook. Will you tell me something?"

"What?"

"Anything."

That was a weird thing to say. What did she mean, *anything?* Then I noticed what she'd drawn on the window. It wasn't a picture. She'd written something:

$$E=mc2$$

It clicked. She'd remembered what I'd told her on the tor, about energy and matter. She'd been interested. In physics.

"You remembered!" I said, grinning helplessly.

"I googled it," she said, "after what you said about mass and kittenic energy…"

"Kinetic."

"Whatever. I didn't understand it. I must be thick." She stared at her feet.

"E=mc2? There's about five people in the world who understand it."

"And you."

I laughed. "No. I'm just interested… it's mind-blowing, some of that stuff."

"Yeah, proper fascinating… I like you, Kook… I like that you're into that stuff."

"But you're not like that," I said.

"What I am and what I like's two different things. You want mind-blowing? Do you like the Chemical Brothers? They're old school, but their music… *that's* mind-blowing." She pulled her iPod out of her jean-jacket pocket. She put one ear in. My heart dropped. We'd only just got talking and now she was going to put her headphones in? Great.

But that wasn't what she was doing. She offered me the other earphone. And the only way I was going to listen was by coming and sitting right by her, wedged in between her and the boards and bags.

My heart thumped in my throat.

I climbed over the stuff and squeezed in. We sat, with our legs just touching, and our heads close, connected by this tiny white cord. If I looked at her, or she looked at me, we'd be almost kissing, and if I moved away, the earphones would come out, so I sat there feeling her body next to me, like it was radiating sex.

The music started. A whooping sound, not music at all really, electronic, and soft and strange, like hippy tunes you'd hear in a crystal shop. Then the drum started, and the bass. It was dance music, but not like any dance music I'd heard. It took ages to get going, but when it did it had this heavy power. Deep, pulsing waves of music that swam in and out of my head. Music that got into my bones.

"Like it?" she said.

"Yeah, loads."

"Great. You should download some." With one ear in each, we could listen and talk at the same time. "Now tell me some more science stuff. Something. Anything." She turned her head to talk; I felt her breath on my cheek.

I had *no* idea what to say. So I just opened my gob and started babbling.

"You can't really destroy anything. You can't destroy the atoms stuff's made from... You can only recycle stuff... Everything there is... everything... is made up of bits of other stuff that's always been around... The amount of matter in the universe is the same as it's been since the big bang..."

"What's that?" She knew I was uncomfortable. She was enjoying it.

"The birth of the universe, when everything there is now was crushed into something smaller than a ping pong ball, a pinhead, infinitely small, infinitely hot, infinitely dense and it... exploded..." I almost cracked up.

"Everything there is was squeezed into a really hot ping pong ball?"

"Yeah."

"Holy fuckerama. No wonder it went bang."

We laughed, turned our heads, took a sly look at each other. We were both nodding in time to the music. We laughed some more.

She took my earphone out and whispered into my ear. "We should have some of that weed. Payment, like. We can get bombed on the way home."

I looked down the bus, to make sure the driver wasn't checking us in the mirror, then got the weed out. The packet was really warm from being down my pants. She took it off me, opened it, took some of the weed, wrapped it back up and handed it back. I had to put it back down *there,* while she watched. It was more than awkward, because I was showing that I was pretty *physically* pleased about sitting so close to her.

Just feeling her there was like having this liquid energy running out of her and straight down to where I was hiding the weed. And she had this badass smile on her face, like she'd seen the growing lump in my trousers and was stopping herself laughing.

Shit, I thought. *How's it possible to be this awkward* and *happy at the same time?*

19

THERE WAS NO ONE in the water at low tide, so we went hunting for them around the town, carrying our boards under our arms and our wetties in rucksacks.

St Wenna looked like it would be packed in summer. Lots of rent-out cottages on a hill, with fudge shops and cobbled paths, too steep and tight for cars. There weren't any tourists now though, not in autumn; just seagulls crying and the wind howling. Somewhere near I could smell a Chinese start its day's cooking.

It was so empty, it was kind of creepy. And every time we went round a corner I was expecting to see the police waiting with a pair of handcuffs, which was bonkers, but my heart believed it and was thumping the whole time.

We found a gang of them in The Raven, a skanky pub, with a fag-yellow ceiling and beer-smelling carpets. They were out back in the 'garden', a walled-off area with a patch of grass, benches, a couple of tables and one lonely looking palm tree in a pot. Billy was there, and his mate Mick, the guy we'd seen at the beach who'd had been so nice to Jade. Billy sat up, tensed, making ready for whatever was coming. But he relaxed when he saw it was just me and Jade.

All the rest were in their late teens, or older. Girls as well as boys. It hit me how pretty the girls were, California style with long blonde hair, shining teeth and brown legs. Not as pretty as Jade, but honestly, not that far behind.

There was one guy who stood out. He was old, maybe in his forties. Wiry and tanned, with wild brown hair and watery eyes. He sat by himself, with a couple of empty pint glasses in front of him.

The others – the younger ones – were really friendly, and that knocked me sideways. Not what I was expecting at all. The girls swarmed around Jade. Kissed her, hugged her.

"Hey, Jade."

"All right, youngster."

"Nice beanie. Where'd you get it?"

"Who's this?"

"This is Sam," said Jade.

A guy, maybe nineteen or twenty with short blond dreads, stepped right up. He wasn't friendly like the girls were to Jade. But he wasn't *un*friendly either. He wasn't giving anything away. He looked me up and down.

"I'm Tel. That Old Faithful?" he said, nodding at my board.

"Yeah."

"I nicked it from under the lifeguard hut at Gwynsand once. For a bet. That caused a scrap." He smiled, and nodded, like it was a good memory. "Whatcha doing up this way? Surf'll be better at Gwynsand?"

"We've come up to talk about Big G."

"Oh, that. Right." He rolled his eyes. "You'd better come and sit down."

Jade was getting all the attention, but as I walked over to the bench with Tel, I knew I was being watched. I don't know if Billy even recognised me. I ignored him, but I could *feel* him staring. And I was thinking any one of the others could be the guy who'd run his hand across his throat. The guy who'd slashed the tyres.

"You want a drink, Sam? I can get you one," said Tel, starting to roll a cigarette.

"No, thanks." I didn't want us to hang around longer than we needed. But over the other side of the garden, I saw someone had handed Jade a pint of lager.

"Billy told me about what happened in PZ," said Tel. "That G's asking for it, isn't he?"

This wasn't right. I didn't want this just to be about G. He wasn't the only one that had done wrong.

"Did Billy tell you about Ned's tyres?" I said.

"Ned... Ned the shaper? What's this got to do with him?"

I told Tel about Ned's slashed tyres. Tel didn't know about that, or did a good job of pretending. He let out a long breath and lit his roll-up.

"Dude, I seriously don't think that had *anything* to do with Billy, or any of us. I'd know about it." He blew out a stream of smoke. "But let's say, if, for any reason, it did have something to do with Billy, then he's a tit, because we do *not* want any of that kicking off again. Know what I mean?"

He looked me hard in the eyes. It was like he was saying we had a choice. It could go either way.

"Ned told us to sort it," I said. "G started it, and we've come to say sorry."

"Billy's extremely pissed off, Sam. Sorry might not do it."

I looked around, then put my hand down my trousers, pulled out the weed we'd brought and showed it to Tel under the table.

"Will this do?" I said. Tel's eyes lit up like the pub's fruit machine.

"Billy. Come over 'ere!" he called out.

Billy came over. Tel showed Billy the weed under the table, then, after a quick look round, reached over and shoved it into Billy's jacket pocket.

"This thing in PZ with the guitar," said Tel. "And slashing Ned's tyres. Whoever you put up to it. And don't make out you don't know what I'm talking about. You're even. Right?"

Billy just stood there, looking at me. It was hard to tell what he was thinking. He shrugged.

"I said, right?" said Tel. Billy shrugged again, and walked off. But this seemed enough to satisfy Tel.

"You can tell Ned and Rag we'll have some more of that, if it's any good. We'll pay."

He sat back, took a long slug of his beer, and wiped the

froth off his mouth with the back of his hand. He was all smiles now. Business was done.

"Waves will come up on the push, maybe two and a half feet. Bit mushy, but fun. Specially after a pint and a spliff, right? Heh heh. You learning to surf then, Sam?"

And that was it. What I'd been worried about all week was sorted. I made nice to Tel, chatting away about surfing, but inside my head I was breathing a tidal-wave-sized sigh of relief and itching to get out. I hadn't had a fight, hadn't got busted. I had sorted things. I was a fucking hero.

Wolf? What wolf? This was easy. All we had to do now was scarper. Go and have a victory surf.

But Jade was in the corner, sat with Mick, looking settled in. Drinking.

Mick. I didn't even know him and I hated him. He looked pretty much as he had done at the beach. Smart, clean threads, perfect blond hair. And very, *very* interested in every word that came out of Jade's mouth. Bastard.

I didn't want to go and demand we left. So I waited, talking to Tel and his mates.

They all talked about surfing. What else? And were going on about some trip they had planned to Morocco. I don't remember who, but someone had the mag with the pic of the Horns on its cover.

"Don't need to travel to Morocco this winter," said Tel, grabbing the mag off the table and pointing at the cover. "We got this right here!"

"Yeah, but you have to find it," said one of the girls.

"I'll bet we find it and surf it before you lot," Jade shouted, coming out of the little Jade-and-Mick bubble that existed in the corner.

The older, wiry guy spoke up then. He spoke slow and quiet, but everyone listened.

"I been in a boat all round every island between here and the Scillies, fishing like. Spooky, some of those spots. You any idea how many ships and boats are lying on the bottom? Any case, there's no island looks anything like that, not with a lighthouse on it. Take my word for it. And anyways, that's not an English wave. Ireland at least, maybe Portugal."

"We'll find it," said Jade. I noticed her glass was almost empty. She must have necked that pint. "Me, G, maybe Skip," she said.

But she didn't say "and Sam". Why not? I didn't have the years under my belt like the others, but I was learning fast. Why not me too?

"It ain't real," said Billy, scoffing. "You heard Bob."

"It's real," I said, loudly.

"Yeah, cuz you'd know," said Billy.

Mick was pouring some of his drink into Jade's glass. Then he patted her thigh with his hand. She pulled her leg away, pushed his hand away. But gently, smiling.

"We're going to surf it. Right, Jade?" I said, loudly.

She looked up.

"Right on, Sammy boy. I'll drink to that…" She picked up Mick's lager and swigged it. She sounded a bit pissed.

"This is all bull," said Tel. "It's not real, and if it was, no one's going to surf it."

"We are," I said, louder still, staring at Jade. I stood up, grabbed my board and bag. I didn't want to hang out there any longer, watching Mick get Jade drunk. If she came with me, great, but if she stayed, that was her choice.

"Got a map, have you?" said Billy. There were a few laughs at that. I kept looking at Jade.

"A chart. Yeah."

They stopped talking, stopped laughing. No one had expected me to say that. Jade looked at me, saw how serious I was. She got up. She'd suddenly forgotten all about Mick. She'd suddenly forgotten about everything. It was like we were the only ones there.

"Hey, where you going?" said Mick.

Jade walked over, till she stood right in front of me. Close. She whispered. "You got a chart?"

I nodded. It was like on the tor, when I told her about energy. But it wasn't just a switch that had gone on now. I'd lit a fire. And it was raging in her eyes.

Jade picked up her kit.

"Let's go," she said.

I walked out of there buzzing. My skin was on fire I was so happy. We'd made the peace. We were going to surf the Horns.

Everything was sorted.

20

WE DIDN'T GO surfing in St Wenna. The waves weren't good enough to distract Jade from what I'd told her. All she wanted to do was get home and see the chart for herself. On the bus she talked about it non-stop for five minutes, firing questions at me. But then she was quiet, pretty much the whole rest of the journey.

When we got back, I went and got the chart and the book, then went and joined Jade in the den. She was pacing round. Tess too. Poor dog thought we were going for a walk.

"Well?" she said.

I unfolded the chart, and laid it down on the floor. Carefully, because it was fragile. Jade got down on her hands and knees and looked over every inch of the faded ink and sun-washed paper.

"You're sure?" she said. "DH. Devil's Horns."

I knelt beside her, showing her the book, then pointing to different bits of the map. Her hair trailed over my arm. Her breath brushed the back of my hand.

"The initials are islands," I said, my voice wobbling a bit. "The names are shipwrecks. I've looked up everything I can on the net too. I wanted to be sure before I told you. There's records of the wrecks, *and* there's mentions of some of the islands and rocks. I can't know for certain, as they're just nicknames fishermen and sailors gave them. Sometimes two different islands have the same name, or one island has two names. There's lots of mentions of Devil's Horns, but no exact location. But my dad, he was a scientist. That's what he was trying to do, put some proper mapping down. Sort truth from myth. For some reason, he thought the ship that went down at the Horns was in that exact location. Maybe he found something off the wreck."

She sat back, kneeling. I did the same.

"Wow, you're a one, ain't you?" she said, wide-eyed, with her mouth open.

"What d'you mean?"

"You go and rescue a dog when you can't even swim proper. You learn to surf, by yourself. In secret. You're some kind of science professor. You don't bottle smuggling weed, sorting a fight... And now you find the one thing everyone round here is looking for. Anything else I don't know about you, Kook?"

I just smiled.

"Did you see their faces, when we walked out of that pub?"

162

she said. "Shit, that was cool. It's gonna start some talk. I'd look after that chart, if I was you. And don't tell *anyone* where the Horns are. Only us. Swear." She spat on her hand and held it out. I spat into my palm, and we shook. We looked hard into each other's eyes, holding on to each other's hands a moment too long. Then we let go and both turned away, a bit embarrassed, and wiped our hands on our jeans.

"We're really going to surf it?" I said.

"Dunno. Now it's real… actually happening, I don't know if we're ready," she said. "We can tell the surf mags though. They'll send some pros, cameras, jet skis. We'll get a mention as the kids who told them where it was. Hey, maybe they'd let us come and watch?"

"Um, really?" I said.

She rolled her eyes. "No, shit-brains. *Not* really. Course we're gonna fucking surf it. And… what? *What?* Why you looking at me like that?"

Jade all fired up. She looked hot; I couldn't help it any longer. I put my arm round her, pulled her in towards me, and kissed her.

At first she looked terrified, eyes wide and staring. She raised a hand and put it on my chest, keeping me where I was, stopping me getting closer, looking up at me. But she didn't push me away.

I kissed her again.

I felt her soften, the hand on my chest coming up, round my shoulder.

163

Her mouth opening.

For a moment, our tongues touched... Then she pulled away. Breathless.

"I got to take Tess. I'll see you later, yeah?" And she was gone, running away from me as fast as she could. Down the steps, out the door, over the moors. Leaving me wondering.

★

The following morning, me, Jade, Rag and Skip sat in the Old Chapel cafe, fuelling up for the day's surf on toast and mugs of tea. Only Big G was missing. I was glad about that. It was always that bit less intense when he wasn't around. Jade was drinking Red Bull as well as tea. Gallons of it. She was fired up about the Devil's Horns and begging me to show the chart to the others.

Apart from that, she wasn't any different. There was nothing in the way she looked at me, or acted, that said... *We kissed yesterday*.

I laid the chart out carefully on the table. It seemed so fragile it might break up like dry leaves if I didn't treat it right.

"Wow," said Skip, "that's the real deal. Where'd you get it?"

"In my dad's stuff," I said.

Jade looked at me, when I said about Dad. Her eyes were sad, but she gave me a little smile and squeezed my leg under the table. And suddenly it was like we were together again.

I decided not to say anything about what had happened to my dad right then. I didn't want to freak Skip out. I didn't want to scare anyone, or spoil the mood.

Jade and Skip leant over it, reading Dad's writing.

"DH. Devil's Horns," said Skip.

"Told you," said Jade. "Rag, take a look."

"What? Yeah, sure," said Rag, lazily. He didn't even glance at the chart. He just looked round the cafe, smiling stupidly at the families eating their breakfasts.

"Well we don't *know* it's the Horns, do we?" said Skip. "Not for sure, not till we go and have a look." But even if he had doubts, he couldn't hide how excited he was. He drummed the table with his fingers, then he put his glasses on, leant right over, so his nose was almost touching the paper. "That land bit, that's Nanjizal, just south of Land's End. These islands are a few miles south. Surfwise, it's looking good."

"What do you mean?" said Jade.

"See these?" He traced lines on the chart that ran to the islands in long curves. "Those are contours on the seabed. See where there's a load bunched together? That's a trench. Most swells would go over it, sideways. But say there's a storm bringing in a swell from south-south-west, a mean mother that sits out there for a week, kicking up twenty-foot waves. The coastal shelf takes the punch out of it. Saps it. *That's* why Hawaii gets big waves. No coastal shelf, see? Same size storm in the Atlantic, we're lucky to get six foot. But this –" he tapped on the chart – "this trench is a swell funnel. You wouldn't know it was there, but, like I say, if you had the right angle…" His fingers walked up the trench, then he made a cup with his hand like it was a wave. A wave that buried the island.

"Hawaii?" said Jade.

"On our doorstep."

"We can do this; we can totally fucking do this," said Jade. Her eyes were busting out of her skull. She was high as a cloud on Red Bull and sheer stoke.

Skip laughed. "I dunno about *doing* it. I might come and just watch you, make sure you don't kill yourself. What about you, Rag?"

"Yeah, whatever," said Rag. He was still looking round the cafe, not looking any one of us in the eye when we spoke to him. Under the table, one of his legs was bouncing up and down like it had a motor in it. I figured he'd smoked too much weed that morning. Maybe being in this public place was freaking him out a bit.

"I think we should check out the island," said Jade. "Take supplies out there and leave them. Get ready for the day."

"It needs the right kind of storm," said Skip, "and we'll need the right kind of kit. Big wave boards, proper guns, GoPro cameras to get proof. We'll need a couple at least, so we can film the surfing in the water *and* from the island. Some serious camping gear, cans of food and bottles of water, firewood… Oh, and we'll need to get there a day before the big swell hits or the waves'll smash up the boat and spread us over the reef like jam."

It was tricky, but we could do it. If we were lucky, it'd be a weekend when the big waves came. If not, we'd bunk off school.

None of this worried Jade.

"I'm going to ride a big wave and get filmed doing it. That's it." She necked some more Red Bull.

"What do you mean, 'it'?" I said.

"We put the place on the map, and I get famous. Mag covers, sponsors. I'm made."

For Jade, it was that simple. I don't think she was too worried about GCSEs.

"Dunno why you don't just enter contests," said Skip. "You're good enough."

"Too slow," said Jade, waving away the idea. "Takes forever to get cred. But if we surf this place… just one wave, that's all it takes. From now on we're chasing big waves every time a storm hits. We don't run away from swell. Screw surfing sheltered spots, we go full-on wherever there's decent size waves, right? We've got to get in shape. We've got to get used to taking big wipeouts. Get ready for the day." She banged the table. She was totally serious, totally fired up about the plan.

Rag checked the clock on the wall, then stood up. "I'm going for a slash. When someone comes in looking for me, I'm in the bogs."

"What do you mean when…?" Skip looked at me, frowning. Worried. "You're doing a deal, aren't you?" said Skip through his teeth, kicking the table leg. "Shit!"

"No biggy," said Rag. "The St Wenna lot liked the gear; they want some more." He shrugged, and walked off quickly.

I was as pissed off as Skip. I'd gone all the way to St Wenna with a bag of weed stuffed down my pants. But I'd chosen to do that. This was different. I didn't like how we were suddenly involved in Rag's 'business'.

Jade shrugged. "Nothing to do with us," she said. She didn't give a shit. She was all about the chart right then. She had another good look at it, like just staring at it would make the storm come. Like it was a piece of magic that would make all her dreams come true.

She kept asking me and Skip questions, getting into how we'd follow the weather reports, the surf forecasts, stuff like that. But I only half listened. Now I was constantly checking the door to see who'd come in. And so was Skip. I told myself it would be okay. At least Rag wasn't doing the deal at the table.

Who was it going to be? Tel, Billy, someone else?

We waited.

One minute.

Two minutes.

"I don't like this," said Skip. "This isn't our shit to deal with. What's Rag playing at?"

Then the door opened.

It wasn't Billy that walked in. It wasn't Tel. It was two policemen.

21

EVERYTHING RUSHED IN at me. Everything was razor sharp. The step of their boots on the flagstone floor. The ticking of the clock on the wall. The coffee machine gurgling. The bright yellow strips on their jackets. Their calm, serious faces as they talked with the woman at the counter. Looking at us, back to her, back to us. I felt and saw *everything*, but at the same time was totally out of it, like I wasn't me any more.

It was Rag who was in trouble. But we'd all get searched and questioned. We were all involved. And I didn't like it. I didn't like it at all.

Everyone in the cafe was looking at the police, then at us, but pretending not to.

"It's probably nothing to do with Rag, right?" said Skip. But I knew. I just knew. And so did Jade.

"Sam," said Jade. Her voice was soft and clear. "Sam. Don't look at them; look at me. Look. At. Me."

The police were still at the counter, still talking to the woman. I forced myself *not* to stare at them in wide-eyed horror; forced myself to turn and look at Jade.

"Go and warn Rag. Flush the gear. Don't look at them. Just go."

I tried to stand, but my legs didn't want to. I was heavy and cold, made of stone. I got up. Somehow.

It was dreamlike, walking to the bog, thinking I was going too fast but walking in slow motion too. I had no idea what speed I was walking, or how I looked. It was hard just remembering *how* to walk, without falling over or banging into anything.

In the bog, Rag was standing in the corner. The world got real again, super fast.

"Police," I whispered, "two of them."

Rag's face fell apart. "Pigs! What do we do?"

"What do you mean *we*? *You* flush it. Get rid, Rag. Quick."

Rag shook his head. "No way. They're probably not even here for me."

I couldn't believe what I was hearing. I properly could not believe it. "You reckon? You've been set up, Rag. It's obvious. Flush the fucking drugs. Now."

He pulled the stuff out of his trousers. A packet like the one I'd taken to St Wenna. The size of a large green pebble, held in his hand. He offered it to me. I held my hands up, backing away from him, shaking my head.

"What you doing?" I said.

"That favour. When we gave you the board, the suit. You *promised*." Rag begged me. "You owe me, Sam. Shove this down your trousers. They're looking for me. I'll go out there, keep 'em busy. You follow in a minute, sneak out the door."

"No way, Rag, no way."

"Please, man, come on." He was holding it out to me, jabbing at me with it, desperate for me to take it.

There was no time to argue. I grabbed the packet, deciding I'd get rid of it the second he was out of the bog. He walked straight out.

What was I going to do? Flush it? Chuck it out of the window? Wash it down the sink?

The window was quickest. But it was too high for me to reach. You needed some kind of pole to open it.

The toilet, then. But there was a piece of paper stuck on the door, and on it, written in biro:

Broken. Please use staff toilets.

Never mind, I thought. *I can shove it down the pan.* They couldn't pin it on me, even if they found it.

A man with his kid came in. He looked at the cubicle door and the sign, then he looked me up and down. I had the weed in my hand, but held tight, behind my back.

I looked suspicious. No doubt about it.

He took his son to the urinals. And I just stood there staring at their backs. I couldn't go in the bog now, could I? The man turned, looking at me out the corner of his eye.

I had to get rid of it properly. Quickly. But I was frozen to the spot.

There weren't any other options apart from washing it down the sink. But unwrapping it and breaking it up would be pretty obvious. And I couldn't just stand there, waiting for the man and his kid to finish pissing and go.

If the police came in, I was screwed. I was surprised they hadn't come in already. I was almost crapping myself. I couldn't think straight, only, *This can't be happening*. But it was.

For one crazy moment I even thought of eating it.

There were no other choices. The man and his kid were busy at the urinals. I walked a step so I was directly behind them, then shoved the cellophane-wrapped weed down my boxers and under my nuts, with a cold, heavy hand.

I took a deep breath, checked myself in the blotchy mirror. I was white as the bog walls.

Fear makes the wolf look bigger. You can do this, I said, silently, to the guy in the mirror who wasn't me. Then I opened the door and walked out.

The police were all over Rag. They had his arms spread and were going through his pockets. One of them had his face an inch from Rag's ear, and was firing questions at him. And Rag was smiling, cocky as shit.

"Can't a dude have breakfast without police harassment?"

he said. Cheeky bastard. I had to give him cred though. He was playing his part, getting their full attention, so I could scarper.

Poor Skip. He just stood by the table, staring at the floor, looking embarrassed. At first I couldn't see where Jade had gone. Then I saw her by the cafe door. She was hiding behind a family of four who were clearly getting off on this whole scene, with their two young sons grinning like their favourite TV police show was happening, live, right in front of them.

Jade was pretending to play on her phone. She saw me and nodded. I nodded back. I guessed she knew what we'd done. She'd worked it out. I headed for her. Not straight at the door. Too obvious.

It was all happening fast. It was all happening too slow. There was no air. I couldn't breathe. It was like being down deep, held under. And the door was like the light and air above the surface. All I had to do was hold on, make it back to the top.

Rag grinned, turned to face the policeman who was going through his pockets.

"You're enjoying this, aren't you?" said Rag. The man had a go-on-make-it-worse-for-yourself smile on his face. The other one took Rag's bag off the floor and emptied it on the table, sending the salt-shaker and an empty cup flying.

That was our chance. When I was sure all eyes were on Rag, I poked Jade in the side, and we slipped out the door.

Our boards and bags were on the ground outside. We didn't pick them up.

There was another policeman, on the phone, with his back to us, leaning against their van. Next to him was a dog, an Alsatian. It saw us, sat upright. Staring at us. It looked like a wolf. A big one.

We walked straight past.

Ten yards. Twenty. Jade put her hand in mine, squeezed it. I started to breathe.

Holy shit, I thought, *holy shit*.

Another few yards, and I'd chuck the weed. We could come and get it later. Or not. I didn't care. I just wanted rid of it.

I felt light. Cool. Free.

I thought we were out of there.

I didn't hear him sneak up behind us.

"Hold on," he said. I turned. The policeman was coming right at us. He had the dog-wolf on a leash. It was almost pulling him over. And it was looking right at me.

The dog sniffed around my junk. The policeman put his hand out.

"Hand over, son. Unless you'd rather a strip search."

22

THEY TOOK ME to the station and left me, sat at a table in the interview room.

There was a small, square, black machine on the table, probably some kind of recording device, and a cup of tea they'd given me, going cold. Opposite me, on the other side of the table, an empty chair.

Nothing to do but think. I guess that was the point of leaving me alone.

Questions fired through my mind.

What was Mum going to say? Was there any way I could stop her finding out?

Would I get suspended from school?

Would I get fined, or community service?

Would I get a record?

I was stupid for taking the stuff off Rag; stupid for not

getting rid of it.

A man came in after five minutes. He was about Mum's age with short, dark hair. He was dressed smart-casual, shirt but no tie, smiling.

"Hello, Sam. I'm Detective Jones," he said, shaking my hand, like he was my new best friend. "Now, Sam. Hmmm," he said, smoothly, "this is the first time anything like this has happened to you, isn't it?"

"Shouldn't I have a lawyer or something?" I said, looking at the machine. No lights on. It wasn't turned on as far as I could tell. "Shouldn't I be interviewed with an adult present?" Jade had told me that once.

"This is just a friendly chat between you and me. Of course we'll get someone if we interview you, and if we charge you. But I was hoping we might avoid that."

"But I thought…" I stopped myself. I didn't want to give anything away. He'd said 'if'.

He shook his head, kept on smiling, like he was being really patient with me.

"We haven't *charged* you. Not yet. We *will* charge you –" he paused – "if we know for a fact that the bag you were carrying was yours. We'll charge you with possession –" another pause – "with intent to supply. In plain English: dealing drugs."

Fear tore at my gut. My head had already gone haywire thinking about fines and community service. Stuff I could handle if I had to. But dealing. That was different.

I was thinking, *There wasn't that much in that packet*. But then

I hadn't really looked at it. I had no idea how much there was, or how much you had to have to get done for dealing.

"Maybe –" Smiley Detective Jones started, slowly, like an idea was coming to him as he spoke – "maybe… you carried it for someone else?"

That was it then. They knew what had happened. They knew it was Rag they were meant to bust. Rag had been set up.

"How did you know about… us being there?" I said. "Did someone tell you?"

He just smiled at me.

I knew Rag had been in trouble before. Maybe he was on his last chance and they *really* wanted him. And Smiley was threatening me. No wonder this 'friendly chat' wasn't official. They weren't interested in me, not as long as I gave them Rag.

He looked at me hard, for a reaction. I didn't give him one. I wanted to punch him. I hated what he was doing. But truth was, I wasn't going to take the rap for dealing. I wasn't prepared to go to a young offenders' institution, just to cover Rag's arse.

Smiley waited. I hadn't been charged. All I had to do was tell him what had happened.

I thought, *He knows I'm going to tell him. That's why he's smiling.*

I thought of Jade. Imagined her saying how I'd done a lot for Rag, and how it wasn't my fault.

And Skip. He'd say Rag had it coming.

And G. He'd say he'd have done the same as me.

They'd say how I'd had no choice.

They'd say it had been the right thing to do.

I mean. *Anyone* would have done the same.

And Rag… I didn't want to think about Rag.

"Do you know what it's like at a young offenders' institution, Sam?" said Smiley. He was trying to scare me. Bullying me. I didn't like it.

I thought, *What if I don't tell him?* Fear makes the wolf look bigger, and I had a sure-as-shit feeling he was playing me. Else, why were we having this off the record 'chat'?

Yeah. He *knew* I was going to tell him, all right.

The smug twat.

"It's mine," I said, sitting up straight.

He was still smiling. But he was forcing it now. He sat up straight too, clasped his hands and put them on the table. He leant forward.

"What did you say, Sam? And think carefully before you open your mouth again; think for a while before you…"

"It's mine. The weed I had. It's mine." I sat forward too, copying what he did. That wiped the smile off his stupid face. It made him angry. I felt good about that.

"You're in a lot of trouble, Sam. I don't think you know how much…"

"It's mine," I said.

"Where did you get it from?"

"Are you charging me?"

"There's no need if you…"

"Are you charging me?" I said.

I had this wild, hot tingling all over my body. It felt good. Like jumping off the cliff, or taking on a big wave.

"Yes, Sam," said Detective Not-Smiling-Any-More. "We're going to interview you with an adult present. You're going to say it's yours, on record, then we're charging you. Possession of a suspected Class B controlled substance."

*

There were a lot of forms.

And they did get hold of an adult.

The door opened.

Mum stood there, staring at me with sad, angry eyes.

23

"DRUGS, SAM. DRUGS." Mum said, through her teeth, as she stirred sugar into her tea.

She'd been quiet driving home from the police station. Hadn't said a word, not even to answer Teg's endless questions. But soon as she'd packed Teg off upstairs and sat me down in the kitchen, she made it clear she was going to make up for it.

"Drugs." She kept saying it. Slowly, quietly, like I didn't know what I'd done. Like I didn't know what 'drugs' were. She was calm, in that way people force themselves to be when they're really furious.

I looked up at the clock. Three o'clock. I had a whole evening of this lined up. Joy.

"Drugs. Not shoplifting. Not drinking cider till you throw up. Not something normal. Oh no. *My* son has to deal drugs."

"I wasn't dealing," I said, with my arms folded, staring at the table.

"Then how come you had so much?"

I shrugged. I hadn't told the police anything. I wasn't going to tell her either. I didn't want to tell the truth; I didn't want to lie.

"You heard what that policeman said," she said, after a long, dragging silence. "If you'd had a bit more, they'd have done you for dealing."

It was true. Rag's little package was as much as you could claim was for 'personal use', and even then, only if you were one dedicated puffer. But I'd been right about Smiley, threatening me. They couldn't have done me for dealing.

"I *wasn't* dealing," I said.

"All for you, was it? Or were you giving it away? Making yourself popular with your new friends." She was glaring, staring, accusing, sarcastic. But her bottom lip was trembling, and her hand was shaking when she picked up her tea.

I felt nervous, awkward. I *hated* this grilling, but I felt sorry for Mum too. This was hard on her. All she wanted was the truth. But I couldn't trust her not to tell the police, or go round to Rag's house and bully him into fessing up. Because she *knew* I was covering for him. The police had pretty much told her. They knew what and who they were looking for when they came into that cafe. Someone *had* set Rag up. Billy, probably.

"Jesus. I thought taking you away from London was a good

idea. I thought bringing you down here would keep you away from all that crap... and... and..." She stopped halfway through her sentence. A tear was rolling down her cheek.

There was a knock at the kitchen door.

"Are you all right, Mummy?" Tegan's voice said through the keyhole. Teg opened the door. She stood there, in her giraffe onesie, toy rabbit hanging at her side. Seeing Teg made me feel worse than anything.

"I told you to stay upstairs," said Mum.

"Are you bad, Sam? Are you going to prison?" said Teg. Mum got up, knelt down, holding Teg gently by the shoulders.

"Listen, Honey-bundle. Sam's made friends with some bad boys. The police think he did something the other boys did. But he didn't and he's not going anywhere. Do you understand? He's not going anywhere."

"Promise?" said Teg.

"Promise," said Mum, kissing Teg on the cheek.

"Promise, Sam?" said Teg, to me. I nodded. Mum took Tegan back upstairs.

Long moments passed.

Mum came down. She had a magazine in her hand, rolled up. For a second I thought she might whack me with it. But she opened it, and started reading. "*What is skunk doing to our teenagers?*' You're a science geek, Sam. You like facts. Well here's some for you. Marijuana is twice as strong as it was twenty years ago. It can affect short-term memory and a developing teenage brain in 'irreversible ways'. It says here there is a high correlation between schizophrenia and smoking skunk. Smoking it can give you lung cancer. One joint is the same as smoking eight normal cigarettes, or something." She looked up. "Shall I go on?"

I shrugged.

She threw the magazine at the wall. But that wasn't enough. She picked up her teacup and threw that too, smashing it to pieces, leaving a massive splodge of brown tea dribbling down the paintwork.

"It's because you haven't got a father, isn't it? That's why you've gone off the rails!" she shouted. She put her head in her hands and started crying. Properly sobbing.

I hadn't expected *that*. It was so wrong.

"I'm sorry, Mum. I'm really sorry."

Mum wiped at her eyes, trying to get it together.

"I won't do it again, Mum. I'll never touch it. Nor anything else." I meant it too. I wanted her to believe it.

It was a good minute before she could talk again.

She banged her fist on the table. "This surfing nonsense stops right now." She pointed her finger at me like it was a weapon. "You can kiss goodbye to that board and your idiot druggy friends," she said, through angry tears. "In fact, if you don't stop surfing and hanging with that crowd, I'm taking us all back to London."

"What?" I said. She had to be saying it just to hurt me. Had to be. She couldn't mean it. "Mum, you can't do that."

"Get rid of that board and that wetsuit. If you don't, I will."

I kept calm then. I forced myself.

Like she said, I was a science geek. I did like facts.

And this is what I knew.

Mum meant what she said.

Me giving up surfing had zero per cent probability.

Those were the facts.

24

THE SILENCE WAS painful then. It went on and on. Mum had delivered her killer punch. No more surfing. She didn't have anything else and she didn't need it.

I wasn't going to give up the truth, so she was going to punish me. As hard as she could.

And I was pissed off. More than I had been at anything, ever, but I wasn't going to start arguing. Or worse, begging. So we sat in silence.

There was a knock at the front door.

"You get that, Sam," she said. "It's probably the police. I expect they've talked to your drug dealer friend Stephen by now."

Stephen. I went totally blank for a moment. I'd forgotten Rag even had a real name. Perhaps they had talked to him. Perhaps I was off the hook. Or not. I'd still tried to smuggle away the 'evidence', hadn't I?

I dragged myself out of the kitchen and into the hallway, wondering in what new and twisted way God was about to make my day worse. The day had that kind of vibe about it.

But it wasn't the police. It was Jade, with Tess.

"You look like shit," she said.

"Thanks."

Mum came up behind me. "Hello, Jade."

"Hi."

Jade stood there, waiting to be asked in. But Mum didn't do that. She stood behind me, not saying anything. The world had changed. And in this new world, I was no longer friends with Jade. But what was Mum going to do? Tell Jade that, right there and then?

"Is Tegan okay?" said Jade. The sound of Teg crying was coming from upstairs. I hadn't even noticed. Mum left us. I walked out of the door into the cold and wind.

Jade threw herself at me and held me tight like she was never going to let go, standing on tiptoe, pressing her cold cheek against mine.

"Are you okay?" she whispered.

"Yeah, kind of. How's Rag?"

"Crapping himself."

I pulled her away, so she could see my face. She had a hold of my jumper on either side of my waist, gripping tight.

"Listen. I didn't tell them anything," I said.

"I know you didn't."

"How?"

"Because you're you."

And then she kissed me.

On the lips. Full on.

I was blown away. Not just from the kiss, but also at the wonder of how the shittest day ever can turn into the best one in a second.

We hugged, our bodies tight together. Tess came and nuzzled at our legs, trying to get in between us.

"I need to get out of here," I said.

"Let's go see the others."

"Not a good idea right now. We should let Rag know he's in the clear though."

"Nah. Let him stew. He shouldn't have let you take the blame, should he? How about the tor?" she said. The sky was dark, boiling with grey clouds that looked like they would burst any second.

"What about the den?" I said. She shook her head.

"I need to get out too. Dad knows what's gone on. Sort of. I can't take you round mine, not unless you want a load more questions."

I didn't. Mum came out of the door then. She must have sneaked back down. Had she been listening? How much had she heard?

"We're going out," I said.

"No you're not, Sam," Mum said, hanging on to the door like it was holding her up.

Stalemate. Again. I didn't want to just run off. But I wasn't going back inside. I think Mum could see that.

"All right," said Mum, sighing. "All right, go. Go and see your grandma. You can't get in trouble there." Mum had had enough of arguing with me. For that day at least. She went inside.

"You coming?" I said to Jade, as casually as I could, but really hoping she could see how much I needed her to say yes. How much I needed *her*.

"Yeah, course," said Jade, softly. And she kissed me again. On the cheek this time.

We went to get our bikes, before Mum could change her mind.

★

We stood at the front door, waiting.

"Woooow, you're proper posh, aren't you?" said Jade, looking up at the blue-framed windows and cloud-white walls. She had her hood up, to keep off the rain that had started up. I leant over and pulled it off her head.

She was about to complain, but then the door opened, and there was Grandma.

Sometimes she seemed small and grey. Other times busting with life and energy, not like a sick person at all – this was one of those times. As usual, she wore a scarf on her head and one of her smocks, covered in flecks of paint.

She held a hand out for Jade to shake. Jade held a hand out too. She was like a mouse, small, and holding back, suddenly unsure of herself.

"You're Jade?" said Grandma.

"Yes."

"Ah, the siren," said Grandma.

"Um… what?" said Jade.

"The girl who has led poor innocent Sam into so much trouble." Jade looked scared for a second. It was the only time I ever saw it. Grandma put her hands on her hips and looked down at Tess. "And you… a foul, scraggy mutt to mess up my clean house. Hmmm. I suppose you want a biscuit too?"

Tess was cowering a bit. She wasn't sure what to do either. But she wagged her tail when she heard 'biscuit'.

"I know all about it, Sam. Your mother rang ahead. I think to make sure you did actually end up here and not go off getting into more trouble. Now come in. I want to know *everything*. But let me assure you, I am with your mother on this."

She disappeared, leaving us to let ourselves in. I'd been hoping for a soft landing, letting Grandma know in my own time, in my own way. I had hoped Grandma would be less uptight than Mum; she seemed to be about most things. Clearly not drugs though.

Jade was bug-eyed. "Maybe this wasn't a good idea," she whispered. But Tess slipped in the door, looking for that biscuit.

"You can go if you want," I whispered back.

"Nah. I ain't leaving you to face any more of this shit alone."

We went in, glad to be out of the wind and the rain that was now lashing down. Grandma was walking up the stairs.

"I'm going to lie down. I don't need to, I just feel like it. You make the tea and biscuits and bring them up."

Me and Jade and Tess went to the kitchen and I got busy with the kettle and teapot.

Jade was like Alice in Wonderland, curious and more curious, nosing around the kitchen, then going into the lounge with me following her, checking out the paintings, the furniture, the books on the shelves, picking up vases and little statues on the shelves and examining them.

She knew all about Grandma, and the whole family situation. But I hadn't really told her about the house. Everything about it was so different from the cottages. More space. Cleaner, fresher. More expensive. I was a bit embarrassed about it, really. Jade and her dad weren't ever going to live anywhere like this.

When the kettle whistled, we went back into the kitchen.

"You won't want to know us lot when you move in here," said Jade. "Posh boy."

She said it like a joke, teasing me, but she wasn't smiling.

"Yeah, I will," I said. We looked at each other. Each of us dead serious about what we'd said.

"Kettle's whistling," she said.

★

Grandma lay on the bed. There was a wicker table and two chairs next to it. It was like she'd planned us coming round and having tea in her room. Perhaps she had. She patted the bed beside her, and Tess leapt straight up and snuggled up by Grandma, waiting for her first biscuit.

"So, Sam, what happened?"

"What did Mum say?"

"Everything she knows. But I suspect that isn't the half of it."

I told her about the cafe, and the police station, said I'd tried weed a few times. But I wouldn't do it again. She put her cup down and shook her head.

"You're no drug dealer. You're not a troublemaker. Not like Jade here. She looks like trouble on a stick." Jade smiled weakly, then found something on the floor to look at. I was hoping for the Grandma I was beginning to know. Mischievous, sarky, but warm-hearted. That was the Grandma I wanted Jade to meet. That Grandma wasn't there today though. This one was pissed off, and she knew Jade was one of the gang of mates that had got me into trouble.

Grandma sighed.

"Well. At least you took the flak. You have been loyal to your friends. Some small consolation."

"Mum's not very happy."

"Of course she isn't. Any mother would be the same."

"She says I have to stop surfing. Or else she might take us back to London."

"Noooo!" said Jade in horror. "What about the Horns?"

"The what?" said Grandma.

Jade shot me an *oh shit* look. Grandma glared at me for an answer.

"It's a surf spot, down the coast."

"Horns? Devil's Horns?"

"Um. Yes. You know it?" I said, trying to sound calm.

"It rings a bell. Your father mentioned it a couple of times." Grandma sighed again. "Anyway. Look. Your mother is very upset right now. She may say things she doesn't mean. And as for the surfing… She lost her husband to the ocean, Sam. This little drama is the perfect excuse to get you out of the water. I'm sure she will relent, because if you don't do this, it'll just be some other sort of stupid thing teenagers do. I mean, there are no more wolves to kill, are there?"

"What, Grandma?" What did she know about wolves? I'd never told her about the graffiti.

"Rites of passage, Sam. In old times, you became a man by killing a wolf, or a tiger, or some such beast. That's how you proved yourself. Well, there are no more beasts to kill. You have to make your own wolves. Or travel to find them. Listen, I'll talk to Jean when she's calmed down. But you have to prove to her that you won't do anything else stupid or dangerous. Do you think you can do that?"

Me and Jade looked at each other. Surfing the Devil's Horns was pretty high on the list of stupid and dangerous things we could do.

"I'll look after him," said Jade. Grandma put her hand on Jade's arm. She gripped it like her hand was a claw.

"You'll keep him safe?" said Grandma, suspicious.

"Yeah. I promise," said Jade.

25

I DIDN'T SEE the others till I was back at school. Jade had got a text telling me to meet them in the boys' bogs.

Big G was leaning against the sinks; Skip and Rag stood by the far wall, under the frosted window. They all had downer looks. Arms folded, frowns on their faces. Rag looked like he hadn't slept for a month.

"Well?" said Rag.

I waited, holding out for a few seconds, just for a bit of sick pleasure.

"I didn't tell them anything," I said.

Rag came away from the wall. He put his hands on my shoulders, stared into my eyes.

"You took the blame," he said slowly, to make sure we both understood what was being said. And what it meant. "They think it was yours? Seriously?"

"Yeah," I said, "they pretty much knew I was covering, but I said it was mine."

"You know what, Sam. I fucking *love* you and I want to have your babies!" He threw himself at me. "You are a *legend*, Kook!!!!!" His stubble rubbed my cheek. "Thank you, Sam. Thank you."

"Jesus, Rag, you are a massive pussy," said Big G, then patted me on the back like I was a good dog. "Well done, dude. Seriously, that's huge; you didn't have to do that." Skip came and patted me on the back too.

The sound of laughing brought Jade in. She rolled her eyes at the sight of me being hugged by Rag, and the others, almost joining in.

"You lot are cosy," she said. She pulled a face. "Ugh. Stinks in here."

"So what happened?" said Big G, ignoring her.

Once I'd peeled Rag off me, I told them. How I'd been charged with possession. How I had to go to juvenile court, but I'd probably get away with a warning, and a bit of community service. How they knew I was covering. How it was really Rag and Ned they were after, and that they'd made threats as to how bad it was going to be for me if I didn't grass.

"Rag was set up then," said Big G, punching the wall. "Billy's dead already."

"Sam," said Rag, "come round mine tonight. I've got a present for you. A big one."

"If it's a bag of weed, I don't want it," I said, laughing.

"No, Kook. It's way better than that."

★

I texted Mum that I had to stay back after school to talk to a teacher about science homework.

If me and Jade weren't too long at Rag's, we could get on the next bus and be home an hour later than normal.

I didn't know if Mum would buy it or not. I didn't care.

Above the garage was that choice bit of art-graffitti I'd seen before. Fear makes the wolf look bigger.

Ned was in the Aladdin's cave garage, working on a board with a sander. He was wearing a kind of mask over his nose and mouth, and was covered in white dust. He took it off, put it on top of the board. He wiped his hand on his jeans and offered it to me.

"Rag texted me, told me what you did, Sam. That's big. I've got a bit of form and Rag's been in trouble too. Police, school. We can't afford any more aggro. So you taking the heat... it means a lot, yeah? You didn't have to do that."

"What about this present then?" said Jade, sounding excited, like it was for her.

Ned went through the rack, till he found what he was looking for.

He handed the wetsuit to me.

The suit was sheer, matt black neoprene. It had a fresh rubber smell, a gleaming chunky zip. There were no holes, no worn patches. It had a big square tag on it, with a picture of a guy riding a thick winter barrel of near-black water.

It was new.

"Try it on," said Ned.

There weren't any changing rooms in this shop. Jade turned away, getting very interested in the boards. I kept my boxers on. I wasn't about to get naked in front of Ned and Rag, even if Jade hadn't been there.

The wetsuit was a nightmare to put on. I had to squeeze myself into it, pulling and stretching at the rubber, inch by inch. It sucked at my skin, not letting me in unless I really heaved and pulled. When I was in it, I couldn't get the zip at the back up. I had to ask Ned to do it.

I started getting hot, even though I wasn't moving. It was tight, but not too much. Ned nodded his approval.

"Good fit. Don't piss in it unless you really, really have to," said Ned, "and if you do, do it right at the beginning of a sesh."

He stood back then, sizing me up, just like when him and Rag had given me Old Faithful.

Ned asked me a bunch of questions. About how I rode a board, what kind of waves I liked, what turns I could do. When he was happy he knew what he needed, he went and got a board from the ones lined up against the wall. He handed it to me.

"What are you doing?" I said.

"I'm giving you this board."

I stood, wondering at the thing I held, wanting it more than I had ever wanted anything. But feeling guilty too. It was a reward for not grassing. And it was too much.

I wanted to say, *I can't take it*, but the longer I held it, the harder it was to get the words out. Or let go of the board.

I was on fire, I was so happy.

It was a different beast from Old Faithful. Shorter, lighter. It had a pointed, upturned nose.

It wasn't new. It was covered in dirty wax. But it didn't have loads of fixed dings. It was more like the boards the others rode. In my head, I was surfing it already, imagining what it could do, how fast it would go, how it would carve up the wave.

"It's thick in the middle, plenty of volume, so it catches waves easy," Ned explained. "Not a high-performance board, but you'll be able to do proper bottom turns. Off the lip too. It'll take a bit of getting used to; don't expect much in your first session."

"I dunno what to say," I said, standing there, grinning like a kid at Christmas who got his dream present. "It's too much, Ned. I can't take it."

"You don't mean that," said Jade. And she was right.

Rag and Jade took turns to hold it, feeling the weight of it, feasting their eyes on its lines and shape, comparing it to their own boards, talking about what it could do.

"You could surf the Devil's Horns with that board, if the waves weren't too big," said Jade.

197

Ned shook his head. "I heard about that. You're chasing a myth. Not that you groms'd be up to the job, even if you *could* find it," he said.

"Really?" said Jade. "Ned, do you know anyone with a boat?"

26

NED DID KNOW someone with a boat.

A rotten-toothed, leather-skinned old fisherman called Pete.

He picked me and Jade up at Penzeal harbour the next Saturday morning in his fishing boat *Sunrise*. It was even older and more knackered than he was, and stank of mackerel and creosote.

"Nice," I said to Jade. "Reckon it'll get us home?"

Pete helped us aboard. Us, our boards and bags, and two plastic barrels filled with firewood, bottles of water, blankets and cans of food that we planned to leave at the islands. If we found them.

My old board and suit were still at our house. Not chucked out, but not being used either. I'd told Mum we were going fishing.

"Staying there long?" Pete said.

"We're looking for a surf spot," said Jade, giving him a photocopy of the chart. "We might go back there sometime."

She showed him the surf mag. The lighthouse, the massive wave.

"I seen those islands," said Pete. "There ain't no lighthouse there. The light that keeps boats away from them rocks is a mile further off. Southwest."

"What? Where?" said Jade. "Show us on the chart." She glared at me, eyes blazing. "Maybe that's it, Sam. The one he's talking about. A mile off the islands."

"Nah," said Pete. "It don't look anything like that one. It's a modern thing, sat on a tiny rock, not a proper island. Nothing like that picture."

"Take us anyway," said Jade, sounding flat. She dumped her board with the barrels and went and stood at the front of the boat, with her arms crossed, looking out to sea.

"It's thirty quid," Pete said, with his hand out. I gave him a plastic bag full of notes and coins, a lot of it loose change from Jade's money box.

He started the engine. I went and joined Jade. She was staring into the mist, looking for something that wasn't there.

"You heard him," I said. "What my dad wrote on the chart, it could mean anything, not Devil's Horns at all. You'll be disappointed."

With the chart, I thought. *With me.*

"We *have* to know. We won't *know* till we go."

Jade was quiet after that. She wouldn't talk. The only sounds were the chug of the engine and the odd gull crying out. The sea was green-oil calm. Misty, with no wind.

★

The mist cleared when we got near. We could see the islands. A circle of them. Three islands at the further edge of the circle, the biggest about a quarter of a mile long, the other two a bit smaller. Between them and us was a scattering of rocks, sticking out of the ocean like shark's teeth. The smaller rocks were bare, apart from strands of seaweed. They'd be covered by water at high tide. But the three larger islands had tufts of grass and rocks stained white and grey by gulls' shit.

I couldn't see any lighthouse.

I looked at Jade. She shrugged and spat over the side.

The sun began to shine through in columns, lighting up the sea. In the water, in front of the boat, I could see smooth, almost white rocks, like round tables under the surface, and gardens of seaweed and turquoise sandy shallows. Pretty. But around the circle of islands and rocks, nothing but deep, dark-blue ocean.

Pete put *Sunrise* in reverse, then killed the engine. He came and joined us at the front of the boat.

"This is as far as I can go. See them rocks? More'n a few boats gone down 'ere. It's a graveyard, see. Lot of bones ground into the sand… I've never put a pot down there. Nor cast a line. Never will. I stay clear most of the time."

I thought about Dad. Not for the first time, I played with the idea that this was where he died.

But he'd have known about this place. He'd have known the dangers. He'd never have come here.

But then Grandma had said he'd been caught out in…

"What's it like in a storm, Pete?" I said.

"I never been near it in a storm. I ain't stupid. I only come 'ere today as it's mostly calm."

Mostly.

There was no wind, no swell rocking the boat. But there *was* a wave. It was breaking on the other side of the smaller of the three islands, twenty yards offshore. Not huge, no more than shoulder-high, but peeling smooth and even into the shallows.

A reef break.

"Up for a surf?" I said to Jade, thinking it might help her get over the no-lighthouse disappointment. Thinking it might stop me thinking about my dad.

"Do bears shit?" she said.

Jade found some deep part of the boat to get changed, away from Pete's eyes. Mine too. I got into my suit. Plus boots, gloves, hood. The only bit of skin showing was my face. Jade appeared, looking exactly the same.

"You look like a surfing penguin," I said.

"Right. Never heard that one before."

We threw the boards in the water and jumped in after them.

I expected a shock of cold but felt nothing. The suit was

tight, and warm. It didn't leak like the old one. It was weird. I was in the water and I was totally dry. I had to get my head under just so I could connect with the fact I was in water at all.

The board was easy to get on, not like Old Faithful. But harder to *stay* on. If I didn't keep moving, it sank underneath me.

We paddled through the rocks and blue-green shallows, then between the two largest islands, then on to the edge of the reef where the wave was. The water got colder on the edge, darker. It was like going over a cliff. A cliff with nothing at the bottom of it. Just darkness.

We moved out and round, coming to break from behind.

The waves were good. Glassy and slick, hollow and fast. Problem was, I struggled to catch them. When I did get one, the board skipped and skated underneath me. I couldn't manage more than a couple of seconds before I fell off.

Jade was all over it. Wave after wave, while I flapped around.

"Didja see that?" she said paddling back into the line up, misty eyed and grinning, then turned and hooked into another one before I even answered.

"I ain't going till I get some," I shouted after her.

I meant it. I was going to get some proper waves. Even if it took all day.

I learned. Slowly. After an hour, I was getting rides. Long, walled up, clean, green beauties that started fast and got faster. Trick was not to do anything fancy, just stand, turn, glide.

Watch the wall of water jacking up by my head. I could almost run my hand along it, it was so close.

"Oi," Pete shouted, from the boat. It was a hundred yards away, on the opposite side of the islands and rocks we'd paddled through to get to the surf. Any wind and we wouldn't have heard him, but the day was so still, his voice rang through the air like a bell. "Time's up!" He was waving his arms, calling us.

"Shall we head back?" said Jade. Another peak was rising up.

"Nah," I said as I lay down and started digging for the wave.

We ignored him. We weren't going anywhere till the surf died, the tide ruined it, or we got too knackered.

When bigger sets came along, we paddled over them, so as not to risk getting creamed. Sat out back, I saw a wave was breaking off the largest island, about thirty feet offshore. There was a column of rock there, sticking out of the water. The wave was breaking off its edge. Small though. When a wave broke head-high where we were, the wave there was just an ankle-biter. I pointed it out to Jade.

"I'm checking it out," she said, heading over.

"Why? It's tiny."

"It's got potential."

I didn't follow. No point. The waves were good right where I was.

Like with the reef we were on, Jade didn't go straight up

to it. She paddled right around, into deep water, then made a right angle for thirty yards, round the rock column, so she'd come to the break point from behind.

When she was ten yards off the break, she froze, stopped, sat up on her board.

She was staring at something on the far side of the island, something I couldn't see.

I headed over. As I came round the second island, I lost sight of the boat. That meant Pete couldn't see us either.

"Oi!" Pete shouted. "Where you going?"

"Jade," I shouted when I got near, "you all right?" It was odd how she sat there, not checking for waves, just staring at the island.

She raised a hand and pointed.

And I knew. I just knew.

When I came round the column of rock I saw.

A ruin. At the top of the island, set in a half-moon of rock. A square grey building, built into the stone. On top of it was the broken stub of what had once been a tower. Most of it was long gone, fallen into the sea, or maybe knocked over by one of those legendary ghost storms. But the square storage room at the base still stood, and the base of the old tower.

The ruins of a lighthouse.

The back of it was cut into the rock, so you wouldn't see it from the other islands, or the sea between the islands and the mainland. From out to sea, the base of it – what was left – was hidden by the rock. Boats stayed well clear of this place, but even if you sailed right by, with the tower gone you wouldn't see it unless you were either really close, or looking hard.

In front of it was a slope, leading down to a shingle beach.

We paddled to the beach, ignoring Pete's cries. I heard the boat engine start. He was either going without us, or was going to bring the boat round the islands so he could get us. I had to hope it was the second option.

We left the boards on the beach, and walked up to the lighthouse.

"Holy fuckerama," said Jade.

The door was iron, rusted. It took all the strength I had to get it open.

There was a small anteroom, like a hallway, then an open door to the base room. We walked into the cold and dark.

It was a storm-trashed wreck of a place. The roof was intact, apart from a hole where a rusting stairway led up into the sky. Patches of blue paint on the walls. In the corner, an old hulk of square metal, so far gone I couldn't even tell what it had once been. And on the stone floor, sand and shingle. And rocks. From the beach. Brought up there by storms. By waves.

Jade's excited voice echoed round the room. "The hole could be a chimney. As long as the rain's not heaving down, we can make a fire against the wall and sleep around it. We can leave the wood and food in the corner. It's amazing. It's perfect."

We went back outside and climbed round the back, till we stood on the highest point.

We shouted and waved at Pete. He was already bringing the boat round the islands to come and get us.

While we waited, we walked round the edge of the island, till we were facing west. Looking down at the reef.

"See those white-green shallows – that's rock. It'll peel nice off that, if the swell's big and coming from the right direction. And…" Jade squinted, and cupped a hand above her eyes, looking into the distance.

"What is it?" I said.

"There's a reef out there, another one. See where the water's a lighter blue? "

I did. It was a few hundred yards off. A long way out to sea.

"That's it," she said. "That's where it'll break when it gets big. Not now, but a big enough wave will jack up there. That's what's on the mag cover!" Jade was grinning and started bouncing like an excited rabbit. She held on to me, gripping my arm tight. "We discovered a surf spot, Kook. They'll name it after me… us. We'll be in the mags. There's at least three breaks, more probably, in the right swell. All we have to do is get footage, pics…"

I looked at the reef, and the endless pit of dark water beyond it. I couldn't feel the same stoke Jade did about the place.

This was where my dad might have died. It was where *I* might die, if I didn't know what I was doing.

"…and we can come back, with the surf mag and… You okay?" she said.

I nodded. I felt her hand, squeezing my arm. She wasn't letting go. I put my arm around her waist. I felt dizzy.

From the surf, from finding the place, from her.

Jade took off her hood, letting her hair fall on her shoulders. I took mine off too. We stared at each other.

I put my arm around her waist again. I pulled at her, gently. She moved into me.

We kissed.

She held my neck; I held her. Our bodies stuck together with just the wetsuits between. Wet sea creatures snogging. Our tongues exploring, tasting of the sea.

I don't know how long we kissed. A long time.

It was proper this time.

I would have taken her to the lighthouse. Gone further. A lot further. Right there, right then. But Pete had brought the boat round the islands. He shouted out, "All right, lovebirds, time to go." Jade let me go, laughed, and ran back to the beach.

We set about getting the waterproof plastic barrels in the water. We tied them to our leashes and pulled them behind our boards.

We left them in the storeroom. Ready for the day.

27

THE NEXT DAY we met Skip, Rag and Big G at the Old Chapel cafe to tell them about the islands.

The last time we'd been in was when I got busted and the woman who owned the cafe wasn't too happy to see us. She worked hard at not smiling, clanking and banging the cups of hot chocolate and plates of scrambled eggs as she put them on the tray.

We sat down with our food and told the others — where the islands were, how we'd put the firewood, blankets and tins of food safe inside, how we'd surfed, how we'd checked the reef. I sat back, waiting to be blown away by how impressed they were. Jade was grinning.

"Well?" she said.

Big G let out a really long sigh. "Holy shit. This is real." Big G never looked floored by anything. But right then, even he was a bit in shock. Wide-eyed about the thought of us doing it.

"That's it then," said Skip with a long sigh. "We're going to surf the Horns."

"Yeah," said G, quietly. "We are."

"You not excited, Skipper?" said Jade. "This is massive."

"Yeah, but we don't *have* to do it, right?" said Skip. "I mean, we can get there and then check it out. See if we're up to it? Depending on what it's like."

I waited for the chicken noises, the cries of 'puss-ee'.

But Jade put her hand on Skip's shoulder, making sure she had his attention.

"Look at me, Skip. Listen up. *No one* has to do anything they don't want. This is an adventure. We ain't going there to kill ourselves. Right, Rag?"

"Yeah, man," said Rag, laying into his eggs. "We'll only take on what we can handle. *And* we'll get in as much surfing as we can before the day."

"You going to do it, Kook?" said Skip.

"Dunno," I said. And I didn't. Not really. But I thought, if Jade did it then I would. I didn't want to be sat on the rocks watching those fuckers get the waves of their lives, thinking, *If only*. But I didn't say that.

It was a weird moment. Suddenly we were talking seriously. Not taking the piss, or bigging anything up. But weighing it up, *thinking* about what we were getting into.

We were a bit grown-up about it.

But there was only so much being grown-up Rag could handle.

"I think we should celebrate," he said. He reached into his jacket pocket and pulled out a handful of brightly coloured, leaflet-sized pieces of card. He waved them in our faces.

Jade poked Rag in his side, making him flinch, giving her a second to snatch them. She passed me and Skip and G one each.

It had a picture on it. A really old photo of a girl in petticoats, sitting on a swing, under a tree. But the picture had been messed with. The girl's eyes had been replaced by sparkling blue diamonds. Streams of burning blues and acid greens flowed out of her skirts into an ocean that filled the bottom half of the flyer. On the trippy sea was printed:

World Famous Crystal Collective
Black moon party – All nighter
Friday 29th November
Tregiffian Peninsula, Cornwall
Venue TBC
Text yr number on the night to 07987 XXX XXX
Musical mayhem guaranteed
Ticket No 573

"What's it a ticket to?" I said.

Jade rolled her eyes. "*Crystal Collective!* They're DJ's, surfers too. They put on parties. Bali. France. Hawaii. They're legends.

You can't just get a ticket. You have to know someone who knows someone. People go mental. It's a one-off. The chance of a lifetime. We *have* to go. Where'd you get them from, Rag?"

"Ned's got a pile of 'em. He sorted the Crystal guys out with some boards. I nicked these before he counted them. We all in?"

"What if the St Wenna lot are there?" I said.

"Then we'll get a chance to talk things through with Billy," said Big G, with a sick grin.

"Um, Rag..." said Skip. "Never mind Billy. You don't think Ned might notice we're there?"

Rag waved this small problem away. "He won't give a shit. We'll turn up late; he'll be on it by then."

I'd never been to a rave before. Not a nightclub. Not a warehouse party.

I liked the look of this, just from the ticket.

Musical mayhem guaranteed.

"The 29th," I said. "That's my birthday."

"Birthday!" said Jade. "I *love* birthdays. We can get a cake and presents and shit. Yeah. We can get you presents!" She was grinning. It was sweet. She was really into it.

"What you going to get me?" I said, laughing.

Rag put his arm round my neck, pulled me tight and ruffled my hair with his other hand.

"What am I going to get you, Kook? I'm going to get you off your face. *That's* what I'm going to get you."

★

I had to lie to Mum. Again.

"But, Sam," she said, stood by the sink, peeling potatoes, "I thought we'd do something as a *family* on your birthday. I've got Brian at the pub to reserve a table."

Mum kept mentioning this Brian guy. She didn't say anything *about* him, but she kept mentioning him.

"Right. Well, maybe we could do that during the day," I said. "But there's a stargazing convention on at Plymouth Uni. Because there's no light on the moon that night. A black moon, a one-off. The chance of a lifetime… You know I'd love it. Mike and Harry are up for it. It goes on all night. Then we're staying at Mike's."

It was a perfect excuse for a geek like me. The geek I used to be. And as far as Mum knew, it didn't involve Jade or 'Stephen' or any of the others.

"But I booked a table at the pub," she protested. "I mean, I'm not sure, not after… what happened. I don't know if I can let you go a whole night. And what about Teg?"

Teg came in the door, bang on cue.

"What about me?" she said.

"Sam doesn't want to spend his birthday with us," said Mum. That was harsh. That pissed me off.

"Why, Sam?" said Teg, her voice rising, heading for 'upset'. I explained to her, said we could make a real fuss the rest of the day, I'd just be gone in the evening, after her bedtime, she wouldn't miss anything.

"It's okay," Teg said, to Mum, doing a good job of hiding her disappointment.

"Please, Mum," I said. Mum looked at Teg, like she was checking her face, and whatever it told her would make up her mind.

She put her peeler down, turned and faced me, suddenly calm, suddenly serious.

"And what will you do if I say no?" Her eyes were all accusing. The way she said it was sarcastic. She was testing me.

I should have just said *well that's fine*. But I didn't like how she tried to use Teg.

"I'll go anyway," I said. She raised an eyebrow.

"Really?" she said, quietly. She wiped her hands on her apron, then took it off. The potatoes wouldn't get finished till this was over.

Me and my big mouth.

"Saaam!" Teg whispered, pulling at my hand. She was warning me not to upset Mum.

I had to change tactics, and quick. I walked over, picked up the peeler and started on the spuds.

"Look, Mum, all I'm saying is I really, really want to do this. There'll be more stars in the sky than I've ever seen. Ever. They've got telescopes I can only dream about. I'll never get the chance again, and it is *my* birthday. I really want to go." I smiled. Sweet as I could manage. I was making myself feel sick, I was sucking up so hard.

"And then he can tell us all about it?" said Teg, suddenly on my side, now I was making nice.

Mum didn't look overly impressed. Hands on hips, eyebrow still raised.

"And…" I was searching now, looking for a trump card, "well you could get a sitter for Tegan, and go out anyway. She deserves a night out, right, Teg?"

"Yes, Mummy. That's okay," said Tegan.

Mum paused as this idea sunk in, and her mind chewed it over.

"Okay," she said, "but we go to your grandma's for an early evening drink. And you get back the next morning at a reasonable time. Stargazing. You really want to go?"

"Best stargazing experience ever. Guaranteed."

She went to watch TV with Teg, leaving me to finish the spuds.

I'd done it. By lying.

Lying to Mum was normal by then. Lying was something I did every day.

28

WE WERE ALL IN. Me, Jade, Skip, Rag, Big G.

We got a bus to the Tregiffian Peninsula. It dumped us at a village called St Barts at half past ten.

The place was dead and dark.

There was no sign of any rave, or anyone who looked like they might be going to one.

That included us. We wore coats, jumpers and woolly hats to keep out the cold. And we were carrying sleeping bags, for wherever we ended up sleeping. We hadn't planned that bit. We'd just see where we ended up. Chances were we'd be up all night anyway.

I wondered about Jade, about what she was wearing underneath her massive army coat. It went down to her knees. I could see she had bare legs, so had to be wearing a dress, not jeans. She wore a beanie that covered most of her head. She looked more like a tramp than a raver.

"We'll get a text soon, saying where the rave is," said Rag. Right on cue, his phone bleeped. He read the screen. "Port Barrow."

"Port fucking Barrow," G complained. "That's three miles away."

"Four. We'd better get walking," said Rag.

We headed for the cliff path. It was a short cut. Apparently.

We walked heads down, using torches to find the way. G had a bottle of vodka. He poured a little on the ground.

"Libations," he said.

"Libations," the others echoed back at him. Not me though. I wasn't into superstitions. We passed around the vodka as we walked. There were spliffs too. No one said anything about it being my birthday.

"So," I said, "anyone been to one of these before?"

"Nah, not this lot," said Big G.

Silence. I thought everyone would be more excited than they were.

But then I figured maybe none of us had been to a full-on warehouse party or rave before. They just weren't letting on. Maybe no one had been to a party that wasn't in someone's front room, when their parents were away. This was new. In some ways it was as big a deal as surfing the Horns. At least we – or the others – knew what we were doing when it came to surfing.

On this trip we were all out of our depth. For once I wasn't the only kook. G passed me the vodka. I took a long slug.

As we walked I kept thinking about what Rag had said in the cafe. *I'm gonna get you off your face.* He meant drugs. Not just spliff, something to get us dancing like bug-eyed, shape-throwing loonies. Dancing like monkeys. Till dawn probably. I wasn't exactly scared, just aware I was getting into something I'd never done. I had butterflies in my gut. I didn't like them being there. So I drowned them with more vodka.

*

We walked for hours.

After a leg-knackering climb from a tiny beach to the clifftop, Skip stopped. I stopped too, took the chance to veer off into a field for a piss.

I looked up. Stars. Billions of them. Not staying still though. I was dizzy. *No more vodka for a bit*, I thought.

"Rag, what we doing?" said Skip, when I came back to the others.

"It's just round the corner."

"You say that every time we—"

"Shush!" said Rag. "Can you hear that?"

"I can't hear anything," said Skip.

Jade cupped a hand to her ear. If the rave was near, she'd hear it. Or sense it. "Wait. Yeah. Listen," she said.

I could hear a very faint, distant thudding above the gentle wind and shore break. Deep bass. The heartbeat of something.

"Right," said Rag, digging in his pockets, "who's up for sherbet dib dab?"

He produced a small bag with some kind of white powder in it. He opened it, licked a finger, put it in the bag, covered it in the powder, then rubbed the stuff into his gums.

"Jesus," said G, shaking his head and walking off.

Rag offered it to Skip. He looked at it, really wary, and shook his head. Jade went straight in, with two fingers.

"Hey!" said Rag. "That's got to last. Leave some for Kook."

I watched them, heart hammering, not knowing what to do, not knowing what I *wanted* to do. Not now it was right in front of me.

Rag offered it to me.

Would I regret it if I did some? Would I regret it if I didn't?

"What is it?" I said.

"A few hours of pure fun," said Rag, waving it in my face.

Even in the dark the powder sparkled and twinkled, like a bag full of tiny stars, fallen from the sky.

I was drunk from the vodka and that helped me make my mind up. Plus it was my birthday. I licked my finger, put it in and took a dab. Not a lot.

It wasn't sweet like sherbet. It was bitter; chemical tasting.

I took another swig of vodka to wash it down. I didn't feel anything. I knew I wasn't supposed to, not straight off. But I'd sort of expected to.

219

"Come on, G," said Rag, waving the bag at his mate. But Big G kept his distance, and folded his arms.

"I'm not even smoking weed any more, let alone that shit."

"Please yourself," said Rag, shrugging.

We all walked that bit quicker then.

Once we got to the top of the next valley we could hear the rave properly, and see it too.

Near the old mines, down a track, was a big old stone hall, with a couple of smaller, half-standing ruins attached. To the side of the ruins were three marquees: two small ones, one massive. They were throbbing with music and lights. The deep sides of the valley blocked the rave from the rest of the world perfectly. It was hidden. Secret. Another world.

We followed the track, down into the valley.

My heart was beating in time with the music.

Three bouncers stood outside the entrance. They wore hoodies, jumpers, beanies. They looked like surfers, but they had big yellow patches on their chests saying 'Security'. One of them was wearing shades.

Rag did the talking. The rest of us hung back.

He showed them his ticket. But instead of opening the tent flap the bouncers walked across the entrance, blocking it. That wasn't good.

Rag talked to them for a bit. Eventually he called us forward, looking for support.

"Look, we've all got tickets," he shouted, to be heard over the music. We held them up.

The bouncers didn't move, or speak.

Rag did his best Obi Wan Kenobi impression. "Let us through. These are not the droids you are looking for." We all laughed. Nervously.

"What are you lot... twelve?" said the shades guy.

"This rave probably isn't even legal!" Rag complained. "How can you say we're too young?"

All three of the 'Security' found this hilarious.

"You're not coming in," said Shades. "It's past bedtime. Go home. Now." And he folded his arms, staring at Rag through his glasses.

We put our tickets in our pockets and limped into the dark like a pack of beaten dogs.

I'd never felt like such a loser.

"What now?" said Big G. No one had an answer.

"The gear will kick in soon," said Rag.

"So," said Big G, "me and Skip are in for a night walking clifftops in the dark, with you lot off your faces. Great. Just great."

We stood in a circle. Looking up at the path. Looking back at the rave.

The tent flap opened for a second. A guy rolled out. Inside, hundreds of bodies swayed in a sea of green smoke and blue light.

"Sod this," said Jade. She walked back down the path, but before she got near the marquee, wandered off into the shadows. We all followed.

We clambered around the lowest edge of the valley, sneaking round the marquee and ruins, till we got round the back. There were lorries parked up, with their engines running, and massive cables running from the back of them into the smaller of the two marquees. There were a couple of guys in the front of the vans. But they were facing away from the rave.

We sneaked up between the wall and vans till we got to the edge of the marquee attached to the small building next to the main hall.

"What now?" said Big G.

I felt brave. Heady. Maybe from the drugs, maybe from the vodka. Maybe just from *being* there. I crawled up to where a cable led into the tent, and stuck my head under.

Inside were generators, stacks of speakers, and a desk with buttons and dials on it. There was one guy in there, a thin dude with a pile of dreadlocks on his head, leaning over a laptop and smoking a roll-up. I thought maybe I recognised him from somewhere. Like I'd seen him in the surf sometime.

"Who are you?" he said.

"Sam."

"What you doing, Sam?"

"Trying to get me and my mates in." There didn't seem any point in lying. "We've got tickets." I pulled mine out of my pocket and showed him.

"Then why are you crawling in the dirt?"

"The bouncers said we were too young."

"Too young, eh. Well you'd better piss off then, hadn't you, Sam?" He turned back to his laptop.

That was that then. Game over. But I didn't move. I couldn't face telling the others, never mind the long trawl home. So I just lay there, melting into a puddle of disappointment. I wondered... what if the St Wenna lot were there? What if they'd got in and we hadn't? We'd never live that one down.

"Didn't you hear me, Sam?" said Dreadman.

"How old were you?" I said. He stopped fiddling on the keyboard and looked at me. I carried on. "I mean, your first rave."

"About fifteen."

"I'm sixteen. It's my birthday. Today."

He put his laptop down, took a long pull on his roll-up, thinking. Then he came over, and lifted the canvas to get a better look at me.

"How many of you?" he said.

"Five."

He sighed. Rolled his eyes. Then a wide grin spread over his face.

"Get a move on then. I sodding hate bouncers anyway."

I crawled in, then put my hand back under the canvas and waved the others in. They crawled in too, one by one.

A curtain blocked the entrance. Behind it was the hall and the main marquee. I could just see the back of the decks where the DJs were.

"Quick then," said Dreadman.

I dumped my coat and sleeping bag. The others filed through, one by one, keen to get in before anyone stopped us, patting me on the back and punching my shoulder, as they went. Me and Jade were last.

She took off her coat.

I stood. Dead still. Staring. Just like the first time I'd seen her, that autumn afternoon, with her dad outside our cottage.

"What?" said Jade.

She was wearing a dress. Jade. A dress! Summer-ocean blue, shimmering and thin, curving over her body. She wore white glowing trainers. A chain of flowers on her head.

She had eye make-up on too. Her eyes shone like diamonds. Like the girl on the ticket.

"What?" she said, again.

"You," I said. "You look… different." I was kicking myself. That was the lamest thing I'd ever said.

Jade offered me her hand. I took it. We crouched down, snuck into the rave behind the curtain.

And walked hand in hand, into the sea of bodies.

29

A FILM WAS PROJECTED on one of the walls: a surfer deep in the barrel. It was slowed down so much he was hardly moving. But the wave was caving over him. Explosions of light and water.

On another wall, a projection of a girl, on a longboard, hair down to her bum, swaying as she carved a line on a crystal-green wave.

And the lights on the crowd. A sea of jade green and acid blue, with the sunlight dancing on it.

Waves of arms were rising, falling, swooping, crashing, rising, falling.

And all of us. In the middle of it. Whooping. Screaming with happiness.

The DJ put on the deepest tunes. Tracks that built, paused for a bit, slowing, then increasing the rhythm, the beats per minute. Getting into us with small electronic beeps, long whistles that started in our heads and ran down to our feet. Filling us up till the music was pouring through our blood and thumping in our heads.

Rag stood on a speaker waving his arms over the crowd.

We were below him, in the ocean.

The music went… higher. Higher.

The music… tweak, tweak. Tweeeeeeeeeaaaaaaaakkkkkkkk… k…k…k…k…k

A second pause… then…

BOOM. BOOM. BOOM, BOOM.

BOOM. BOOM. BOOM, BOOM.

Arms raised to the sky, saluting, praying, thumping the air.

Everyone went bonkers. *Everyone.* Hundreds of us.

A kaleidoscope of lights, music, arms and smiles.

And in the heart of it, in her own space, but the centre of it all, soaking up the energy and spitting it right back out…

Jade. Her body swaying, her hands over her head.

We all danced around her, with her. She was the centre of it all.

★

We danced for hours.

When the music wound down after one really mad, long tune, she held a hand to her throat and stuck her tongue out to let me know she was thirsty. She turned, ducked under whirling arms. I followed. But the crowd was thick. A surge of bodies swayed into me, blocking me. I had to squeeze, to push. By the time I found space, Jade had vanished. I went back to the others. She'd be back soon enough.

But apart from Rag, the others had gone too. We carried on for a bit, but it wasn't the same. After a while we decided we'd go and get some drinks ourselves.

It was only when we came out of the crowd that I noticed I wasn't wearing my T-shirt. It was tucked into the back of my jeans. I didn't remember taking it off.

I was cool with it. My body had changed. I had muscles now. Surfing does that to you. I was dripping with sweat. I was pissed. I was high. On the music, the vodka and… spliff? Or the sherbet dib dab? If this was it, I liked it. I didn't feel *out* of it like I'd expected to, just totally happy, and really into the place, the people and the music.

There was a 'bar' in the smaller marquee, selling bottles of water for stupid prices. People – beautiful people – stood around, smoking and drinking. You could even hear yourself talk in there. Everyone was smiling, but looking like they'd done a few hours in a heavy swell. Super happy, but kind of stunned.

I used the T as a towel to wipe the sweat off my face, then put it back on. Rag passed me a bottle of water. I necked it in one go.

"You getting anything off the gear?" said Rag.

I felt great. Happy, dizzy, head spinning. But now I was out of the crowd…

"Dunno," I said. "I think so."

"You *think* so? Let me look at your eyes." He looked into

them like a doctor checking for something. And he looked disappointed.

"Nothing. Thought so. I've been sold actual sherbet. Or something else. But it *tasted* proper! Shit. Bugger."

So I wasn't on anything after all. No biggy. I was having a *great* time.

Skip and Big G appeared. No Jade. Skip put his arms round mine and Rag's necks.

"This is mental!" he shouted, his head nodding in time to the music. I'd never seen him so happy.

"You on something?" I said.

"Skip?" said Rag. "You're kidding. He's just high on life. Always. Annoying wanker."

Skip laughed. "So what, we're having a blast, right?"

"Yeah," I said. "You seen Jade?"

"Nah, not for a bit. How you guys getting on? You don't *look* out of it."

"We aren't. Might as well do it all," said Rag, sounding sad. "It's probably just weakened down; there could be some in there. We might get something off it if we take enough."

Rag dug in. He didn't bother to hide what he was doing. No one seemed to mind, or even notice. He offered it to me. But I was fine as I was. It probably wouldn't work, and now we were inside and having a good time it seemed a bit late and pointless anyway.

I saw Jade then, weaving through the crowd, moving fast. Guys were looking at her, noticing her. Not leering, just doing a double-take at this gorgeous girl, skipping through the crowd. She was hopping and running, almost bumping into people, but dancing round them, weaving like a dodgem at a fair.

"Hi, what's happening?" she said.

"Want some?" said Rag, offering what was left in the bag.

"That shit? It doesn't work, Rag," said Jade. "The St Wenna crew are here: Tel, Billy, Alice, Pig, all that lot. I been dancing with them!" She was blurting the words out, speaking super fast. She sounded ecstatic about finding them.

I wasn't. She hadn't said Mick's name. But he had to be there, didn't he? I didn't want to ask.

"Right," said G, a twisted grin on his face, rubbing his hands. "Time for a chat."

"No," said Jade, wagging her finger in G's face. "No, no, no, no. Noooooooooo, big hairy G. Only peace and love tonight. Don't spoil it. Bad G. Baaaad."

"All right. Just with Billy then," said G, standing straight, puffing his chest out. "He set up Rag."

"Not tonight, man," Jade begged. "Come on, let's just have a good time. Get even, sure, but not now, not here. This is too… special. Pleeeeeease." She grabbed his wispy beard and pulled it.

"All right," he said. She could even charm that miserable git.

"You okay?" said Big G. Jade was bobbing about like she needed a piss. She couldn't keep still. She put an arm around my neck, pulling me away from the others.

"Smile, Kook, come and dance." I caught sight of her eyes

then. Her pupils were black saucers. Massive. I put my arm round her waist.

"You okay?" I said.

"More than okay, it's like… like…" She was struggling to get the feelings out of her head and into words. "Us, together. Now. It's the best. And I'm gonna be a surfer, Kook. A pro, free surfer. I can do it. I know so. And this… THIS. It's gonna be us." She pointed at a projection on the tent wall – surfers riding waves on a beach, at the edge of a jungle, in front of a ruined temple. "That. This. Us. Right?"

"Us?" I said, squeezing her waist.

"I love you, Kook…"

Love. Had she just said *love*? I zoned out, not even hearing what she said next. I could see her lips moving, but I couldn't hear.

Love.

Then I zoned back in. I *did* hear.

"…you're the sweetest, cleverest dude I know. You're not like that lot. I love them too but I've known 'em forever and you're, well, you're different, aren't you? And Jesus, you can even surf, good too, for how long you been doing it. And… science, you know about science, and facts and things like water and energy, and I read that we're mostly water and so is the earth's surface, Kook, so we're like the earth, right? Or the ocean really, and when we surf we're part of it and it's inside us and it's insane and makes sense all at the same time, which is like I am right now. And time. It's not even real… and… you get me, right?

230

Grrrrr…" she growled with frustration, taking her arm off me and grabbing at her hair. She was fizzing and bubbling, talking a thousand words a minute. It was hard to keep up. "It's like it's like it's like it's what I was born to do born in the water and we come from water all life does, I looked it up, you've got me into it, Kook, made me think about shit like that. I looked it all up on Google and the whole universe was tinier than the tiniest thing and there was no time before and… what was I saying? Oh yeah, when we surf we're just going *back* into the water. Made of it. In it. Part of it and born in the water and… and…"

She'd said she loved me. But could I believe her? Trust her? She hadn't even remembered it was my birthday. And she was rambling. Did she even know what she was saying? Maybe she was like this because…

"Are you on something?" I shouted into her ear, thinking, *Something. Not Rag's sherbet.*

"Yes, Kookasamasamakook. Hey, there's an old singer called Sam Cook my dad likes and you're Sam Kook, that's funny, and yes…*YES*… I am on something. I'm on drugs. I'm the girl in the swing, Kook. My eyes are diamonds. I see *every*thing." Her eyes *were* diamonds, bright and fierce in the shadow of her face.

This was Super Jade. Believing she was ready for anything. But when she stood still she was swaying. Unsteady. Like she'd got off the fairground ride of Super Jade for a second and was feeling dizzy. Like she was too much to handle, even for herself. Like if she stopped moving, she'd fall over.

So she started dancing again. Heads turned. She looked a

231

bit odd, madly going for it in this small marquee. People were standing chatting, not dancing. They'd gone there to chill out.

I reached out to hold her hand, to steady her a bit. She brushed me away.

"Having a good time then?" I said.

"Yeah, this stuff the St Wenna lot gave me is amazing. It's a class A drug. I mean, why do they call it that if they don't want you to take it? It's class A, amazing, top-drawer, dead brilliant. They don't tell you that, do they? Makes you wonder what else they're lying about."

"Who?"

"I dunno. You know. Them. The government, the police, teachers. I think they're lying about a *lot* of stuff, like wars, the economy and shit. Shall we start a revolution... or just say fuck it all and go surfing forever?"

She was on one. She was intense. Making no sense, and *knowing* she wasn't making any sense, but believing every word.

It was scary. It was hilarious. It was awesome.

Super Jade.

"Do you want some? Mick'll sort you out," she said.

Mick. Shit. He was here. And he'd given her the drugs. And no doubt he'd want to cosy-up to her. They'd be in their drugged-up little world. I'd be in mine. Shit.

"Come on, come on." She pulled at my T-shirt, trying to get me back into the main marquee. I was worried she was taking me to see Mick. Looking at her I didn't think I wanted to be on what she was on. Although...

But she just wanted to dance.

We were joined by the others. She danced with me, with them, with groups of people. Alone. With friends, with strangers, with girls, with guys. She never stayed with anyone for long. People got a quick light beam of Jade, before she moved on, leaving them blinded.

Like I said. Taking all the energy, spitting it right back out.

Jade was getting off on all the attention, high and happy.

It was great to see. But at the same time, I had a gnawing pain in my gut. Because all of a sudden we weren't enough for her. I wasn't enough.

After a specially mind-mangling bit of music, she stopped, seeing me looking at her, hypnotised by her. I felt embarrassed. Like she'd caught me looking at her naked.

She hugged me tight, shouted in my ear, "See you in a bit, yeah?" She ran off, into the ocean of bodies.

It was clear what she was saying.

I'm Super Jade. You can't stop me. I can't stop me. Even if I wanted to. You can't join me. Don't follow me.

I didn't follow. I didn't want to make a tit of myself. But the state she was in, it worried me a bit. At the same time, I felt angry with her. Why had she said *see you later*? And jealous. I didn't know what I felt jealous *of*, or why. But that's how I felt.

I spent some time with the others. Dancing. Standing on the edge of the main marquee looking at the rave. Dancing again. Pretending not to be thinking about where she was, who she was with, what she was doing.

After a bit I couldn't stand it any longer. I wasn't going to follow her, wasn't going to interrupt anything. Didn't want to be a sap. I just wanted to check she was okay.

I couldn't find her. Not in the sea of bodies. So I walked around. She wasn't in the chill-out tent. She wasn't outside. I even went back to where we'd got in, where we'd left the coats and sleeping bags. Dreadman said she hadn't come back. And her coat and sleeping bag were lying there, with the others.

I was sure she hadn't left. There were a lot of people and she was likely in the middle somewhere, raving her perfect arse off.

But I had a nightmare image of her in my head, running off into the dark with Mick. And it was hard to get rid of. I hated feeling like that.

About twenty minutes after I'd last seen her, I saw Billy, Tel and some of the others from St Wenna. Behind them, right on the edge of the tent, was Jade, standing talking to Mick, holding on to his shoulder with one hand, and holding a glass of something with the other. She wasn't hopping around any more. She was swaying and rocking. He had her round the waist, and was talking in her ear. Just like I'd been. Shit.

A girl passed her a spliff. She downed the rest of what was in the glass, dropped it on the floor, took the spliff, took a drag. Then another. She didn't pass it on.

As I worked my way towards them, I saw Mick unwrapping a small foil package. Getting something out. For her? He stopped when he saw me, put it back in his pocket.

"Koooook," Jade shouted out. "Here's Sam. Youallknow Saaaam, right? He's gonnasurf the Horns with me."

I walked straight up. Right up so she could see me. She and Mick kept a hold on each other. Like they were a couple.

"I bintellingMickaboutislands," said Jade.

"You really got this chart then?" said Mick, shouting over the music. "You know where they are?" He was friendly, trying to chat.

"Yeah, *we* are," I said, looking at Jade, trying to get her to look at me.

"Not if we get there first," he said. How much had Jade told him? I took the spliff off her, just so I could grab her hand. She slipped out of my grip.

"Whayadoing? I'm fine," she said.

"She's fine," said Mick.

"I'm fine. I'm havingnicetime," she said.

"Come on, the others are looking for you." I got her wrist. Mick got her other arm. It was like a tug of war with Jade as the rope.

"I'm fine, I'm fine, I'm fine, I'm fine." She was singing it, staring round, trying to focus.

"What's your problem, mate?" said Mick. "I'm looking after her."

"I'll talk to him," Jade said, she pulled her arms out of our grip, then patted Mick on the cheek. She pushed me away, to the edge of the tent. Now it was me she was using to help her stay standing, with her hand on my shoulder, shouting into my ear.

"What'syerproblem, Kook?"

"Let's go get some water."

"I'm having fun. These guysrokay, partfrom Billy, he'stwat. Mick'sallright."

Maybe that was it then. It hit me like a cold wave. Sudden and clear.

Mick was 'all right'. Course he was. So was I. But I wasn't enough. No one was. Anyone was okay till she found someone else more fun. She'd hang out with any of us. She wasn't fussy. Till she got bored. Then she'd move right along. A better wave. Some drugs. A rave. A new guy who fancied her.

"I'm girlinswing," she said. Her eyes had been diamonds before. They were dead now. Great, dark pools of deadness. Her skin was scary pale. She was sweating.

"He's getting you out of it," I said.

"So what, Dad?"

"Are you with him? What about us? You said you loved me."

She sparked at that. She was shocked. "Did I say that?"

"Yeah. You did."

She looked straight suddenly. Sober. Afraid. Then she smiled. Mask back on.

"I love*everyone,* Sam."

"You coming or not?" I grabbed her hand. She stood away from me. And behind the dead eyes, anger.

"You don't fucking own me, Kook," she shouted. She yanked her hand away, turned, went back to Mick. He moved in, pulling her towards him. Talking in her ear. Pressing. His body against hers.

I felt sick. Hot, and sick.

Jade clocked my face. She laughed.

I didn't know her then. This was some other Jade.

I hated her. I hated myself too. I went up to her. Looked down at her.

"Fuck you," I mouthed, right in her face.

"Fuggoff yourself," she said.

Mick pushed my shoulder.

"Watch it, mate," he said. It wasn't much, just a nudge. I pushed him back, in the same way. But I pushed a bit harder. He pushed me again. Harder again.

"You heard her," he said.

"You're coming," I said to Jade. He pushed me again. Right in the chest. Not just messing about now. "What you given her?" I said, thumping his shoulder. "What you doing to her? Arsehole."

"Fuck off back where you came from. Kook." He gave me a final, hard push. Sent me back a foot or more to make sure I got the message.

I did the same, straight back at him.

He beckoned at me, curling his finger, like he wanted to talk to me up close. I guessed to stop the pushing before it turned into a fight. I put my head forward, nodding.

"What?" I said.

When I was right up close, he slapped me under the chin. Hot anger flooded into my head.

I punched him. Hard. In the face. I felt his nose crack.

30

IT KICKED OFF.

One second it was eyeball to eyeball and sarky smiles, the next a storm of fists, lashing out, kicking.

I couldn't see what I was hitting; I didn't feel anything; I was still drunk. I didn't have any sense of what I was doing. I was numb to any pain, lashing out, arms flying. I'd keep doing it till he was off me. I wasn't going to stop. I hated him. I wanted to kill him.

Then I was on the floor. I don't know if I fell or slipped or was pushed. But there were feet kicking me. More than just Mick's feet. I tried to get up, but they just kept on coming. I put my arms over my head, like when I got thumped by a wave. I was in a ball, rolling around trying to avoid the kicks. It was all happening above me. I was locked down. I kicked out with my feet. They didn't hit anything.

It was dark down there. Dark, under the surface.

But all I had to do was hold on, come up for air when it stopped.

I rolled about, counted. One, two, three…

Ten…

And then it did stop. Suddenly. I looked up.

Rag, Skip. They were stuck in. Pushing, pulling, hitting, shouting in faces. Spitting with fury. Yeah, even Skip. I couldn't tell who was fighting and who was trying to *stop* the fighting.

I couldn't hear the music, just this high-pitched whine.

I looked around. For Jade. I couldn't see her.

I tried to get up, but I only got to my knees, then fell back. I tried again, managed to get up this time. Just. I was looking for Jade, but for Mick too; I wanted to hit him again. To finish him. But I couldn't see him either. Then I saw G, wading through the gobsmacked crowd, eyes fixed like a dog after a rabbit.

Billy was shouting at Rag, being shouted at *by* Rag. Rag had his hands up, not surrendering, just saying he wasn't going to hit anyone any more, trying to stop it. Billy was squaring up, wanting to fight, trying to *make* him hit him. He didn't see Big G's fist coming. He went down like he'd been hit by a truck.

Then G sat down on top of Billy, quite casual, and began punching him in the face. Again and again and again.

People tried to pull him off. It didn't make any difference. He was too strong. Too determined.

I weaved around people, looking for Jade.

I saw Ned and Sue. The looks of horror and pain, as they took it all in.

Ned saw one of the St Wenna lot holding Rag by the throat. Ned didn't like that. He waded in. He got this guy by the neck, lifting him, pushing him. Then he saw G trying to kill Billy. He let go of the guy and threw himself at G instead, got his arms round him. Squeezing. He shouted out, and I heard him, just.

"Stop. You're going to kill him. You're going to kill him."

G got off, stood, shaking Ned off him like he was a blanket. He'd done what he needed to. Billy was on the floor, eyes closed, blood pouring out of his nose. Ned went back to the guy who'd had Rag.

The bouncers turned up. They looked lost, confused. One got Ned by his arms, trying to wrestle him out of the fight and pull him away. Not easy, as Ned was now trying to hit the guy who'd had Rag by the throat. Sue was screaming in the bouncer's ear, pulling at him to leave Ned alone.

The more dudes got involved trying to stop it, the more it kicked off. I stood, head numb, feeling hot *and* cold, vaguely aware of blood trickling from my nose. The iron taste of it in my mouth.

All this had started because of me, and I'd started it because of…

Jade.

There she was. Sat on a speaker stack, kicking her legs like the girl on the swing, looking at the floor, trying to focus, not even noticing the madness in front of her.

I saw shades man speaking into a walkie-talkie. A girl waded into the middle of it all, arms up, shouting, "This is a rave, this is a rave, this is a rave."

Because if she repeated it, loud and often enough, they'd all see sense. Right?

It was too late for that.

I pulled Jade away, just to get her away from the fight. She stumbled. I put her arm around my neck so I could carry her.

The music was still playing. But everyone had stopped dancing. They were stretching their necks to get a good look.

Then the music *did* stop. The lights came up. Not flashing now, not oceans and rainbows, but hard and white. I could see the sweat. The blood on the faces.

And the police, marching through the crowd. Smiley.

Shit. He knew how old I was. If he saw me, he might leave the other police to sort out the fight and come straight for me.

I snuck Jade out of sight, behind the desks, right back where we'd started at the rave, what seemed a million years ago.

Dreadman was there. He was busy stacking up records in boxes. Like luggage for a holiday. He ran out with one under each arm.

I helped Jade put her coat on, holding her up and helping her put her arms in, hurrying her up.

"Wherewegoing?" she said. "Why leaving?"

"Police are here." I wondered about Smiley. What he'd say if he saw me.

The others stormed in then, grabbing their coats and bags.

"Insane," said G, grinning, like it was the most fun he'd had in months.

"Mad," said Rag. He wasn't grinning. "How did that fuck-up happen? Who started it?"

I kept quiet.

"Mental," said Skip, shaking his head, "just full-on mental." But weirdly, he was smiling like G. Skip. Nervy Skip. High as the sky. On the rave. The fight. On life.

We got out where we'd come in.

Dreadman was in the shadows, with his pick-up truck, one just like Ned's. He was loading his boxes of records on to the back.

"Got any room?" I asked. He turned, took one look at the stumbling mess that was our gang and shook his head.

"Come on, man," I said. "She's in a bad way, and I really need to avoid the police."

"You and me both," he said. "Anyway. I can't fit you all on the back."

"Just me and her then. We're underage, ain't we?" I said glaring at him. Dreadman had helped get us in. Maybe it wouldn't be so good for him if the police knew that. I didn't like putting pressure on him, but I was desperate.

"Not all of you," he said. We looked at each other. Big G

didn't look happy, but he had to see the sense in getting Jade away, and in me avoiding the police.

He pointed at Jade. "Get her out of here then," he said, to me.

The others vanished. I helped Jade into the back of the pick-up, laid her down gently as I could, then helped Dreadman get the rest of his stuff. Quickly though. I didn't want to leave Jade.

I came back, lay down in the back, with Jade.

I thought what she'd had was meant to make you buzzy and awake. But she was only half with it. *God knows what she's on*, I thought. Or what happened if you mixed it with loads of vodka and spliffs. I guessed I was going to find out.

Dreadman started the engine. As we drove off, I peeked over the edge.

We went straight past the police cars, pulling on to the verge to get round them. There was only one policeman, all the others were inside the marquees. No one came after us.

We drove into the night, leaving the marquees and the crowds and the police behind. The lights on the cars flashed in the dark, like they were part of the rave.

Jade sat up, looked at me without seeing me, then put her head over the side and threw up. I held her hair.

She came back up when she'd finished, gasping, but looking way better.

Sick glistened on her chin.

"Mayhem guaranteed," she said, smiling weakly.

31

I HAD A BOTTLE of water in my bag. I poured some into her cupped hands. She washed her face, then drank the rest.

"Are you okay?" I shouted, above the engine. She nodded.

Then she lay down, using her sleeping bag as a pillow and burying herself in her giant coat. I laid down too. Down there we couldn't feel the rush of cold air. The record boxes and our bags protected us.

She pulled the beanie down over her forehead and her coat collars around her, so I could only see her nose and her eyes. She stared up at the stars.

She stayed like that as we drove. A good half-hour. Longer.

As the time passed, the glaze on her eyes melted, and I could see she was really looking, seeing the stars. She looked calmer now, better. Being sick had done her some good.

I tried to imagine what she might be thinking. But I couldn't.

"Thanks," she said eventually, turning to me. "Thanks for looking after me."

She was back, not slurring her words, not speaking like a motor-mouth either. Still wide-eyed, but seeing me.

"You all right?" I said.

"Better now, Kook. I was right out of it and I felt… I feel…." She stopped, to check how she *was* feeling. "I still am. I'm on one. But it's different. I'm like… here… now. Really here, really now. But I was gone back there." She paused a second, rewinding whatever memories she had of the chaos we'd just left. "What happened?"

What happened? Had she really asked *me* what happened?

I told her. Dancing. Mick. Fighting.

"That's heavy," she said, and let out a long whistle. "I think I fell over when it started. I was on the floor, trying not to be sick. I crawled through all these legs. Then… I dunno."

"You *don't know*?" I said. The way she was talking; it was casual. She didn't seem that bothered.

"What were you doing?" I said. "What was all that with Mick?"

She frowned like she didn't understand.

"Dunno," she said.

That made me mad. I was angry with her. I was worried about her. I hated her. I wanted to get away. I wanted to be with her. All at once.

I didn't know *what* I felt. A whole storm of things. But she was just cool. As ever. And that made it worse.

I was straightening up by then, not so drunk. But I wished I was out of it. I wished I could knock back more vodka.

"You don't *know*?" I said, again.

"What do you want from me, Kook?" She glared at me, challenging.

"After the island… when we kissed…" *I give up*, I thought. *I just give up.* Whatever I wanted, she wasn't going to give it. "Look, it's okay," I said, "if you like Mick. I just… got it wrong, that's all."

"You didn't. He's nothing. I dunno what I was doing. Can't remember. Just having a laugh."

Having. A. Laugh.

She smiled and put her hand on my head, and through my hair.

"Then why…?" I stopped myself saying any more. I pushed her hand away. She put it back.

"I don't know, Sam. Pushing you away, maybe. Seeing how much he liked me? Trying to make you jealous? I don't know about you, Sam. You're posh… You're… you're not like us and you'll leave us behind one day, won't you? And… I don't always know *why* I do things. I just do them. Look… I like you, okay. Is that what you want to hear, you annoying, fat pain in the bum? I like you; I *really* like you… but… I'm not who you think I am. You don't want to get involved with me. I'm a fuck-up."

"Too late," I said.

"Do you hate me?"

"No. I don't know. No…"

"Happy birthday," she said, and leant over and kissed me. There was still a faint reek of sick off her. I didn't care.

"Pretty freaky birthday," I said.

"Oh yeah." Jade started fumbling in her coat pockets. "I meant to give you this at the end of the night. Didn't think it'd be like this though." She gave me a small box wrapped up in paper. It was Sellotaped tight. I had to tear at it with my teeth to get it open.

Inside the box something was scrunched up in tissue paper.

A cold, smooth stone, like a small pebble.

We passed through a village. Quiet, cold and asleep. In the orange glow of the streetlights, I could see the soft green stone.

A piece of Jade.

Of course. What else?

I kissed her then. She kissed me back. We held each other tight. It was more than a kiss. It became something else. Something that had me breathing hard, with my hands inside her coat, finding the dress, and the soft skin beneath it.

32

WE HAD TO STOP when the van stopped.

Dreadman dropped us on the road, a few miles from home.

We had our sleeping bags. But we didn't have anywhere to sleep. We couldn't just pitch up at home, not with Jade like she was. We'd have to walk all night. No bad thing, maybe. I was still a bit drunk, maybe a bit stoned, though nowhere near as much as I had been. And Jade? She was still high as the stars.

We went to Penford beach, just round the corner from Tin-mines. It was what we needed. Somewhere quiet and dark, well away from any houses or people. A good place for Jade to run off her craziness. We needed to keep moving too. It was bone-biting cold.

She was still whizzing from whatever it was Mick had given her. That was okay. She was safe, she could go as nuts as she liked, but she *was* being a headcase, now she'd got over the booze. The stuff was stronger than drink and spliffs; it was going to last a while. Turbo-charged Jade. Super Jade. She ran around on the sand, arms spread out, spinning, dancing to whatever bonkers tune was playing in her head.

"Look, Kook, look," she said.

"Yeah, I see you," I said, shaking my head and laughing.

"Not me, *this*!" she said, opening her arms to the beach, the black sea, the night packed with stars.

"Yeah, it's cool."

"Cool?" She marched right up to me, held me by the coat collar, putting her face so close to mine I felt her warm breath on my mouth. Hot metal liquid exploded in my stomach and filled my whole body. Were we going to kiss again? I was still going from the snog we'd had in the back of the van. It had been getting even better when Dreadman stopped and booted us out.

I leant forward. She pulled away. No more than a breath away. But enough to give me a 'not right now' signal. Maybe she wasn't that out of it. I wanted to kiss her so bad it was hurting. And the booze and spliff were still working on me and making me that little bit hornier, and braver too. I took her hands off my coat and held them.

"It's beyooootiful, Kook, and… and sooo intense, but *good* intense," she whispered. "Why is it so intense, Sam? *Why?*"

"Cuz you've had a bucket of drugs, Jade."

"Oh. Right… Sam?"

"Yeah."

"Let's get some *more*?"

We were on the beach, at fucked-up o'clock in the morning, with Jade off her face. And she wanted more. I laughed. Yeah, that was funny.

"What's cracking you up?" she said.

"You." I pulled her a bit, towards me, but just as our lips touched, she laughed, slipped away and was off, running to the shore and back again, playing chicken with the tiny waves.

She stopped suddenly, up to her ankles in the freezing water. I don't think she even felt the cold.

"Come in, Kook. Let's go swimming!" she shouted.

I'd had enough. I went and grabbed her hands and pulled her out of the water.

"No way," I said, speaking to her like she was a kid – a really stupid one. "That would be mental."

"Jesus, Sam. I'm just *kidding*!" She rolled her eyes, adding, "And you're being mean."

"You're off on one.*"

"Am I being a dick?" she said.

"Honest?"

"Yeah."

"Unreal. Off the scale. But pretty funny."

"And you're looking after me."

"Someone has to."

"Sorry." She frowned and bit her lip, trying to look cute. It worked.

"It's not your fault," I said, thinking, *It's Mick's.*

She tried to pull away, but I kept hold of her hands. When she sussed I wasn't letting go, she leant away from me, arching her whole body backwards so she was facing the sky, with her mouth wide open.

"Wooooooooow," she said.

There was no moon. No clouds. Just stars. Thousands of them. Like someone had taken handfuls of white sand and thrown them over a black sheet.

It was minutes before she spoke again.

"Science stuff, Kook. Now."

"What do you want to know?"

"How many stars are there?"

I pulled her upright, leant down and picked up a handful of sand, then I took her hands, opened them and put the sand on her palms. I spread the sand around with my finger. Then I got my phone out and used the display as a torch.

"How many grains of sand in your hand?" I said. She shrugged. "As many as in the sky?" She looked up again. The sky wasn't a dark thing. It was blue-white milk, it was so thick with stars. She looked back at the sand in her palms, leaning right over them. I swear she was counting the grains.

"I dunno," she said.

"There's more stars than grains of sand."

"More than the sand in my hands?"

"More stars in space than all the sand on all the beaches in the world."

She screwed up her face, and looked me in the eyes, suspicious. "Is that true, Kook?" she whispered.

"Yeah."

"Holy fuckerama."

"Yeah, holy fuckerama." In the phone's light I could see wonder in her wide eyes. She smiled, like we'd shared the most amazing secret.

We were close, huddled around the phone like it was a candle. I leant my forehead on hers and that hot metal liquid flooded through me again.

I put my hands on her cold cheeks and kissed her. She just stood there for a moment, frozen. I thought I'd blown it. But then she dropped the sand and was kissing me back, pressing hard with her lips. Jade holding my coat. My hands in her hair.

She broke away. "Let's go to Tin-mines," she said. She was breathy now. Breath*less*. Nervy. "We can make a fire."

I knew what it meant. I knew what was going to happen.

We kissed again. We picked up our bags from the beach and walked hand in hand across the sand to the cliff path.

★

The key to the mines was hidden in the rocks.

We got into the den. It was dry and warm. And totally dark.

I didn't know what to do, what to say. I'd suddenly run out of words. So I got busy making the fire.

Behind the boards and wetsuits I found driftwood. Piles of

it we'd collected from the beaches in autumn, and dried over the weeks. Then newspaper, then matches. And rugs, and blankets.

She held the phone, giving me enough light to make the fire.

It was only when I lit it that I realised how cold I was. My hands were shaking. But maybe that wasn't just the cold.

I knelt, feeding the fire, watching the smoke rise and creep along the ceiling and out of the mine entrance, while Jade got some of the rugs and blankets and heaped them by the fire. She got our sleeping bags and opened them up. For us to sit on.

To lie on?

The fire flared up quickly. Soon there was a wall of orange flames and smoke between us and the world. Home, school, Big G and the others, the fight, Billy and Tel. It was all gone. Mick was gone. There was just us, now, here, locked into our own little world by the wall of flames. And as the flames got higher, the inside of the mine was lit up. And we could see each other.

We sat side by side, not speaking. We didn't look at each other much, apart from just to give quick little smiles. We didn't talk. And we *never* didn't talk.

She hugged her legs, hiding most of her face, so her green eyes stared at the flames over her knees. She watched the fire like it was hypnotising her.

She'd calmed down. She wasn't out of it any more. She wasn't Super Jade.

The silence was deep as the mine. Deep as the sea. I wasn't used to Jade being shy. But she was. She was quiet. Straightened out. A different girl from the one on the beach. A different girl to the one I knew.

What now? Was it too late?

"Sam…" she said, quietly, turning towards me, resting her head on her knee.

"Yeah?"

She didn't say anything else. Shadows and golden light danced in her eyes.

I edged closer, shuffling. Just the sound of me moving toward her was killingly loud. My heart was thumping through my whole body.

Closer.

We kissed. And kissed. I tasted the salt on her lips. And kissed. More and more. We couldn't stop.

"But you're…" I started. I was going say "out of it". But she shut me up with kisses.

"It's okay, Sam. I'm okay."

Then…

Her stretching out and lying down, us getting closer, not just our lips, our bodies. Together. Hands fumbling through clothes, looking for warm skin. My head spinning.

She pulled at my clothes and at me. And I did the same. Fiddling with belts and buttons, shuffling out of jumpers, T's, jeans. Her dress.

Soon there wasn't any more fumbling with clothes, and

there was a lot of warm skin. Feeling the places where there'd be bruises. Her hands across them. Hurting.

Then it was just a whole storm of kissing and tumbling.

"I haven't got any—" I started.

"It's okay, Sam. I do," she said.

I looked at her. "Oh. Oh, right."

She punched my arm. "Not like that. Just… I was thinking of you. You know?"

I didn't know if it was true, but I wanted it to be.

She got one from her bag. I put it on. Then…

I thought it would just happen, by itself, like we'd just fall into one another. Just magically get it together.

But she helped me, put her hand down my chest, my stomach. Lower. Guiding me, letting me know what was happening.

Jade wasn't shy. She looked at me the whole time.

The hot metal liquid burned me up.

★

Afterwards, we lay by the fire, in a mess of rugs and sleeping bags, holding each other tight.

Lots of giggling, lots of kissing. We couldn't stop.

"Holy fuckerama," I said breaking away.

"Yeah, holy fuckerama," she said.

And we smiled, and grinned and laughed, like we'd shared the most amazing secret.

"What was *that*?" I said.

"Don't you know?" she said, smiling, with her arms tight around me, playing with the hair at the back of my neck.

"We…?"

"Go on, what?"

And it wasn't just about Jade right then, it was also that I'd…

Done It. Lost my virginity.

"We had *sex*," I said, sounding way more pleased, and way less cool, than I meant to.

"No. We didn't," she said, seriously, like it was a fact.

"Didn't we?" I said, thinking, *What?*

"People in biology books have sex."

"Oh right." We laughed again. Kissed again.

"We fucked?" I said.

She whacked me on the back of the head. "No, Kook! *Way* too porno."

"Made love?"

"Get real."

"Shagged?"

"Animals shag. And slappers in night-club car parks."

"What. What did we do then?"

She slid down my body and rested her head on my chest, using me as a pillow.

"Dunno if there is a word, Kook. Not a good one, leastways."

We were quiet then, for a long time. The crackling of the fire and the rush of the sea on the nearby beaches – they made a pretty good soundtrack right then, to us just lying there.

"That was your first time, wasn't it?" she said, after a bit, quietly, and I was glad she wasn't looking me in the eyes right then. I knew I didn't need to ask if it was *her* first time. And I was thinking, *Shit, what did I do wrong?*

"Was it... okay?" I asked. Wanting to know. Not wanting to know. She looked up, climbed on top of me. Lying on me, she rested her chin just below my neck, with her whole body on top of mine. Her boobs squashed into me, my hand on her back. That liquid fire was inside me again. Stirring. She smiled. That smile of hers that was kind *and* mean, like there was something about me she always found a bit funny.

"Yeah, Kook, it was okay. It's just... you were pretty eager, weren't you?"

"Is that bad?" I asked, worrying I'd got the whole thing wrong. Maybe I just *thought* it had been great, maybe that was just *me*. But her eyes told me not to worry. That it was okay. That everything was okay.

"Don't panic, Kook. Eager's good. Just slow down a bit next time."

I almost got up and did a dance. There was a next time?

"Happy birthday," she said, kissing me.

★

We started kissing. And that wasn't an end to things, it was a beginning. Over the hours we did it again.

Less eager. More slow.

★

I shoved loads of wood on the fire. Piled up the rest, so I could lean over and put a log on whenever it died down. We wrapped up tight in the sleeping bags, with the fire in front of her and me behind her, staring at the arm I had wrapped round her, stroking the hairs.

"You've changed," she said. "Your body, brown, muscles… fire skin," she whispered, just as she fell asleep.

I didn't sleep. I looked at the fire, and at Jade, breathing.

I was sixteen. And me and Jade were together. And we'd done it.

I was thinking, it wasn't like in porn, it was like… I couldn't say any of those words in my head and fit them to what we'd done.

Jade was right about that.

33

WE WERE WOKEN by the morning light and a fresh breeze.

All the firewood was used up and the cold was getting in the mine and trying to get in our bones, so I dressed and packed up quick. Jade pulled her clothes on, then sat in the mine entrance, wrapping herself in the sleeping bag.

Outside, the light stung my eyeballs. Everything was hyper. More real, somehow. The sea was bluer, the ashes of the fire burned like a sunset, the wind gentle but crisp. And Jade, more beautiful than ever. Even with sunken eyes and crow's nest hair.

We couldn't go home. Not straight away. I needed to make out to Mum I'd been away. I needed to keep that lie going. And as for Jade...

"What time d'you need to get back?" I said. She shrugged, looking away. "Well, what did you tell your dad?"

"Said I was going out. Didn't know we'd be out *all* night, did I?" She laid one of those little smiles on me.

"He'll be worried," I said.

"He'll have drunk himself stupid last night, 'specting me to pitch up later. He won't be out of bed till midday. If he kicks off, I'll just say I was out early this morning."

"Have you checked your phone?" I said.

"No signal. Out of juice, anyway."

"Do you want to go home, now?" I said. She stood, opened the sleeping bag like a cape and put it round my shoulders, then put her arms under and around me, pushing her body up against me, using me and the bag for warmth.

"Nah. Not yet," she said. I stared out at the flat, burning blue ocean, thinking about where we could go. Somewhere warm and safe.

★

It was early. We were the only people in the Old Chapel cafe. We went straight to the table by the wood burner. Our table.

There was one old armchair, next to the burner, and Jade sat in it, curled up in the sleeping bag.

I ordered coffee and a full English with extra toast and marmalade.

My left eye was throbbing. My muscles and bones were stiff from the fight, and sleeping on the mine floor. But I felt good. Sitting by the burner, lapping up the heat. Knackered, but on top of the world at the same time.

Jade didn't eat much when the food came, but I wolfed it. Sausage and egg and tomato. Rounds of toast, melted butter and marmalade. I'd never known food could taste so good.

My phone bleeped. A message from Mum.

Hope you saw lots of stars.

Have you heard from Jade? Her dad's worried sick.

"You'd better read this," I said, handing Jade the phone.

"Shit."

"Do you want to call him?"

"No. Can you get a message to him?"

I didn't fancy talking to Bob, so I took the phone back and texted Mum.

Jade went for surf. Met me and Mike for brek in cafe. His mum treating us.

Jade's phone dead. Cn U let Bob know shes OK? Home soon.

I showed Jade.

"Nice work, Kook."

I ordered more coffee. A few minutes later, as the woman was about to serve it, I heard a car. There was no mistaking the rasping, sick-man cough of the old Volvo. Not any car. Bob's car.

"Shit," said Jade.

We watched the door. Waiting.

Bob rushed in and walked up to us, his eyes frantic-wide.

"You're all right?" he said to Jade. I was relieved. He wasn't angry. Just worried.

"Fine. I got up early," said Jade, "that's all." She was so cool about it. Lying was like a language she could speak better than anyone.

"But… you always leave a note," said Bob, standing over her.

"I didn't bother."

Bob looked at the sleeping bag, piled up in the armchair, and at the two plates, cups and sets of knives and forks.

"I thought you was meant to be with some kid and his mum?" he said.

"Um, they left about ten minutes ago," I said. Bob glanced at the plates again.

"Your bed weren't slept in," he said to Jade, his voice getting harder.

"I made it."

"You? Never. And how come you never took Tess?"

His voice was hardening with every question. He was getting louder too. Now he knew Jade was safe, he wanted answers.

"You trying to make a fool of me, missy?"

Jade smirked. A look that said: *No, you're doing that yourself.*

"Get in the car," he shouted, pointing at the door. "We're going home."

"Me and Sam'll come later."

"Now," he said, quietly. Too quietly.

"No," said Jade. Just as quiet.

"Where were you last night?" he said. He reached out to grab her arm, but she twisted out of his grip and sat on her hands.

"Maybe you'd better go, Jade," I said. She looked at me like I was a traitor. And maybe I was, but I didn't want things getting worse for her right then.

"Look, I'll come too," I said. "I'll just pay."

I stood, and went and threw money at the woman, quick as I could, while Jade sat there, with her dad standing over her. I thought maybe if I came too, it'd help; that things between them might calm down.

"Come on," I said, picking up the sleeping bag and forcing it into its sack. Jade made a *humph* sound, then stood. I picked up our bags and we walked out, in silence.

"So, where were you?" said Bob, soon as we were out.

"Out."

"Where?"

"None of your bizzy," she said, and stopped still. Jade wasn't going anywhere with Bob. She just didn't want a scene in the cafe.

Bob grabbed her, by the wrist. And this time she wasn't quick enough. He started dragging her. She pulled back, digging her heels in the dirt like a stubborn horse. He just pulled harder. Using his strength and weight.

"I said, where?" he said.

"You're embarrassing," said Jade. He pulled her harder then. Too hard. His nails digging into her.

"Hey! Let her go," I said. He stopped yanking, but still held Jade's wrist. A snake, wriggling to get free.

"What?" he snorted.

"You heard me. Let her go." I pushed his shoulder. He looked at me, curious, seeming to notice the bruise on my eye for the first time.

Jade stopped squirming, staring at me too. Unbelieving.

"Or what?" said Bob, mock-laughing.

"She was with me," I blurted. "We went to a party, a big one. We missed the last bus. It was my fault. We haven't slept. We've been walking all night." It was a sort-of lie, but a good one. Like I was speaking Jade's language now too. "I looked after her," I said. I stared right at him, my face inches from his, my nostrils flaring.

He let go of her. The three of us stood there. Bob and Jade, staring at each other, at me. Both of them confused.

Bob folded his arms, smiling. "*You* looked after her?" he said, sarcastic.

"I don't need looking after..." Jade started. I glared at her to shut her up.

"Is that how you got that?" he said, pointing at my eye. "Looking after my daughter?"

I nodded.

"Well," said Bob, smiling, "your mum's gonna be well interested to hear this, isn't she? How you gonna explain that?"

"I dunno…" I said. Then added, "But if you don't back the fuck off, right now, I'll tell her you did it."

Jade sidled up to me, behind my shoulder. I felt her hand slip into mine, squeezing tight.

"*What?*" said Bob.

"She'll believe me too," I said. "I'll say you were going to hit Jade and I stopped you." He knew I meant it. And he knew I was right. "Don't ever touch her again," I said.

"What?"

"You heard me."

"What?" he said, again. I think the only reason he didn't belt me was because I was his neighbour.

"You *heard* me."

Jade stood just behind my shoulder, leaning into me, like we were one body.

Bob took a step back. Then another. He walked to his car, backwards, watching us the whole time. Then got in, and drove off.

"He'll be worse later," said Jade. "I'm in the shit now."

I turned and put my arms round her.

"No. I don't think he will be worse. I think you'll be all right." I don't know how I felt confident about that, but I did. I'd seen the look in Bob's eyes when I threatened him. He wasn't scared of me. But he *was* scared of Mum knowing what he did. Of her believing my story.

"Oh, Sam," said Jade. Her words were heavy and sad. "You don't know much about things, do you?" She kissed me.

"What now?" I said. "What do you reckon?"

"I think we'd better not go back for a while: that's what I reckon."

We picked up our gear, held hands and headed for the clifftop, not knowing where we were going, or for how long.

34

I GOT HOME LATE. I was determined to hide my bruises from Mum. At least as long as I could. I planned to head straight to my room, and stay there, till Mum had gone off to do her barmaid shift at the Admiral.

Avoiding Mum for a while wasn't going to be hard. Even though I'd promised to be back early, the truth was me and Mum not seeing each other much suited us both. Home life had been tense since the bust, especially with me bombing off and surfing every chance I got. And lying about it.

You'd think she'd have been on my case, but we had this unspoken deal. When she worked barmaid shifts, I was home looking after Teg. You can't surf when it's dark, so that was fine by me. As long as I was there for that, and Old Faithful stayed in the shed, she assumed I wasn't surfing, or hanging with that crowd, so didn't fuss about where I was the rest of the time. She didn't know about the new board. There was a lot she didn't know.

Like I said, I'd got good at hiding stuff. Lying was getting easy.

But bruises can't lie.

I came in and shut the door, quietly.

"That you, Sam?" said Mum, from the kitchen.

"Yeah, gonna have a bath, then I've got studying," I said. Long seconds dragged before she answered.

"Okay," she said, from the kitchen. Phew. I raced upstairs and straight into Teg coming out of the bathroom. She opened her mouth to shout, but I put a finger to my lips, glaring at her.

"What happened to you?" she said.

"Nothing. Keep it down," I whispered.

"Have you been in a fight?" she squealed with excitement.

"No."

"Yes, you have."

"Don't say anything to Mum. You can have… crisps… and stay up late."

"And then you'll tell me about the fight!" She bounced down the stairs, certain she had me wrapped up for as long as she wanted.

I went into the bathroom, started the taps and stripped. While the water ran, I looked at myself in the cracked, mould-stained mirror.

I had two corker bruises on my body, as well as a few

smaller ones. One in my ribs, one on my thigh. Purpley-blue as the deep sea. I poked the purple flower on my ribs and sucked sharp air with the pain. It made me feel good. Kind of proud.

Not just from the bruises though. My body, like Jade had said, had changed. I had muscles. My face was weather-browned. Salt-water beaten. My eyes glowed out of a dark face. Like Jade's.

I poked the bruise again. A reminder of the rave. That, and the memory of Jade. Us lying together, in the old mine, by the fire.

What a night. Happy birthday, Sam.

But as well as body blows, a fist or boot had got me in the corner of the eye. A small, hard egg of a bump stuck out of the side of my head. Telltale purple and black surrounded my eye like thick make-up.

I took my time in the bath, letting the hot water get to work. Because it wasn't just the bruises that hurt. My whole body felt stiff and slow, like I'd been run over by a steamroller.

As usual, when I'd finished getting clean, I put my head under, held my nose, and counted.

I could make sixty easy by then. And if I kept calm, even eighty, or ninety.

I did one hundred before my vision shuddered, and my chest spasmed.

A record.

I hoped Mum would be gone by the time I got out. I was drying off when I heard her shout, "Sam, tea's ready." It was a no-messing kind of a shout. It meant: come and get it. Now.

269

We had to do things like clockwork since she'd started working at the pub. She couldn't be late.

I opened the door and shouted down, "Can you put it on a tray? I've got homework to do."

But she shouted back.

"Come and eat with Teg. You can't just disappear to your room. Work downstairs till you've put Teg to bed, please."

I went and put on a long sleeved T and tracky bottoms, and walked down the stairs. Slowly.

Mum was in the hall, coat on, smelling of flowery perfume, doing her make-up in the mirror.

I sneaked past. She didn't look up. In the kitchen there were two trays, with plates of fish fingers, beans and toast.

The kitchen had a hatch, straight into the lounge. I passed Teg the trays, then went into the hall and past Mum. Again, she didn't see.

Teg was sunk in the sofa, already getting into her tea. I grabbed the remote. Not much point. We were going to watch *exactly* what Teg wanted.

Mum's head popped in. I didn't look up.

"Normal bedtime for Tegan, Sam. Lock the front door. I've got a key and... Sam, fascinated as you are by the TV, could you look at me while I'm talking?... Sam!"

I turned my head, slightly.

"Hope work's good. I'll lay out the breakfast things," I said.

"Thank you." She rattled her car keys in her hand. "Got to go... Bye."

"Bye."

"Sam."

"What?"

"*Look* at me when you speak to me, please… Sam!" She marched in and stood in front of the telly. I looked up. Her jaw fell open. Well and truly gobsmacked. "What the bloody hell happened to you?" She put her keys in her pocket. Hands to hips. Double teapot arms.

Excuses raced through my mind. *Fell over. Banged into a door. Did it surfing… No, can't say that.*

"I… er."

"Teg?" said Mum.

"Sam was in a fight," Teg blurted.

"What about the crisps?" I whispered. She shrugged, staring at Mum goggle-eyed. Afraid.

"What happened, Sam?" Mum fumed.

"Nothing."

"Nothing? That's your answer to everything I ask. You go nowhere. You do nothing. With no one. That's all you ever say. Did this happen last night? Where were you? Clearly not stargazing… What *happened*?!"

"You're going to be late for your new bloke."

"What did you say?" She said it quiet, but I could almost see smoke blowing out of her nostrils.

"The bloke you're seeing at the pub. Brian, right? Dolling yourself up, coming home late…"

"I… I'm at work," she flustered.

271

"Not till three in the morning."

Mum looked at the carpet, at Teg. She was a bit floored by how I was suddenly the one being like a parent, and she didn't know how to act. She took her keys back out of her pocket.

"Let's not have this conversation now, Sam. I'm your mother. Just tell me what happened to *you*!"

I folded my arms, focused on the telly. Then I thought, *Sod it, why not?*

"I went to a rave. I got in a fight. I got hurt, but not bad."

"When? Last night, on your birthday? You lied to me, didn't you? Who did it?"

"An idiot."

"Was it your fault?"

"It wasn't anyone's fault. It just happened."

She sighed, put her keys back in her pocket. "Why didn't you tell me?"

"Cuz you'd freak."

"Sam... I'm your mum. You need to tell me stuff."

"Why? There's a load of stuff you don't tell me. Like about your new bloke."

She gave me a not-in-front-of-Tegan look, then sighed, again. About to speak. Stopping. About to speak. Stopping. Like she couldn't decide. To shout. To talk. To stay. To go.

"Look. We'll talk. We will. But I have to go now," she said, quietly.

"See ya then." I said it mean. More than I meant to. I started flicking through channels.

"You know you can be a little sh… git sometimes," she said, her voice wobbling. Teg slipped off the sofa and out the door.

I looked up, at Mum. A jolt of shock. For both of us. I saw it in her eyes and I felt it in my bones. Because neither of us knew who we were looking at. We didn't know each other any more.

It was awkward. Embarrassing. I started flicking channels again.

"Let's talk tomorrow," she said. I tuned in to the TV.

Your Christmas saving scheme. Click.

Burger menu special this month. Click.

"Sam?"

I love you, Rachel. Click.

"Sam. I'm trying here."

Local farmers up in arms. Click.

Mum stood aside, went and sat on the arm of the sofa.

"Turn off the TV. I'll go in late. I'll call them. It's fine. We need to talk. Now. I won't be angry, I promise. Okay?"

I looked at her. "Okay." I nodded.

Giant waves…

I sat up, zoned in on the TV. Turned up the volume.

"Sam, okay? Can we talk now? Perhaps we… Are you listening? Sam… Sam…" She said something else. I don't know what. Her voice melted.

Ken was on the TV. The local celebrity weatherman, with his flapping hands and excited voice. "Right at the beginning of December we're expecting a series of storms, deeper and stronger than anything we've seen for a decade or more, sitting much further south than normal, in the mid-Atlantic. These storms will generate enormous waves…"

"Sam!"

"Just a sec, Mum."

"Fine. You know what? I'm going to work."

I didn't look up.

They showed pics of the last time storms had lashed the coast.

A shot of Whitesands harbour. An explosion of white water against the cliff.

The seafront. White vans, and trucks. Dozens of them. Men in Day-Glo yellow jackets, piling up sandbags outside ice-cream shops. Towns preparing to be invaded.

I turned off the TV. I had to phone Jade.

"Sam?" said a voice.

It was Tegan standing next to me. Mum had gone.

35

JADE DIDN'T ANSWER when I called. She didn't answer texts either. I went to bed wired.

My head was dizzy-full. With the rave, with Jade, with sex. Especially with sex. And those TV pics of waves, battering cliffs.

"A series of storms." That's what Ken the weatherman had said. But when would it be right for us? How would we know? How would we not kill ourselves just getting there?

I fell into a half-sleep, turning and sweating the whole time. Like the storm had begun, and it was in my head.

★

Jade still hadn't answered any of my texts by morning. I didn't much fancy going over to her house, not if Bob was there.

Then I decided, *Fuck it*, I wasn't going to be afraid of him. So, I went over. Turned out his car wasn't there anyway.

The only answer I got when I knocked was Tess barking. So I turned, and started walking. But then – a cracked and croaky, "Hello, Sam."

Jade stood in the doorway, in tracky bottoms and T-shirt. Her eyes were sleepy deep, not really seeing me. Her hair was a mess. She looked like some animal, woken from hibernation.

"Did you see the news?" I said, running back.

"No, what about it?"

"Storms. Loads of them, coming our way. We're on for the Horns."

"Cool, great," she said. But she sounded flat. It was like talking with an answerphone.

Can't talk right now. Get back to you another time.

"Are you okay?" I said. "Has he…"

"He hasn't spoken to me since. I'm okay, just glazed and confused. Took a while for that night at the rave to catch up with me. You?"

"Fine."

"Fine. You're fine? Lucky bastard." She looked up, her eyes beginning to focus. "Oooh, nice bruise. It's come up a treat," she said, putting a finger to my eye. She stroked the bruise, soft like a feather. "Storms then?" she said. Her mouth broke into a smile as the news sunk in. "Storms. Devil's Horns. Yeah, that's cool."

"Where's your dad?"

"Shit knows. He left a note saying he was off though. Not back till tonight. I got to go back to bed. I haven't really slept. The gear I took. I swear it took two days to wear off. Now I'm full-on broken. But that's great about the storms."

"You going to let me in?" I said.

Jade bit her lip, stared at me, like she wasn't sure. But then she opened the door, wide. "You want a coffee?" she said.

"Yeah," I said. We hugged. She was soft and warm from bed.

"Make me one too," she said. "Strong." She pointed to the kitchen, told me where I'd find coffee and milk, and headed upstairs.

While the kettle boiled, I had a nose around.

The lounge hadn't seen a hoover in a while. There was a low table, with a full ashtray, and two beer cans on it. Old newspapers were piled up next to the fire. The rug was covered in burn marks. There was only one picture on the wall: a bad painting of a ship. No photos or paintings, but dark squares where there might have been some. I stood a while, watching the dust in the air, like a billion tiny stars, imagining her dad sunk in the armchair, drinking beer.

"What you doing?" Jade stood in the doorway. The kettle was whistling. I hadn't even noticed.

"Nothing, just…"

"It's okay. I did the same at your gran's house."

"Where's the photos?" I pointed at the empty squares on the wall.

"Dad doesn't want memories," she said. "Kettle's still whistling." She went back upstairs.

I went and made the drinks, expecting her to reappear, dressed. But she didn't.

Was she still in bed? Was she *waiting* for me to join her? She seemed hardly awake, not likely to want to... But still...

I walked up the stairs.

She was in bed, scrunched up in her duvet. I wanted to climb in with her. It wasn't likely to happen, but I *did* want to get in. Shit, I wanted *her.* Badly. But I just stood there like a lemon, a steaming cup of coffee in each hand.

"Put them down here." She sighed, and pointed to her bedside table, then threw back the quilt, and moved over.

"No funny business, Sam. Right?" I kicked off my trainers and climbed in. We kissed. We kissed more. I moved my body into hers. "I said no funny business," she said. Jade sat up and patted the quilt between us. Tess leapt straight up and lay down. A wall between our bodies. That was that, then.

"Storms," she whispered. "We're gonna do it, Sam."

"Yeah. Afraid?" I said.

"I'm not afraid of anything."

I wondered about that. Everyone's afraid of something.

My eyes wandered around her room. Clothes were scattered on the floor, like the laundry basket had puked them up. Cups and plates too. The shelves were crammed with surf mags. And like the den, the walls were plastered with pics of surfers. But there was one photo, part hidden behind the mags. A woman standing on a beach. A woman who looked like Jade. For a second I thought it *was* Jade. But this was a pic of a woman, not a girl.

"Is that your mum?" I said, pointing.

"Yes."

I went and got the photo and got back into her bed. I felt a shock, looking at the woman who was so like Jade. But older. A happy mum, on a beach, with a seven or eight-year-old Jade, cuddling a puppy.

"You. Tess. Your mum," I said.

"I'm the spit. I know. Everyone says it."

"D'you miss her?"

She took the photo off me, and looked at it. Into it. "Course I do, Sam. She's my mum."

I hesitated. Wanting to know more, not wanting her to flip on me.

"How come she left?" I said.

"Still nosy, aren't you?" she said. Jade looked at the picture, stroking Tess's head with the other hand. "It's for the best. I miss her, but I don't miss…"

"What?"

She paused, holding her breath.

"What?" I said, again. "It's all right you know. You can tell me."

Jade bit her lip, looking out the window at the moors. She was dead still, thinking.

"…the fighting." She let out a long sigh.

I sat up too. I put my hand out and stroked the hair off her forehead. She smiled at me, then looked down at Tess. Almost shy. Almost embarrassed. I brushed her cheek, tried to get a smile out of her.

I wanted to know. Maybe to prove I didn't just want Jade the girl, Jade the mad surfer. I wanted to know about her family. I didn't know if I could help. I didn't know if I could look after her like I'd said to her dad. But I could try.

When she spoke, it was mouse-like. Not much more than a whisper.

"She never wanted to live out here, see. Me, Dad, Tess, we'd hate to be shacked up in town. But Mum wasn't... *isn't* like that. She likes pubs, shops, clothes. And people, she loves people. She can't be alone. She loves attention."

"From blokes?" I asked. I thought about Jade, at the rave.

"Yeah. They married young because mum was knocked up with me. I'm the reason she had to give up her party life..."

"And?"

"When I was older, she started going out. That's how it started."

"How what started?" I couldn't stop the questions, I couldn't stop pushing her, no matter how gentle I made it seem. I was getting in deep with Jade. Not just the sex, everything. Everything that was her.

"Well, she's pretty and blokes liked her and she enjoyed it. Too much. But she never did anything, when she was with Dad. I reckon I'd know if she had. She just liked messing with blokes' heads, got a kick from it…" Again, I thought of Jade at the rave… "She lapped it up. Dad was jealous. He'd go looking for her, round the pubs, people's houses. He took me with him once. Christ, it was embarrassing. Last couple of years I was out surfing whenever I could. So one good thing came from it. They didn't even notice. Glad to have me out the way, so they could fight."

She gripped the quilt. She sat bolt upright, looking at me, worried, searching my eyes. She was nervy. I reckon she thought she'd said too much. She sighed heavily and sat back into the pillows. "Dad wouldn't let her go out. He smothered her. And he got worse with the drink… Then… I dunno what happened, not for sure. But she couldn't stand it any more. She went and stayed with a mate. For a bit, she said. But a bit turned into a month. Then…"

"How come you didn't go with her?"

"I reckon I was part of what she was getting away from. Responsibilities, like. I don't blame her but…" Jade put the cup down. She folded her arms, her voice suddenly rising. "Well. She still *bloody* went, didn't she? She still left me… us."

"Left you with him," I said, and I was thinking: *With a piss-head who uses his fists*. Now it was my turn to take a deep breath. "Does he hit you, Jade?" I said. She flinched, turned to look at me.

"No, Sam. You got to believe me. He doesn't." She was pleading, desperate for me to believe her. She was breathing fast, scrabbling for an answer. She looked afraid, really afraid.

"It's been close, that's all. Like yesterday, at the cafe. He holds my arm, tight, like this." She grabbed my arm, digging her nails in.

"Hey, ouch!" I said, but she didn't stop. She shook my arm. She scowled, lowering her voice and tucking her chin in.

"What do you think you're playing at, missy, staying out all hours? What kind of a fucking princess do you think you are?"

It was scary. She acted it too well. Tess cowered.

"You have to get out, Jade," I said. "Maybe you can stay at ours?"

"You reckon he'd be all right with that, do you? Anyway, you got less room than we have."

"Grandma's then. Or with your mum?"

"My mum's in no state to look after me. Even if she wanted to."

"How do you know? You never see her, and…" She turned her head, away, sharp and quick, hiding her face from me. "Christ. You *do* see her, don't you?"

She shrugged, still facing the wall.

"When you seeing her next?" I said.

Silence. A long silence. Then: "Tomorrow. She's in town for a couple of nights," she whispered.

"It's school tomorrow."

"For you maybe."

"Do you want me to come?" I said. I thought she'd turn and face with me flaming eyes, and mean lips. But her eyes were soft.

"She'd like you. I know she would. You'd… surprise her. But no, you're all right, Sam. Believe me, once you got a taste of what my life is really like, you wouldn't want to know."

"Yeah, I would."

"Really?" She looked at me, unbelieving.

"Really. Let me come."

"No. But it might be good to meet up later though, she's…"

"What?"

Jade shook her head. She was saying: *No* more questions. Making it clear. But was that a tear in her eye?

I leant over and pulled her to me, our foreheads touching. She sighed. She smiled. We kissed. I held her head with my hands. She held on to my T-shirt, gripping it.

"I said no funny business," she said. But I kept on.

She didn't say it again.

It was her who grabbed Tess by the collar and pulled her off the bed.

36

I NEVER REALLY meant to follow her. I just did; I couldn't help myself.

We got the bus to school like normal. Only, when we got off at the school stop at the top of town, the crowd of kids went one way, and Jade went the other, with the women and toddlers, off to do their Monday shop.

"Hope it goes all right," I shouted after her.

"Thanks," she said, not looking back.

"I could still come with you?" I said. But she didn't answer.

I watched her disappear into the crowd. She looked smaller somehow, younger, like a kid. I felt a twist in my gut, watching her go. I was about to shout after her, to get her to stop. But hands grabbed my shoulders from behind. Rag spun me round and shook me.

"See the news?" he said. "See the Fur. King. News? Kook? You listening?"

I looked after Jade, but she'd gone. And it was like a knife in my gut. Deep and painful.

"Rag, I'm not coming to school. Tell them I'm ill."

"Sneaky surf, eh?" He winked, and tapped the side of his nose.

"Nah, something else." I ran off, after Jade. If she saw me, she'd be mad as a poked cat. And spying on her wasn't good. It just made more sense than going to school somehow.

I ran down the main street into town: a cobbled walkway of cafes and quirky shops. I couldn't see her. I ran all the way down. If she'd been walking, I'd have caught her. So where was she?

"Shit!" I ran back. Only this time I looked down the alleys that ran off the main drag.

The first one was empty. The second too. She could have been anywhere. But when I checked the third one, there she was, right at the end, turning a corner.

I ran down, peeked around the wall.

She was walking down a thin alley of tall terraced buildings. The backs of shops. It was a bright wintry day, but the alley was deep in shadows. She looked even smaller. And alone.

I didn't call out; I didn't catch her. I followed, like a spy. I didn't want her mad at me, didn't want to interfere. I told myself I'd catch her up and talk. Eventually. But for now…

Down one alley, another street, another alley. She was making her way down town, towards the harbour. Eventually she came out of the maze of alleys and streets and on to the seafront, a row of pubs and cafes near the docks.

She stood outside the shut door of a run-down pub called The Dolphin. It was weird that she was meeting her mum in a pub. It had to be closed. It wasn't even nine yet.

The door opened – I didn't see by who – and in she went.

Not quite opposite the pub, there was a cockle and whelk stall, boarded up. I went and hid behind it. Planning to wait for her.

But then, in the pub window: I noticed a woman was sat down at a table. A pack of fags in front of her, and a half-full glass.

It was Jade's mum. They *were* the spit of each other. But this woman was changed from the woman I'd seen in the photo. She was still beautiful, but she had a face that had seen some weather. Her face was hard. Lined by the years. Damaged.

Then, there was Jade. Her mum stood up and wrapped her arms around her, squeezing her tight. They hugged, rocking. Her mum kissed Jade's cheeks. Lots of times.

They sat, Jade's mum keeping hold of Jade's hands, staring into her eyes.

I kept out of sight, but peeked around the wall of the shack. An old woman walked by with her dog, looking at me, suspicious.

Spying wasn't a good thing to do, but now I was there I couldn't just walk away. And watching them was like being pulled by some kind of magnet. Because it was like watching a vision of who Jade might become. And seeing Jade as she really was now, too. Stripped of all her attitude.

They talked a while. A man brought her mum another drink, and Jade a cup of tea.

I watched them for twenty minutes, maybe half an hour. I thought of going. I didn't know how long they'd be, and the longer I stayed, the more guilty I felt. I'd go in a minute. That's what I told myself. Lots of times.

Jade got pretty active, her mouth moving fast, her hands open on the table. Pleading. Her mum sat there, listening, shaking her head once in a while. Jade banged the table with her fist.

Eventually Jade stood to go. Then it was her mum pleading with *her*, begging her not to go, I reckoned. Jade dug around in her bag. She pulled out a handful of notes and offered them to her mum. I don't know how much. But whatever it was, it was more than Jade could afford, which was nothing.

Her mum shook her head, but eyed the cash, hungrily. Jade pushed the money at her, insisting. Her mum took the money, squirrelling it straight into her pocket. She stared at the table. I reckon she was ashamed. I felt that shame too, watching something I shouldn't be.

Her mum looked up, but not at Jade, out the window. At me. It happened in a second. I didn't have time to hide.

"Shit," I said.

Jade's eyes flared. With shock. With shame.

She said goodbye to her mum. They hugged a long time, Jade looking over her mum's shoulder to see if I was still there. Accusing. I walked off, out of sight, waiting for Jade, and feeling like crap.

She came out of the pub, saw me and – making a point of it – turned, and marched off, towards the harbour.

"Hey," I said, catching her up. She kept on marching, like I wasn't even there. "Hey, I know you're angry. I never meant to spy, I just…"

She walked faster, almost breaking into a run.

"Will you just *listen*?" I said. I took a fast step around and in front of her, stopping her from going any further. "I said, will you just…" She glared at me, hard. Then down, at the pavement, as the tears came.

"Hey, hey, it's all right," I said.

She punched me, hard, in the chest, then dropped her bag on the ground and slapped me, stinging my cheek. She flung her fists, belting me. I grabbed both her wrists. She squirmed and fought, spitting and stamping.

"You don't get to spy on me, Sam… You don't get to do that."

"Why you giving her money, Jade?"

"None of your fucking business. Let me go."

"You can't afford that."

"Let go!"

"Did you talk to her about your dad?"

"Let go!" she said. I realised I was holding her just like her dad did. I dropped her wrists, like they were burning me.

"I never meant to spy, and I'm sorry but…" I was shocked by how angry I sounded. "I wasn't going to leave you to deal with this alone. Right?"

It was like I'd slapped her. She was shocked.

"I said, you *don't* have to deal with this shit alone."

Her arms hung in the air, like I was still holding them. Or like she was a boxer, about to hit me. Her eyes searched my face. Tears fell down her face in rivers. She was trying to stand tall, trying to look angry. But the harder she tried, the more broken she looked.

"But… I… *am* alone," she said, quietly. Her crying breaking her words into sobs.

"No," I said. "You're not." I put my arms around her, kissing the top of her head.

"It's okay," I said. Over and over. Trying to comfort her.

"It's fucked up, Sam. It's fucked up." She choked the words out, getting angry again. "I told her Dad was being a twat. I asked if I could stay with her, like you said. Do you know what? She said I can't. That's what she said. Happy now? Got any other ace ideas?"

"I'm sorry. I was trying to help."

"Well… don't. Don't try and fix things that can't be fixed. Okay?"

"Okay. Okay."

She broke down then. She couldn't talk.

I didn't ask any more questions. I just held her. Ready to listen, when she was ready.

"I mean, Jesus," she said, after a time. "What kind of mum abandons her daughter, Sam?"

I didn't reply. We stood there a long time.

"You ought to get to school, hadn't you?" she said, eventually. I lifted her chin, wiped the tears off her cheeks with my thumbs, kissed her lips.

"Nah. Learning's overrated. Rather go for tea and cakes."

"Tea and cake?" she said, weakly.

"Not cake. *Cakes*. Tons of them. Rammed with cream and custard and jam."

"Okay."

She kissed my face then. Over and over. It was like being licked by Tess. "You'll need to pay. I'm skint." She smiled at the joke she'd made.

"Best get back home. We stick out in uniforms. We can walk Tess."

She pushed her body into mine. "You sure you want to bunk school?" she whispered, her breath and words like velvet in my ear. A promise.

"Oh yeah. I'm dead certain."

★

We got the bus home, carrying bags of wrapped up cakes and buns.

Jade got cider from her house. Nicked from her dad.

We walked Tess on the tor.

We came back down the hill, sneaking around, making sure Mum didn't see us.

We climbed up to the den.

We did it. Like losing my virginity all over again. Tess lay in the corner, watching us. We joked about her being a perv.

We lay in the winter sunlight, under the blankets, drunk and high and naked. Not caring about anything.

We put sunglasses on Tess.

Jade blew raspberries on my tum.

We made lists of stuff to take to the Horns.

We talked about our mums and dads. We talked about how we'd be strong together. We talked about Jade staying with Grandma if her dad got too much. Seriously this time, planning it.

She told me all the places she wanted to surf: Barbados, France, Morocco, Spain.

Me and Jade. Jade and me. Arsing around. Having sex. Being in love.

37

I TIMED IT CAREFULLY, so I could sneak in about the time I usually got home. Then act normal, like I'd been at school all day. Pretty hard when you've spent the day drinking cider, having sex and wondering how the fuck you're going to surf waves big as houses.

I was too cocky. Mum stood in the hallway, like she'd been waiting there a long time. One look told me I was in the crap. And I smelled cigarettes. Was someone else there?

"You were seen," she said. "In town. The school have been on the phone too, asking if you were ill."

"What did you tell them?" I said. Mum sighed, and shook her head.

"Come in the kitchen," she said.

I went in and sat at the table. Everything had been tidied away. No teacups. No tea being made. No dust, no tea stains.

Spotless. There was no sign of Teg, either. I guessed she'd been sent upstairs. There was a pack of fags on the table though. And an ashtray, and a lighter. And a near-empty wine glass. Mum sat down, lit a cigarette.

"You gave up," I said. She shrugged.

"Where've you been, Sam? And if you lie I swear to God I'll go straight upstairs and start packing for London."

Lies raced through my mind. But suddenly I couldn't speak that language any more. The one Jade had taught me.

"In town, then back here…" I said.

"With Jade?"

I nodded.

"Is this how it's going to be, Sam? The surfing. The friends. Jade. Staying out. Drugs. Police. Going out on your birthday and lying about it. Fighting. Now truancy. Anything you want to add?"

"No," I said. "That's pretty much it." She knew it all. Almost. She had my life on a plate and was serving it to me like it was for tea. *Here you are*, she was saying. *Here's the mess you made.*

"Is this going to get better or worse, Sam?" she said, taking a deep pull on her cigarette. "I'd like to know. Because I'm not going to stop you doing anything any more. Nothing I say or do makes the slightest difference anyway, so I'm not even going to try. But I'd like to know what your plans are and I'd like you to stop lying to me. You owe me that much."

I opened my mouth, but nothing came out. I couldn't lie. I couldn't tell the truth.

Jesus, I thought, looking up at the clock. *This is worse than after the weed bust.*

"Well?" she said. Then, to fill the silence: "I thought it would be easier, here. I know what the kids got up to in London. This is worse. This is so much worse. Is it your friends? Is it you? Is it because you haven't got a father?"

"No. It's nothing to do with that."

"What then...?"

…

…

What?"

"Me bunking school... I was helping Jade. She's in trouble."

"I'm not surprised to hear that. What kind of trouble?"

"No, you don't understand. Nothing she's done. Nothing her fault. It's..." I tried to find the words.

"Her dad," Mum said. Not even a question. She knew. I nodded.

"I've seen them arguing," she said. She'd seen them arguing, not fighting. I wondered how much she really knew. Or if she'd guessed.

"We have to help her," I said.

I told Mum some of what had been going on. I made her promise not to barge in, said that we had to talk to Jade, take it slow. But that we had to help her.

It was a trade. I'd get back on the rails. But we had to help Jade.

"All right, Sam," she said, stubbing out her fag. "We will.

But no more missing school. No more fights. And no more lies. Right?"

"Right," I said. And I meant it too. I'd get back on the rails. I'd be around more. There'd be no more lies.

Right after we surfed the Horns.

"Look, Sam. It's nice that you like Jade. It's great you want to help, but… don't try and use it as an excuse for what's gone on."

"I wasn't. I'm not."

"I still can't help but feel it would be different if your dad was here. Like, he'd do something I can't. I've been too slack. Too weak. He'd discipline you. Not that he was much better. Bloody irresponsible, most of the time…" Mum downed the rest of her wine. She gazed at the wall, looking at it like there was something there. A memory instead of a photo. She got lost looking at it. I wondered how much wine she'd necked.

"How?" I said.

"What?" she said, like she had no idea what I was talking about.

"How was he irresponsible?"

"It doesn't matter. We're here to talk about—"

"It *does* matter. Tell me. You *never* talk about him. Why?"

She looked at me. Vacant. Like she'd stared at the wall.

"Why?" I said again.

"Why do you think?" she said, like I was missing something obvious.

"I don't know, Mum. *That's* why I'm asking."

Mum's eyes searched my face, looking for understanding. "Because it *hurts*, Sam… I lost the man I love. The only man I ever really loved or *will* ever love. Lost him for no good reason. It hurts, still, now. It never goes away. And I'm angry with him for making me feel that. All because he was pig-headed, just like you. I see him in you, you know. Every day. He had his head in a book, or was out there, chasing dreams. Just like you… It's what killed him."

"What? Why? He drowned."

"Yes. He did. Because he was stupid."

"What happened?"

"You know. He went out on a boat. He never came back."

"*What happened?*"

Mum sighed. She went and got the bottle from the fridge. Poured herself another glass. A large one. Gave herself time to think.

"We had an argument. He wanted to take you out on the boat."

"Me, that day?"

"Yes."

"Where?"

"Oh, nowhere far out. He wasn't *that* stupid. He just thought you'd like it. You kept asking, you see. You loved the water. But I said no, not till you were old enough. You were bawling your eyes out, wanting to go. He was dead set on it too. Said he had life jackets, a dinghy. That you wouldn't go far out. That I could come too. But I said no. He got your hand.

296

I kept a grip on you. You were crying and screaming. Maybe I should have let him take you. Because if I had, he'd still be alive."

"What? You can't know that, Mum."

"Yes, I can. He was only going to take you out for an hour. A safe trip. But when I stood my ground he said, *Fine, I'm off. I've got to get something from Mum's, then I'm off. Don't know when I'll be back.*"

"Where was he going?" I said, ice flooding through my guts.

"I don't know… He'd been talking about some place with a wreck. Some rocks called the… Demon's Claws. Something like that."

It was like I'd been punched.

"Devil's Horns," I whispered.

Mum's face clouded with confusion "Yes. How did…?"

"I read about them," I said, forcing the words out. "In a book."

I felt the world spinning round the sun. Eighteen miles a second.

38

IT WAS QUIET the two days before the storm hit. No wind. Crisp, wintry air. No clouds.

It was hard to believe it was coming.

But it was. The storm was in the news. The storm *was* the news.

It was a storm that could kill, smash houses, wash away walls. Turn a boat into splinters. Bad news all round. Unless you were a surfer, and you were in the right place, at the right time. Every normal break would be a death trap. But there were places that lay sleeping all the year, never even having a single breaking wave all summer. Bays and reefs, asleep but just waiting for the right storm. Like the Devil's Horns. The surf websites were full of it. But no one was talking about the Devil's Horns.

Apart from us. We were more excited than Ken the weatherman.

A frenzy of texts flew between us.

Is this it?

How do we know?

Will it be safe getting there?

Is this it?

How early do we leave?

Is this it?

This is it. Wait for the call.

★

The night before, I went to the den with Jade.

We lay on the makeshift bed of old crates, twisted up in each other.

We kissed. And the rest. We didn't talk much. We were both thinking about the surf. What it would be like. Hoping it was big; hoping it wasn't too big. I was thinking about Dad. Trying not to think about Dad.

I was afraid. I was excited. There was no difference between those feelings now.

★

Stealing the boat was easy. We told ourselves we were just borrowing it. But we weren't. We were stealing it.

A lot of boats had been hauled on to dry land because even the harbours weren't going to be safe. Down at Cape Kernow, not far from Grandma's house, the gigs – the big rowboats – had been taken from the slipway to a beach just round the corner. They'd been dragged up the beach and on to a field. Well out the way of any waves.

No one had bothered to chain them up. Who was going to steal a boat in the middle of a storm?

We broke into the boat hut at the Cape and 'borrowed' some oars. Then we walked round to the bay and chose our boat – a sturdy fibreglass-hulled thing with two sets of rowlocks, so four of us could row at the same time.

We got the boat down to the shore. Loaded it with the two big wave boards we'd taken from Ned's garage. Our own boards too, the cameras, cooking gear, sleeping bags, some booze. Coats, hats, towels.

We'd been ready for this for weeks.

It was easy.

There was no one to see us, no one to stop us. We'd left notes and messages, saying to our families we were in places that we weren't. They'd figure out we were gone. School too. But by that time, we'd be long gone.

It was late morning by the time we set off, in what was still calm water, on a sunny winter's day. The gig slipped through the water fast. Within minutes we were round the Cape and headed out to sea. Me, Skip, Big G and Rag rowed. Jade sat at the front, like our own ship's figurehead, staring into the horizon. She turned to face us once in a while.

"Okay?" said Jade.

"I'm fine," I said.

"All right, guys?" said Jade.

"Yeah."

"Good."

"Cool."

There was no hiding the fear in our voices. But there was a buzz of excitement too.

As we rowed, the first sharp wind began to blow, stinging my face, blowing wisps of salt water across the sea. It wouldn't be calm for long.

And on the horizon, a smudge of clouds. A low, long, hazy bank of grey.

Nothing more. But we knew what it was. And we were headed straight for it.

How many kinds of shit would we be in?

It didn't matter. Not once we had the footage.

Jade looked into the horizon like there was a pot of gold there, just waiting for us to come and take it.

39

TWO HOURS LATER we hit the islands. Even on the east side it was beginning to get scary-rough, with the seas coming at us from all directions. There was no pattern; it just heaved up and down, with us riding up and down these huge bumps of water, trying to hold our stomachs in. And every now and then a wave broke over the bow. A slap of the cold Atlantic, just to remind us what we were dealing with.

When we finally got round the islands and hit the pebbles, we leapt out, whooping with joy, with relief, and pulled the boat out of the water, as high as it could go, then lashed it secure to the rocks.

The others began hauling the gear up the beach, but I stopped for a second, and looked at what was left of the old lighthouse. Not much. Most of the tower was long gone, taken by the sea, but even half-collapsed, it was something safe and solid in the boiling, shaking madness around us, and I was glad to see it.

Everything was just like we'd planned. There was the first room, pretty soaked, but a good space for the boards; and through the door, the main room, the base of the tower, mostly dry, with space for a fire and sleeping. The barrels we'd taken were there, with dry blankets and food in cans. We'd need it all.

Skip bunked off, but reappeared a minute later, his eyes bulging.

"Man, you gotta see this!" he said and was gone again. We dropped everything and ran.

On the far edge of the island, right where Jade had said it would break, on the inner reef, sheltered from the winds, were freak waves – a stacked-up army of them marching out of the grey mist and smashing themselves over the reef. Freak waves, sure, but here's the thing that put a shiver down our spines – these waves looked makeable, *totally* rideable, with a straightforward take off, long green walls, and...

Tubes. Barrels. The green room.

"Keg time," said Big G, rubbing his hands together.

We ran back to change. Shot through with adrenaline, we fumbled and tripped, racing each other to get in it, and get on it. Skip was still fiddling and faffing when we were all ready. We waited for him at the shore. Impatient. Then he caught up with us and we paddled out. Less than fifteen minutes after we'd arrived on the island, we were outside the reef, sat on our boards, me and Jade to the side of the reef, the others right on the edge.

No sets came for five minutes. And, Jesus, I needed that time to settle my screwed nerves, just to stop my heart banging in my chest like it was trying to get out. But then they came. Walls of water.

Who'd go? We were spread out, Jade too far on the shoulder, in a safe place, the others further along, nearer the point of the reef where all the waves would break. The first wave was threatening to break right *over* them, so they paddled out so as not to get mashed.

I was in between them and Jade. The peak was good for me.

"It's got your name on it, Kook!" Jade shouted.

I turned. Angled the board. Paddled. Felt the pull. Skipped my hands along the surface. Felt it take me. I pushed down, and – *bang* – I was up, dropping down the wave, turning, riding, then stalling, digging my hand in the wall. No tricks, I just rode it. Then watched the thing roll over my head.

Time slowed. For a few dragging seconds I rode the barrel; a cylinder of crystal energy, with me plugged into it, lit up by the thing.

Then I shot down the line, out the tube and flipped off the back before it closed. I tried to shout, to swear, but I couldn't even speak. I was almost crying, struggling to breathe. I headed back out, afraid because a set might come and cream me, but also feeling stupid in the head from what it had done to me. It was joy and fear, focused *and* crazy, electric *and* numb. Like feeling *everything* all at once, but feeling like nothing too, like it – the wave – was everything and I was just this tiny,

tiny thing, smaller than an atom, less than nothing. But a piece of nothing that had got lucky. I'd seen inside this tear-shaped cave of green water. A sight no one had ever seen or ever would see. That wave was mine.

In spite of being freaked with fear I got back out fine; all I had to do was go around the reef. The waves were like clockwork, always breaking in the same place, in the same way, every few minutes. In the time it took to paddle out, I saw Big G and Jade both get barrels. Then I got another. And another.

We all did. Everyone scored. Not once or twice. Relentlessly.

Every wave was a hit, a high, an all-time best-ever. We laughed like crazies, ruled the water like heroes. We surfed our brains out. For hours. It was insane.

*

When dark came, it came quick, closing on the island like a fog. So we paddled in, mad dizzy with joy.

"We did it," Rag screamed as we climbed off the beach and on to the rocks. We helped each other out, carrying our boards over our heads, so as not to ding them.

"We rode the Devil's Horns!" said Skip, like it was a miracle. "I reckon some were double overhead. Whaddya think?"

"Dunno." Big G shrugged. "I guess we'll see when we look at the footage. How was it, Skip. Get much?"

Skip's face dropped. "*I* didn't film it."

"Why not? I thought that's why you got in after us?"

"Nah, I was putting a new leash on."

"You were supposed to film it!" said Jade.

"We never agreed that!" said Skip. "Anyway… there's always tomorrow…"

Everyone looked at everyone else in shock. We'd been so jacked on adrenaline, so smacked to the eyeballs on stoke, we'd forgotten to fix the cameras to the boards. We had no proof. No evidence of our legend status to stick on YouTube.

Then Rag sniggered, and Skip started laughing too. Even Big G. We all did. Apart from Jade. We couldn't stop. We didn't care. Even though we knew they'd never believe us, even though they'd laugh at our stories. We thought it was funny. Because none of that shit mattered any more. We'd know. We'd always know what that day had been like.

Only Jade didn't join in.

"Idiots!" she shouted. "Well, at least there's tomorrow, isn't there?"

*

Back at the lighthouse, we fed on beans and sausages from tins, washed down with cider and vodka round the fire.

"Libations," they said, like they always did. I didn't say it. I raised my cup, but kept quiet. And Jade, seeing me, did the same. I didn't want to be superstitious. It seemed lame.

We didn't know what we'd face the next day. Whatever happened, I told myself I was putting my trust in myself, and in the others, not in offerings to the sea gods.

We talked of the waves, and what might happen.

"I reckon the swell will switch," said Skip, mopping up beans with a lump of bread. "It's a fickle reef, needs the swell right up the channel. The storm'll get worse though; we might have to sit it out for a day. But so what, we've done it, right?" He raised a mug of cider. We banged our cups together and drank. Apart from Big G.

"Have we?" he said. "Maybe it's just getting started." He looked at me, checking how I'd react. I'd handled it today, but what if it got bigger? I just smiled, and raised my cup to him. He carried on. "We surfed the inner reef. Jade said there's another one, further out. It didn't work today. Maybe it's just waiting for bigger waves."

"Bring it on," said Jade, like she was speaking for me. She leant into me, using my knee to rest on.

We all got drunk, but not so we lost it. We were too sharpened up by the waves for that. But we necked the drink fast, and eventually it loosened us up and piled up in our heads and worn out bodies. We had to sleep. Jade got down to her pants but kept her jumper on, climbed into her bag then snuggled up next to me in front of the fire.

"Keep me warm, Kook," she said with her back to me, her voice a little slurry from the booze. After a few minutes she reached out and took my hand and put it round her.

"Let's go outside," I whispered. "In the storm," I said. But she didn't answer. And even above the wind I could hear her gentle, steady breath as she slept.

I went to sleep holding her hand, feeling the warmth off her and wanting her badly.

I listened to the storm, muscles shredded, skin tingling, my mind turned to liquid with the memory of the waves. I drifted off, feeling happier than I ever had.

★

It must have been five or six in the morning when I woke up.

I didn't know why. The wind was there, but it was like a wolf howling on a far-off mountain. Distant. The mad crash of shore break was gone too.

Then it came.

A crack of power, so strong the rock beneath us shook, followed by long, rumbling thunder. Then, after maybe fifteen seconds, the same again, a bomb that shook the air. The dying fire jumped and sparked. Dust fell from the roof.

Jade was curled up in her bag next to me. She turned to face me. In the thin light, her eyes shone like jewels.

"Did you hear that?" she whispered.

"Lightning?" I whispered back.

She shook her head. "Waves."

Before long we were all awake.

We should have sunk deep into our bags; we should have ignored it. After all, we'd done it, hadn't we? We'd surfed the Devil's Horns.

But there was a loud silence between the sets. Like a big,

silent question mark. Had we done it? Really? We didn't have the footage. We still needed that.

What we'd had the day before, it was good, sure. Even special. But I was thinking maybe days like that happened at Porthleven or Lynmouth every year. Maybe a *dozen* times a year. Those waves weren't what had got this island a mag cover. Waves like the one on that cover were happening right now. Out there.

"What if they're rideable?" said Big G, his voice echoing round the room. He was right. How could we say we'd done it if they were and we didn't go? Shit, we'd never look each other in the eyes again. There were only two ways to go: back home with our tails between our legs, or out there. But no one said anything one way or the other.

"Better get some shut-eye," said Rag eventually. The one and only time he wore the sensible hat.

"Right. Right," we all agreed.

I lay down and turned over to face the wall. But I didn't sleep.

★

When the blackness turned into a sick grey light, it was Skip who was first up and out. We dressed, and walked out to where Skip stood watching the sea.

As the thin blue light of dawn crept under the clouds, the ocean lit up.

Long-period four-footers were breaking on the inside, peeling nice but way too close to the cliff. No one wanted

309

to eat rock for breakfast. But outside, further out than where we'd surfed the previous day – a *lot* further out, on the outer reef Jade had spotted when we'd first come – were monsters.

We watched the things emerge from a long way off, just lines at first, creeping out of the dawn sea, slow and deliberate, like waking giants, lumbering towards us, till they reached the reef – and there they changed into nightmares. Grey-green mountains, taller than houses, jacking up fast, mutating into these giant beasts, before exploding on to the sheet glass water over the reef.

The crack hurt my ears. And when the thunder shook the ground beneath us, it felt like my bones were turning to water and leaking out of my legs. I felt so weak I could barely stand, never mind surf.

No one said anything at first. But Rag could only wait for so long before he spoke up.

"Well fuck me… sideways," he said, as another wave faced up, so big I thought it was going to ride over the shore and nail us. But it exploded on the reef in a giant mess of crashing white water. "Who's going?" he teased. "Who's ready?"

"No way," said Skip, shaking his head. "I ain't, and none of you should. We did it yesterday. That's what we came for. Not this."

I was breathing a huge sigh of relief that Skip had said exactly what I was thinking, that I wouldn't have to face those waves, when Big G said:

"Wait, look…"

40

TURNED OUT WE'D SEEN a big set. When they started coming through, one every few minutes, there were a few real thumpers to each one, but long gaps between them, and a deep channel to the left of the reef that would make it easy to get out. The waves were big, sure – really big – but they peeled down the reef steady and even, with plenty of space on the shoulder to get up and riding before the wave got too critical.

We watched it for a good five minutes before Big G made the call.

"It's do-able," he said, pointing at a wave booming over the outer reef. "They ain't breaking anywhere but over that reef. Must be cuz the swell direction's different to yesterday. We can paddle out and get in from the side, then sit right on the edge. If a massive set comes, we'll see it a mile off. We can get out of the impact zone quick."

He was right. It was do-able. *But what if you don't catch it right?* I thought. There were two ways to go then. Drowning, or getting smeared over the reef. The last anyone would see of me would be a red cloud in the water, getting washed away by the next wave.

The thought of that kept me rooted to the spot. And the thought of my dad having been out there, somewhere. That kept me quiet. The others were afraid too. I could see it in their eyes.

"Come on," said Jade after a bit. "You heard G. It's do-able. It is. We can't bottle it now. We gonna find an epic secret spot, and not ride the thing? Nuh-uh, that ain't happening. We'll be famous. Can't you see it?"

"See what?" said Rag.

Jade stared into the next grinding, heaving wave. I knew what she could see. Herself in a video clip on YouTube, plus Magic Seaweed and a dozen surf websites, rushing along the wave, hood off, hair blowing behind her like she was a pigging superhero. Maybe she'd even be in a barrel. One big enough to drive a car through. And she'd be stood in the middle of the thing, wide-eyed and grinning stupid. Doing what she was born to do and making it look easy. That whole film was already playing in her head. She could see it and she wasn't going to waste this chance to make it real.

"G, Kook, you're all in. You too, Rag, right?" she said.

"No way, guys. Sorry. Too fat, too slow," said Rag, laughing, and patting his gut like it was the best excuse in the world.

"What?!" said Big G, right in Rag's ear. He scuffed Rag round the head.

"Good!" said Jade. She was standing on tiptoe, flexing her fingers, twisting her hips. She was wired. "Rag, you can film us." She didn't care who went or who didn't, as long as we got on with it. As long as someone filmed her.

"And you, Skip?" she said. "You fancy it?"

We all looked at him. We knew he'd say no; we already had him pegged as the official trip photographer and video-filmer, we just needed to hear it. But now Rag was doing that.

Skip was grinding his jaw, breathing hard. His voice wobbled when he spoke. "You know what… fuck it. FUCK IT. I'm in."

"You won't regret it, mate," said G, slapping him on the back. "We'll look after you."

Jade winked at me, turned tail and headed back to the lighthouse. Part of me was telling myself to stay where I was. To help Rag. Not to follow them out there. Not to follow my dad out there. But my legs were moving. We followed.

Inside, Rag got busy with the cameras and mini tripod, fiddling with buttons and dials, reading the instructions.

"I thought someone was supposed to work all that out before we came!" said Big G as he squeezed a leg into his wetsuit.

"The take-off is in the same, small section," said Rag, ignoring Big G. "If I set the GoPro vid-cam up on a rock and turn it on, it'll capture everything. Then I can take pics with the stills camera."

313

We put on rashies, suits, hoods, gloves and boots. They were mostly dry. Then we got the boards.

We needed the guns – larger, thick, pointed boards specially designed to handle the speed and pressure of big waves. We had two of Ned's guns. I had my new board. Jade had her biggest, longest board. We'd head out on them and swap in the channel as we needed to, so anyone in the line-up was taking the wave on one of the guns. Riding a wave that size on any other board wasn't an option.

As we walked out of the lighthouse and headed for the water, Big G told us the plan.

"Me first, to test it out. I'm the most experienced and capable." He wasn't being a big head; it was just a fact. "Then Sam and Skip, then I'll go in with Jade. Everyone not in the line-up sits in the channel and watches till it's their turn. If anyone goes over the falls and it goes to shit, we get in and get them out."

Before they drown, I thought, *and that's if they haven't got a broken neck. Or had their face grated on the reef.*

As we waded out and got on our boards, I looked at the sea around me. The wind was chasing thundering clouds across the horizon, but where we were was weirdly calm. The sky and water were steel grey and still, with the odd gap where shafts of light made sky-blue patches on the water. Spooky, but full-on beautiful too.

And every few minutes, on the outer reef… bombs.

Boom…

Boom…

Like God had sucked the chaos out of the storm and dropped it all in one place. The reef. And us? We were like kids running to the biggest ride at the fair.

Paddling out was easy. The waves weren't breaking on the inner reef where we'd surfed the day before. Maybe because of the tide, maybe because the angle of the swell had changed. Shit, it didn't matter *why*. It meant we could paddle out from the island without having to deal with anything threatening.

It was almost too easy. Like the storm, the Horns, were letting us in. *Inviting* us in.

We came at the reef wide and far out, showing it respect. As we got near, I saw waves coming out of the horizon. Just the sight of them punched a fist of sickness into my stomach.

The waves were rising up in a series of walls towards the reef. Almost moving slo-mo they were so big, but in truth moving really, really fast. I thought, *are they bigger than the ones we saw from the cliff, or are we just waking up to how big they really are, the closer we get?*

We were in deep water, in the channel to the side of the reefs. We were safe. Weren't we?

The first one was jacking up, hiding what was behind it. As the unbroken part of the wave rolled towards us, my guts lurched up to my throat like they were trying to escape.

It wasn't going to break on us, we were too far out for that, but it would be close.

It piled up towards the reef, twenty yards in front and twenty yards to the right.

It wasn't like any wave I'd ever seen. A moving mountain, a solid thing, not water at all. The water was just a skin on its raw power. A freak ray of sunlight torched it up. It was beautiful and mind-numbingly terrifying. Then it cranked up and cracked over the reef. The sound of it ripped the air. Liquid thunder.

I got a good look at it as it broke on the reef then rolled past us. An avalanche of white froth on the top, and along the face, as light shone through the crystal water, every blue and green there ever was.

The outer part of the wave was ahead of us, not breaking, but still way big. We paddled up the turquoise face, towards the feathering top, just as it was getting steep. Then...

...over it.

Relief washed through me.

"Holy shit," I said. "Holy shit."

"Keep paddling," Big G shouted, "quick!"

The wave had hidden the one behind. The wave coming towards us was massive, triple overhead. It had already broken at the peak and was screaming down the reef, with the wall pitching up, threatening to crash over us. We weren't far enough in the channel. We were right in the path of a total monster. If it landed on me, it was game over.

I wanted to throw the board and dive deep before it broke. I had to fight that urge. If I dived I might get underneath it, out of harm's way. But it might easily smash the board. I had to make myself believe I was going to make it over.

We started paddling. Fast.

It reared up, with white water whistling off the top of it, threatening to break. It was too big; I was too slow. I was behind the others. I saw them head up and over. I paddled, climbing up. I was vertical, almost upright. I felt the pull as it took me backwards. I closed my eyes, and kept on paddling. Frenzied. Somehow, I got over and dropped down the other side. I felt it yanking me backwards, trying to suck me into it. But I kept on. I looked up. The remaining waves in the set were there all right, but they weren't that big, they weren't going to break on us.

We headed left, further away from the reef and safely over the last waves of the set.

"You okay?" said Big G as I caught up. I nodded.

"That was close," he said.

"No shit."

We'd almost got caught out, thinking we were safe.

Normally getting battered was inevitable in any bigger session. Screwing up waves was part of the fun. Normally. But not here.

Here you'd get your arse handed to you on a plate. Maybe your teeth too.

It was better to take extra minutes paddling out and round to get to the break point, than risk getting smashed before we even got to the line-up.

We'd got too close.

It was good in a way. I'd had a warning. I could see what was waiting for me if I didn't get this right.

★

When we got parallel to the far edge of the reef. We sat on our boards way deep in the channel, getting our breath back, settling ourselves and watching the waves.

Skip leant to one side and puked.

"Okay?" said Big G.

Skip sat up, nodded. "Everyone else all right?"

"Yeah," said Jade.

"Sure," I said, lying. I was shaking, sitting, gripping the front of the board. I looked back at the island. At safety. It was a long, long way off, much further than I'd reckoned when I'd looked at the reef from the shore. A good fifteen-minute paddle.

Rag was a tiny stick figure standing on the cliff. He waved. I waved back.

Big G went first. He was the most ready, the most experienced. No protest from Jade.

Me, Skip and Jade watched him paddle over toward the reef. Ten, twenty, thirty yards.

He backed out of a few waves, let them go under him, testing them.

Bigger waves came, waves that looked like they would close out, with nowhere for a surfer to go apart from down. But G avoided them easy, just by paddling out and over then back into the break point once the set had gone through.

They were big beasts, but predictable, breaking in pretty much the same spot every time.

Then it happened. The dream became real. A set came through and G paddled in, towards the reef. He paddled right into the danger zone, the point where the wave would pitch up and break.

He rose up like he was yanked by an invisible hand. It looked like he'd be pulled over the back. But he paddled, and paddled, and the board cut through the water and was moving, and then the board was going down the wave. He sprang to his feet and rode it smooth and fast, down and along the face, crouching, arms out, keeping his balance. Sat in the channel, we watched his take off, then him riding as the wave rolled by. As it shot past us and towards the island, we could only see the back of it. He disappeared from view.

A moment of wondering. *Is he still on it? Is he okay?*

Then he appeared, off the back of the wave as it got into deep water. He was forced a couple of feet into the air from the speed. The board landed with a smack. So did G. He got back on it and came paddling back out to us.

We cheered and whooped and punched the air.

After all that, he'd made it look easy. It was clockwork. Mechanical. Straightforward. As long as you did it right; didn't do anything random.

I'd already thought I could do it. Now I *knew* I could.

Big G went and got one more, then came and joined us.

I was up next, with Skip. Big G had already decided that. I think he wanted us all testing it – and being tested by it – before Jade got into it.

"Man, I'm ready," said Jade. "How about I go?"

"No," said Big G. Jade didn't complain, but I reckoned she was being crafty. She could let us make all the mistakes, learn from what she saw, then swoop in when it was her turn and do it right.

So now was my time. No more weighing it up, no more thinking. Just doing. I was as nervy as hell, and afraid, but really excited too. I knew I was going to do it. I *had* to know I was going to do it.

I needed to ride one of the guns. Time to swap.

I got off my board and into the water. I swapped leashes with G and climbed on to the gun. Skip was already on the other. He sat, glued to the board, arms folded, looking at the reef.

"Skip," said Big G. "Come on, mate. Your turn."

"I dunno, maybe I'll watch Kook get one first."

"You said you'd go, instead of Rag," said Big G.

"I wouldn't wait too long if I were you," said Jade.

"Um. Maybe I'm not ready yet. If Kook gets a wave, I'll do it, how about that?" said Skip.

"Well," said Jade, "no one goes in alone and I don't like all this sitting around anyway."

G just shrugged. "Why not?" he said. Skip and Jade swapped boards and leashes.

So it was going to be me and Jade, with Skip and G sat on the edge watching in case of trouble. It made sense to me. With Jade with me in the line-up, and those guys keeping an eye on us, I'd feel as safe as I was going to.

We paddled towards the reef. Compared to my new board or Old Faithful, it was like being on a boat. The thing had to be over seven and a half feet long, thin and pointed, but with plenty of volume. It didn't sink under me at all. I'd paddled it before, even caught small waves with it, using it like a longboard, just to test it out, so I was used to the feel of it. This was a whole different scene, of course, but it still felt good. It felt like I could ride it. And that was half the battle. If it felt right, I could do it. I kept telling myself that.

Jade paddled beside me, fast and steady. I stayed out back and on the shoulder, thinking I'd sit a few out, build up to it. But the first wave that came along was shaping nicely. It was big enough to break where I was. Jade was further in, she had to paddle out to get over it or get a pasting.

I did a quick calculation. It looked like it would break before it hit me, but to the right, on the reef. I could get it just after it had started breaking, use the steepness and feathering white foam to push me along the wall.

I was in the right spot, the perfect position.

I turned, pointed, angled the board slightly, waiting as I paddled forward, expecting the pull of the wave as it caught up with me. I tensed, expecting it to get me. But I didn't feel anything. Nothing. Where was it? For a second I thought maybe it had flattened out and was going to roll under me.

There's a moment, just before you get a big wave, when you feel you should be up the face already. Like it's turned up late. For a second you're confused. Then…

Time slowed. Paused. I wasn't going forward or backwards; I was still.

Then. In that second. I was stone-cold certain I was going to get that wave. It was a concrete moment of knowing.

It was happening. Now. All that stored-up energy was about to explode.

Time sped up.

I was rising, up the face of the wave. I paddled hard, to get ahead and get moving.

A valley opened up in the water in front of me, a wrenching, yawning pit. The board was already angled, going right. I looked down the shoulder, hungry to get on it before the wave pitched too steep.

I got to my feet. Slowly. A frozen, tightrope moment. Wobbling. Heart in mouth.

Then.

Whoosh.

I was racing, the board chattering on the water, rushing, my legs fighting to keep it under control.

I was standing on a board, riding down a mountain.

I made a long, smooth, slow turn, pointing the board along the wall of water.

The wave ahead suddenly curled up, towering, teetering. The top of it, way, way above me, frothing, boiling, opening into a giant jaw. Becoming a cave.

Then it was over my head. A ceiling of water. A second. Barrelling. But I was going so fast, I shot out of the cave, screaming along the wave. So fast I got ahead of the breaking part of the wave and shot off the back. I flew along the surface, bouncing like a ball before the power beneath me washed away and I fell off the board.

The whole thing had lasted a few seconds. A lifetime. I got back on and started paddling.

I heard a trembling voice. "Holy shit, holy shit!"

My voice.

My skin was on fire. I was shaking. My shoulders were trembling. But deep inside, in my core, I was solid rock.

G and Skip hooted and screamed, punching the air. As I paddled towards them, I looked to the reef, for Jade, wanting to know if she'd seen. She was right in the zone, by herself, looking out, waiting for a wave.

"How was that, Kook? Tell us about it," said G, grinning. It was almost a joke. He *knew* I couldn't say. Not because I couldn't find the words, but because I couldn't really speak. You can't when you've had that much adrenaline shot through you. He knew that.

All that came out was, "Woah. Holy shit, holy shit. That was… holy shit, holy shit."

"You're next, Skip," said G. Skip stared at me, wide-eyed, like I was a real freak. Something to be afraid of.

"I'll um… I'll go in a bit. You go again, Sam."

Again?

I'd done it.

I'd *done* it.

It had got Dad. But not me. I'd done it. I could sit out the rest and watch the others, then pack up the memory and go home. Why chuck myself into another raging wall?

But truth was, I wanted it again. Bad. I was already crashing from that insane, skin-screaming high and needed to get the same again.

I looked at the reef, at Jade, paddling about, waiting for her first wave.

The wind had dropped completely now; the waves were even cleaner. Seriously heavy, but manageable. The sun was coming out too, burning through the clouds. It was getting lighter. The mood of the place was good. The door was open. This place, which had seemed like a near impossible nightmare from the cliff, was becoming our playground. The storm had let us in. Given us its secrets. We needed to get it while we could. Shit, it wasn't even cold. Not in the winter suits.

I headed towards Jade. I watched her go for two waves, shouting "go, go, go!" at her. But they went under her. She knew waves; she *had* to be in the right place. Maybe she was too light, I thought, too little for the board. Something like that. Yeah, that had to be it. But then, I thought, it would make her faster, *more* likely to get it. It didn't make sense. Whatever it was, sat where she was, she couldn't catch one. She needed a more critical, later take-off, to be further inside. But if she got that wrong…

She paddled around, hunting. She'd look set up for a wave and so nearly get it. But it would go under her, or was threatening to crash so she had to paddle over it. She wasn't getting lucky. Or maybe these waves just didn't behave like normal waves and somehow she was judging it wrong.

As I got close, I saw her mouthing, swearing. She slapped the water with frustration.

I was near her now, almost near enough to talk, but another wave came steaming out the ocean same as before, and I was in the right spot and I *had* to turn and paddle and get the wave. If you get the gift of a perfectly set up wave, you take it. I'd learnt that much.

It was the same as before. Better. I was mad high as I came off the wave, just as I had been with the first one, but more confident, more in control.

I paddled back to the others, planning to either persuade Skip, or have another go myself.

When I got there, me and G put the screws on Skip.

"Do it, man," I said. "Just do it. You can. You're a way better surfer than me."

"S'up to you," said Big G. "But this is like our only chance… and… did you hear that?" G cocked his head, listening in the stillness.

"What?" we both said.

G put a hand to his ear. "Shouting," he said.

"Hey… hey." Rag was a long, long way off, but he was shouting loud enough for us to hear. Just. And waving his arms like a madman.

We'd been so busy talking we hadn't looked out.

Bumps. Little lines. Slight rises in the ocean. Nothing more than that. But way off. Far off. Miles off.

The only wave you see that far off is a really, really big one gliding over some reef or rise in the ocean floor.

"Jesus," I said. "Jade. I'll go." I started paddling. Fast.

I wasn't worried. There was plenty of time to get her out of there, or just further out to sea so the set went underneath us. Even so, the others started shouting and waving. I paddled as fast as my adrenaline-shot arms would take me.

She was sat, up, alert. Had she seen it? Then she started paddling out.

Great, she's going over it, I thought, getting into the deep, away from the reef, before it shows itself. Before it breaks. But before she'd gone too far, she stopped and sat up. Looking. Waiting for it to appear again.

I felt sick.

She'd gone out to meet it. To get in the right spot to catch one when the set came through.

"No way," I said, to no one. "She's nuts."

I couldn't see the waves. They'd gone over whatever they'd found on the ocean floor and back into deep water. Hidden. But they were coming, gathering speed and size.

There was still time.

I reached her, only yards away now.

"What you doing?" I said, sitting up on my board, right next to her. She didn't look at me. She was focused on the horizon.

"Surfing."

A gust of wind ripped across the water. From nowhere.

Then we saw it. A long way off still, but closer, and rising out of the sea.

Behind it, there were clouds, a whole gang of boiling, rolling grey clouds, moving steadily towards us, like that wave was the leader of some gang.

"Set's too big. Come on, follow me." I turned the board, ready to paddle out of danger and back to the others. I thought she'd follow. She didn't budge.

Jade looked out. The wave was nearer now, rising properly. Her eyes jolted with shock as the wave began to form. She could see the steel truth of what was coming at us.

We had seconds to decide. I'd spent weeks following Jade. Now she had to follow me. *Had to.*

"It's too big!" I said.

"No, it isn't."

"Jade, listen to me. You can get another one."

"I'm getting this one."

It was rising. Closer. Faster. She made her choice. Saw where it was, and knew where she needed to be. A final adjustment, making sure she was in the right spot. She got on the board and paddled away from me, right to the furthest edge of the reef where only the biggest wave would break. Getting ready.

I paddled behind her and grabbed her leash. We were stuck there, her paddling, me stopping her. This wasn't good. We needed to get out of there. Quick.

"Let go," she shouted, still paddling, but going nowhere. She turned her head, glaring at me. Her voice and eyes diamond hard. "Let. Go!"

The others screamed.

"Get out of there!"

"Move. Now!"

The wave was coming. It was different from the other waves that day. Bigger. Uglier. Lumbering and lurching. Not predictable. No real shape yet, just a lump, mutating in the wind. It reminded me of her drunk dad, staggering towards her, fist raised.

A hard blast of wind blew across my face, stinging like a whip. Not just the wave coming now. The storm too.

Jade sat up and turned her board. Great. She'd seen sense; she'd come with me. We had to go…

I let go of the leash, she lay down, paddled towards me.

"You don't fucking own me," she said, just like she'd said it at the rave. She sat up and pushed my arm, hard. I wobbled, making a grab for the board. But she'd unbalanced me. I fell off. I got straight back on. But she was away from me already. She took one last look at the wave, turned and paddled towards the island, getting speed, ready to catch the wave.

It came up in front of me. Enormous, finding its shape now, finally showing itself. It was terrifying. It blocked out the sky.

I couldn't catch it. And I couldn't catch Jade. The only way to go was over.

Again I thought of chucking my board and diving, but it

328

was so big, with so much face, I knew I'd never make it under the wave.

So I went up it, vertical, climbing and climbing, ready to be thrown. Knowing it was too late. Knowing. But paddling like fuck anyway.

I waited for it to throw me.

Waited. I was going backwards. I was almost vertical.

Almost.

Then I was over. A miracle. Paddling in a fit, desperate to get forwards. It was sucking me backwards. I kept on. And on. The pull weakened.

I'd made it over.

But...

Behind that wave, another one.

This was a cartoon. A joke. A special effect. It couldn't be real. It wasn't even a wave. It was something else. Something no one sees and lives. Something that filled the sky, eating all the water in its way. A wall of ocean, with rivers of white, wind-blown froth running down it. And a wall, stretching out forever in both directions.

The whole thing was driving at me, teetering. There was no hope of getting over it. None. It was standing up, gathering force, getting ready to kill me.

I fell off the board, pushed it away, hard as I could, then took a huge gulp of air, and dived, deep.

But not deep enough.

It pulled me, right inside the heart of it. Paused for a second.

I put my arms over my head, pulled my feet in, making myself
into a ball.

I was inside it, caught in it.

Then it threw me at the surface, into the pit. Into an
explosion of blue and white.

41

MY ARMS AND LEGS were ripped away from my body. It turned me over and over, spinning and churning, pushing me down, crushing me. It was worse than any kicking, or beating. Unbelievable force was pounding me downwards, turning and twisting my helpless body.

When I stopped spinning, I didn't know up from down. It took me a second to realise I was being dragged.

The board was right in the wave. The wave pulled at the board; the board pulled at me. Like a giant trying to pull my leg out of its socket.

It had me and wasn't letting go. It dragged me, fast, for long, long moments. There was no fighting, no way of dealing with it.

It went on. And on. I was waiting to hit rock. Expecting it but not able to do anything about it. My lungs were getting tight.

I held on.

Desperate to breathe. Getting more desperate.

The second I felt the wave weaken, I started swimming. Up.

I broke the surface and sucked air.

I looked around, frantic.

Where was Jade? Had she got the same beating? Or had she got the wave?

The sea had changed. Just in the time I'd been under. A sharp wind blew thick rain across the surface. The sea was now rolling and lurching, sick from the punch of the wave.

"Jade!" I shouted. I spun around, looking for her. For the others. For the island. Where the fuck were they? How far had I gone? Froth and sea spray blew hard, stinging my eyes, blinding me. I looked the other way, but all I could see was rain and heaving water.

The whole sea was rising up; rollercoasting, making it impossible to get a grasp on where I was or what was happening.

Something was floating near me. Something jagged and broken.

The board. The wave had snapped it like a twig. Shit. There was about three feet of it left, still attached to the leash. To me.

It was a lifeline. Under the surface it was air that kept me alive. Up here, it was the board. Or what was left of it.

I swam over and got on it. There was enough left to float me. I looked around me, just to make sure there was nothing looming out the ocean, making sure I had a few seconds at least so I could get my bearings. But I couldn't see.

Had Jade got the wave or not? If she had, she'd be in the channel. If she'd wiped out, she'd be near the inner reef. Or would she be washed so far she was over both reefs, in deep water, and safe? I had no idea. But I reckoned the others were near, they'd have seen, they had her back. They'd have found her. Rescued her.

Wouldn't they? But then... They hadn't found me. Not yet at least.

I wanted to know where she was. Where the others were. Wanted to get there. But I couldn't see anything, not with the foam, not with the wind blowing water in my face. I didn't *know* anything.

The sea and the sky didn't give any clues. The storm was confusing me, hiding everything.

I felt swarming water against my legs. I watched a lump of foam streak by me. I was moving, fast, caught in a stream of water. It had to be a rip. Tonnes of water had smashed on the reef, now it had to go somewhere. Out to sea. That meant I was being washed quickly *away* from the reef, and from Jade too. The island had to be in the opposite direction to the way I was going. I tried to paddle the half board, tried to get out the rip. But the board wasn't steady beneath me. I couldn't paddle it. The rip ran away with me like a cork in a river.

The rain and wind suddenly got more intense. I paddled in a frenzy, trying not to swallow the water being blown in my face. If I could get out the rip, make it to the channel, find the safe place…

But as the wind got faster, screaming in the air, I began to think there was no safe place any more. The sky was darkening by the second, full with rain and mist and cloud.

No safe place, no shape to the waves, no order. Chaos was in charge. The sea was rising into hills. Ten feet high. Twenty. Not breaking, but heaving up and down. Seesawing. And the wind was screaming like a million drowning sailors, slowly becoming one voice: a throbbing, deafening hum.

A wave came out of the gloom. Not breaking, but big. Really big. The wave took me high, right to its top. At the peak I saw down a corridor, through the rain and mist. It was like the storm was letting me see, just for a moment. Torturing me.

Waves. Lots of them. Ugly, twisted and massive. The whole horizon was rising up. An army of lines of water was stretching either side, as far as I could see.

What had got me hadn't been a freak set. It had been a taster. The storm was just getting started. And these waves looked like they might break. Like they might kill me.

I bobbed around, waiting. I couldn't even see in the direction of the waves for more than a couple of seconds. I wouldn't have any warning when they hit.

Then…

The first giant loomed out of the rain. I gasped. Hyperventilating. Shocked with fear.

But I rode up, up… up and over the first.

And the second. Pitching down, riding up. I clung to the idea that they weren't breaking, so all I had to do was hold on to the board. Up and over, down, into the pit. Up and over.

Inside my head I was saying, *Here we go again*, with every wave. I couldn't think straight then. Not of getting away, not of Jade, but only of the wave, in that second. Surviving it. Waiting for the next one.

I clung to the board, tighter and tighter.

"Here we go," I said, out loud. I couldn't hear, but I said it, over and over, through lips that were getting number, and slower by the second. Somewhere in my panic-seized mind, I knew I was getting dangerously cold. From the inside, from the core. I could see my gloved hands gripping the broken board. But I couldn't feel them.

"Please. Please," I cried, praying for a break from the madness.

I was sick, throwing up seawater, and foul-tasting bile. Again and again. Dizzy. Sick. Repeating. The storm was relentless in its hate and violence. Punishing me for being stupid enough to take it on. And all the time, I was heaving, up and down, up and down. It went on. And on.

After a while I got angry. Really angry. Because each wave was torturing me. Big enough to make me think it was the last one – that I'd lose the board, give in to the cold, get smashed under and not come up – but not big enough to finish me off. The storm was keeping me alive, but with no hope.

"Come on then, you bastard!" I shouted. *Do it*, I thought. *Go for it. If you're going to try and kill me, just fucking do it! Give me your worst hammering.*

The wind dropped. Just for a second. Like the storm was listening.

"Come on then," I shouted.

Then it answered. With a wave.

A wave? A wall, eating the sky. Caving over me.

The sky vanished.

I didn't even try to dive. I clung to the board.

It hit me. Grabbed me in its fist and pushed me deep and fast into black hell.

42

I LOST THE BOARD. The storm pushed me into the silence, beneath the rolling anger of the wave, to a place where there was nothing.

It wanted to keep me there. I knew that.

I felt, or heard, a wave rumble over me.

My arms were twisting and flailing, trying to swim.

Currents like an invisible octopus were snaking around me. And the more I tried to swim, the tighter they pulled.

I tried to swim up. I couldn't. Another churning monster landed on top of me. It pushed me down again, deeper this time.

I was down. A long time. My lungs were singing with the ache of not breathing. My head was becoming a block of ice. My face stinging sharp with the cold.

A crushing weight was on me. I had no air left.

Panic rose up my neck and into my brain.

If I was above the surface, I was alive. No matter how bad it got, I was alive.

Down here I'd die.

My heart was beating fast; I was fighting with every muscle, trying to swim, arms windmilling, using my air up. Fighting the storm…

…and losing.

Fear was rising like sick. Impossible to fight.

I opened my mouth and breathed a cold shock of water into my lungs.

I had to fight my own body then. My chest was wobbling, forcing me to breathe water. I had to conquer it. If I tried to breathe, I'd drown, quickly. So I forced myself not to breathe. To hold on.

My eyeballs were freezing. My face was numb.

I was swimming, struggling. Flailing.

Going deeper.

Deeper.

There were no waves above me now. I was in blackness and silence.

No, I thought. *Not now. Not here. Not me.*

Please.

Darkness was waiting for me. A cave. Silent and patient.

There was nothing left of the world. I was somewhere else.

I stopped swimming, stopped fighting, trying to think. Forcing myself.

Don't be a kook.

Think.

I had a flashback of the day tombstoning, with G and Jade. Jade's voice, "You can hold your breath a long time. Don't fight. Don't use up your oxygen."

All that training. All that holding my breath. For this?

I heard a voice, deep inside me… Sure and certain.

Stop fighting. Hold on.

I might die.

Hold on.

I reached down, took off my leash, because the board was caught in the havoc and was dragging me. I let go. I let go of hoping.

It wasn't up to me now. I was in the grip of the storm. It might let me live; it might kill me. There was nothing I could do.

I didn't swim; I let the water take me.

I went deeper, further, under.

I sealed off my mouth, my throat. I closed them to the sea trying to get in. I put my arms across my chest.

I counted. One, two, three…

Kept on counting. Focused on that.

Twenty…

Thirty…

The fear was rising in me again, trying to make me breathe water. I wrestled it. Struggling to get control.

Count. Count. If you can make thirty, you can do another thirty.

I started again.

One, two…

Twenty…

One, two, three, four…

Impossible.

Only ten, go to ten. Just ten seconds at a time.

One, two, three, fooooour…

Just five.

One…

Two.

I stopped.

The darkness was coming. I was inside myself. As deep as I was in the sea, I felt no cold. I had no body.

I was half dreaming, almost asleep, but with clear, strong thoughts.

Hold on.

I could die now.

I went to a rave. Lights flashing, an ocean of arms.

Mum and Teg, unpacking boxes at Grandma's house.

I rode that wave. A lot of waves. Surfing with Jade. Blue walls.

We had sex. Her fire-lit body in the mine. Her eyes.

I am dying now.

Please let her live.

Darkness.

…

…

Jade on the tor, holding her hand over my mouth.

"Hold on, Kook. You can do it."

…

…

Nothing.

Where was I?

A star in the endless night. A dying light.

★

Then… hands pulling and pushing me.

And voices. Far off, but dead near. And clear.

Dad: "Come on, Sam; it's only water."

Jade: "Go on. Go on, Kook."

I felt her hands. I felt her arm around me. Her hair washing against my cheek. I *felt* them.

"Someone's gotta make that mag cover, Kook. All those waves, Sam. Someone's gotta ride them? Come on. Come *on*." The way she said it, the way she always said it when she wanted me to do something. To jump off a rock. Take a smoke. Ride a wave.

"Come on, Sam," said Jade. "Let's see what you're made of."

43

I WAS SHOCKED awake by cold and light. Coughing water and air.

I moved my arms, my legs. They were numb with cold, but moving. And swimming. My chest was convulsing; I was gasping air, fighting half to suck air in and half to cough water out.

I puked. Blood was running down my nose, into my mouth.

Around me was swirling, violent, chaos. But not hell. Hell was in the deep, in the silence.

I felt pain. Pain was good. The pain of making arms and legs move in the frozen sea.

I was alive. Wind and cold and stinging rain were life. Down there, beyond the voices and the dark, was death.

The storm hadn't killed me. But it was still full-on raging. The wind was shrieking. The rain was whipping-harsh. Froth was choking me.

I was retching.

Lungs fluttering, convulsing.

Keep going, I said. *Just keep going. Keep swimming.*

I was fighting the storm, fighting my body, fighting to stay awake. To stay alive.

In the clouds I saw a face. A huge, ugly, sagging face. Angry, but raging blind.

"Thuss noooot real!" I slurred with a mouth that could hardly move with cold.

I kept swimming.

Then I saw ahead of me. A huge, shapeless darkness. The heart of the storm, some dark beast coming to take me back down.

No. Not real.

It was rock. An island.

I came to. Awake.

I swam towards the island. Used the last of my strength. I put it all into one push.

The sea was throwing waves at a small bay of rocks. A wave washed me in. I put my arms over my head, into a ball again. I bounced over the rocks, swept along by a wave. Then I stood, chest deep. Just ahead of me, only feet away, was a rock. I could hold on to it if I could just…

The wave sucked back into the sea, trying to pull me with it. I swam, trying to go to the rock, but getting pulled back.

Another wave rushed me along, and smacked me into the

rock. My head banged. Pain exploded inside me. A bomb of pain.

Stay awake. Awake.

I wedged a leg between two boulders. When the sea rolled back, I stayed with the rocks.

I pulled my leg up, and grabbed a ledge.

I climbed, pushed, struggled to get my legs and arms up and over the rock, on to another. Then another. I pulled and pushed and climbed till I was beyond the waves, above the sea. I was breathing now. Puking and coughing.

Sea out. Air in.

Warm blood rivered down my face and into my mouth. Feeling it was knowing I was alive: I was glad of it. I looked down at myself. Half my wetsuit was missing. Torn and shredded. I was cut all over from the rocks. I got to the top, on to flat land. I stood. Fell over. Threw up. Nothing came out. I stood again. I stumbled forwards and saw…

A shadow in the rain. A figure. I staggered towards it.

The shadow had a shape.

It was a girl. A naked girl. Standing, staring at me.

"Jade!" I shouted.

I ran, shaking violently. She was there. Standing there, still, looking at me.

I fell again. Got up again.

I ran and ran, to where she had stood.

There was no girl. No Jade. Nothing but rain and sea spray and shadows.

"Jade!" I span around, searching in the rain and darkness. I looked at the raging sea. Then back at the land. Looking for her.

I saw the ruin of the lighthouse then. A grey square in the mist.

A hunched figure stumbled out of the dark of the doorway, running towards me. There were others behind.

It was Rag.

I fell on him. I grabbed his shoulders.

"Jade…" I shouted. He shook his head. Tears ran down his cheeks.

"Where is she?" I said.

He looked at the ground.

"Where is she?"

He spluttered, choking on words like I'd choked on water. Trying to breathe. Drowning.

"She's…"

"What?"

"She's gone, mate… She's gone."

44

MEMORIES GOT LOST.

Flashing lights. The thunder of the helicopter's engine. An oxygen mask forced on to my face. The wetsuit being cut off my body. A silver blanket.

That was all.

Then the hospital room. A blur of blue and white. Walls and screens and nurses' uniforms.

I don't know how long.

Then...

My hand was being squeezed. I slowly focused on who was doing the squeezing. Mum was by my bed, holding on to me, hard, like if she let go I'd slip away.

Slowly, I noticed things. A drip running into my arm. Pads on my chest, with wires running off them. A can of coke on the bedside table. And by the table, the nurse, leaning over me.

"How are you feeling, Sam?" said the nurse. I felt like I'd been run over by a truck. But I nodded. *Okay.* "Sam, you've been unconscious a long time. You've had a serious knock to the head. You've lost some blood. You've broken ribs too. We're giving you painkillers. They'll make you feel quite woozy and..."

"Jade?" I whispered.

A memory. Fighting Rag, to get back in the water. Howling. Like an animal.

I tried to lift my head. Pain rushed through my chest. But it was dull, thudding. Distant, somehow. Like a storm heard through thick walls.

"How much pain are you feeling? On a scale of one to ten," said the nurse. "Ten being the most you have ever felt."

"Jade?" I said, to Mum.

Mum's eyes were hollow with darkness and fear. She forced a trembling smile.

"Sam," she managed to say, before she started crying. "You're... going to... have to be very brave, Sam." She choked on her words. Just like Rag had.

I turned my head away, stared at the wall.

Everything was cold and white and silent.

45

THAT COLD WHITE SILENCE was there the whole time. When the morphine wore off. Under the sound of trolleys and nurses' chatter. Under the wind and rain, as the tail of the storm swept through the days and nights.

It never left.

I waited for news. Every day. Every minute.

But there wasn't any. She was gone.

I didn't cry. I didn't howl. I was just numb.

★

Mum stayed at the hospital with me. She even slept there.

While she was at the hospital, Tegan was at Grandma's.

Mum and Grandma were strange in how nice they were with each other. I thought it was for my sake at first, but then I guessed Mum and Grandma had had to deal with each other

348

a lot. Something had happened between them, because there was no arguing or point-scoring now.

A day before I left, they visited me together.

"You're coming to live with me," said Grandma.

"All of us, Sam," said Mum. "We're moving in with your gran." She put her hand on Grandma's arm.

"You see... I'll be around a while yet," said Grandma, smiling.

Her cancer had gone into remission. She was headed down the same road as before, and it ended in the same place. But the disease had slowed right down, even stopped getting worse. For now. The doctors couldn't explain it. All their scientific knowledge couldn't make sense of it.

I was pleased — course I was — but I couldn't feel much of *anything* at that point. Even that news didn't really get through the numbness, through the slow and steady horror of Jade not being there. But I *did* think it was a good thing we were going to live with Grandma. I wanted to get out of that blue and white hospital room. It was a prison cell by then.

Then I thought of Bob, and Tess, alone in that tiny cottage. And I felt like shit.

"There's plenty of room," said Grandma.

"Right," I said.

"You won't be going to school for a bit, while you... adjust," said Mum.

I knew what she meant by 'adjust'. To life without Jade.

I guess she meant 'grieve'. But I didn't. Not then.

That silence was everywhere still. I couldn't *feel* anything. At first I thought it was the painkillers. I was on heavy ones. Morphine. Other shit too. But in the gaps between them wearing off, and taking some more, it was still there.

It was like I was in a dream. I surfed through it. Numb. More numb than I'd been in the freezing waters.

★

They let me out a few days later.

Outside, a light grey sky. An endless slab of cloud blocking the sun.

We drove along the seafront. Whole sections of the promenade lay on the rocks below.

In front of one shop a wall of sandbags had been ripped apart. The bags lay half open. Trails of wet sand covering the road, all the way down to the shore.

A car was on the beach, its windows smashed, half submerged in water. It seemed no one had cleared much of the mess up yet. Like the whole town was still in shock after the storm.

We parked up at Grandma's house – our house.

Grandma opened the door. I saw there were boxes inside. A professional moving company must have done it because all the boxes were the same size and neatly taped up.

Teg came to the door. She looked at me, cautious at first, checking to see how I was. She hadn't visited me in the hospital.

We hugged. Gently, softly. I think she'd been warned about my ribs.

We went inside.

"Would you like some tea?" said Grandma. "Watch some TV? Check out your room? Some toast maybe?"

I shrugged. I didn't know what I wanted. I didn't want anything.

"Think I'll go upstairs," I said.

Maybe there *was* something I wanted. To be alone.

My room was Dad's room. All his stuff had gone. Even the charts on the wall.

My stuff was in there now. In boxes. I opened them all, had a look inside. All my clothes and books, neatly packed.

I noticed my rucksack on the back of the door. I reached in the pocket, and pulled out the small box, then the pebble of jade stone inside it.

I got ready to get hit by a wave of emotion. But it didn't come. That wave didn't break.

Still, I was glad to have it, to hold it. That stone was all I had of Jade, other than memories. This was real, something I could touch. I gripped it tight. I wanted more, something else. But I didn't have anything.

I sat on the bed. I zoned out.

★

I was woken from this zombie trance by the grunting of a lorry coming down the lane. The heavy whine and sigh of hydraulics as it stopped.

A bin lorry. I looked out of the window. The green wheelie bin was full. There were bin bags piled round it too.

Looking round the room, I suddenly had the idea something was missing, but I couldn't think what. Then I thought, *I wonder what Mum did with that old wetsuit, and with Old Faithful?*

She'd have chucked them. The bin men were coming to take them away. I didn't care. I couldn't see the board, but I thought it could be buried under the bags.

But what else had she thrown away? Something. Something not in the boxes.

I got up, and hobbled downstairs, feeling a pinching pain in my ribs with every step.

Mum came straight out of the lounge.

"Are you okay, Sam?"

"Did you chuck any of my stuff out?"

"I had to, Sam. A few old books, some clothes full of holes, that old sleeping bag of yours..."

The sleeping bag Jade and me had slept in. That night, after the rave.

"It stank, Sam," said Mum. "It was filthy. I'll get you a new one."

I went to the door, opened it, ran out.

I couldn't run properly: the pain was in my chest, needling. Then stabbing. I didn't have shoes on. My socks got soaked in the puddles left by the rain.

The lorry stopped. One of the men leapt off the back. He put his hands on the green bin handles.

"Hey," I shouted. I grabbed the bin off him and dragged it away.

"Oi, kid, watcha doing?"

I pushed the bin over, upended it. Everything inside slid to the ground with a squelching thud. Then I pulled the bin off and knelt in the mountain of black bags.

"We ain't gonna wait," said the man. "You'll have to put all that back in. Hey, son, you listening?"

I pulled the black bags apart. Stinking tins and rotten food scraps scattered over the ground. I opened another one. Old clothes. And my sleeping bag. I yanked it out and walked back to the house.

"You gonna clear that up?" shouted the man.

Mum stood at the top of the drive, her mouth and eyes wide open.

I went past her, past the house. I ran, half hobbling, down to the sea.

I followed the narrow path along the cliff, till I reached the end, the point where the land didn't go any further. I left the path, and climbed down the sloping rocks. I went to the edge. There was nothing beyond but a deep drop to the water below. I sat, with my legs over the edge. I took the sleeping bag out.

Suddenly I felt like an idiot. It was just a dirty old sleeping bag, and I'd made a stupid mess and run off with it, like it was some precious treasure my mum had chucked out. I felt bad about that. Like a brat. It was just a smelly old sleeping bag.

It *did* stink too.

I lifted it up, and smelled it proper.

Time stopped. The world upended, just like that bin.

I was spun like I was in a wave.

I smelled the earth. I smelled the damp, old mines. I smelled the smoke from the fire. Sweat. Us. Me. Jade.

I buried my face in the sleeping bag. I shut the world out.

I began to cry. My shoulders shuddering, my whole body shaking.

"Jade. Oh fucking Christ. Jade."

Teg found me. She hugged me. I cried like a kid then. On Teg's shoulder. Full on. I couldn't stop.

46

I WAS A MESS AFTER THAT.

The world *had* upended. I was back in the storm, in the water. Hit by a wave so big I'd never get to the surface again.

I didn't know what was up, or down.

I couldn't breathe.

I couldn't sleep; I couldn't stay awake.

I spent all my time in my room.

★

After a few days, when I couldn't stand Mum and Grandma's kindness any more, I started going to the Cape.

At first Mum followed me, I think to make sure I didn't chuck myself over the edge. I hated how she couldn't leave me alone, like she and Grandma and Teg were the nurses now. But I had to get some space. The Cape was the only place I could manage to be, right then. It was where we'd set off for the Devil's Horns.

After a while, when the worst had passed, I spent my time reading about drowning, storms, stuff like that. I got obsessed with it. Trying to make sense of it all.

Every time a kid makes a sandcastle on a Cornish beach, there's at least one piece of bone in it.

I read that.

People are taken by the sea. Their bones are ground to sand in the tides. They become part of the land, part of the sea. Eventually, the atoms inside them spread all over the world, into different things, even different people. It's the same for all of us.

I read about a lot of things while I was 'recovering from my ordeal' (that's what the doctors called it).

I stuffed my head with facts. About drowning, about wrecks, about the ocean.

I couldn't get enough of it. I was trying to process what had happened. The geek in me needed the facts.

If a wave takes you deep enough, the weight of water above you holds you down. That must have been what had happened to me. If I hadn't been taken up by some odd current...

If the water had been a couple of degrees warmer, I'd have died. Cold water brings your heartbeat down, and your mouth and throat close up. Your body survives on a fraction of the oxygen it normally needs.

If I'd lost a bit more blood. If I'd taken on more seawater. If I hadn't – somehow – been washed back to the island.

If. Lots of ifs.

I got a handle on all the facts.

Even hearing the voices could be explained. Seeing and hearing the dead, thinking you're being helped by them. It's a 'well-recorded phenomenon'.

So bit by bit, piece by piece, it all made sense. What had happened.

But it all-making-sense really doesn't fucking matter, does it?

Because Jade is gone.

She's dead.

And I killed her.

All that time I thought I was following Jade, but it was me that led her to her death. It was me that found the chart. Me that told the others about the Horns. I could have pulled out at any time, I could have stopped it, tried to persuade them it was a dumb and dangerous idea. But I didn't.

I killed her. I have to live with that.

47

THERE WAS AN INQUEST. And, after a time, when they finally gave up looking for a body, a memorial service.

The inquest came first.

The verdict was 'accidental death'.

It had been the biggest storm to lash the coast for nearly fifty years. It had destroyed boats, harbours, even parts of the coastline.

It was Billy and Mick who'd told the coastguard about us. Once we'd been missing a day, word got out. They'd made the calls, probably to stop us surfing the Horns. Otherwise, we'd never have been rescued.

The currents had been strong and fast. By the time the coastguard got to search for Jade properly, it was too late.

She was gone.

There was nothing left.

★

I didn't mind the inquest process. I kind of sailed through it. But the memorial service at the old church in Penford put the fear in me. Big time.

For a wimp's reason too.

Because I didn't want to face Bob. How could I look him in the eyes?

I was afraid of that. More afraid than of any wave. Because he knew I'd taken Jade to her death. All that had come out at the inquest. And I felt it every moment of every day.

Right then, if you'd given me a choice of being back in the storm or being in that damp, wintry old church, I'd have taken the storm.

After the service, outside, Bob came up to me. I had the urge to scarper. But that would have been a shitty thing to do. Besides, before the Horns I'd decided never to *not* face up to that bastard. I'd have been letting Jade down if I backed away now.

Bob was thinner than when I'd last seen him. Weirdly, he looked *better* than he normally did. I wondered if he'd stopped drinking.

His eyes were loaded with sadness.

I had an urge to start babbling, to say how sorry I was. But I didn't. I stopped myself. I let him do the talking.

He put a firm hand on my shoulder.

"I know what she was like, Sam. I don't need to say you shouldn't have done what you done. You know that. I can see it on your face. The only thing I got to say to you, is… it weren't your fault." That almost set me off crying.

"I tried to stop her, Bob. I tried."

"No one could stop her, lad. No one could stop her doing what she wanted. She was like her mum."

It hit me then that her mum wasn't there. Her own mum, not turning up for the memorial service.

"Where is she, today?" I said.

"She couldn't face it," he said, shrugging.

We stood, a while longer, not saying anything. There was too much to say. And maybe we'd talk about it all one day. Maybe. Though I had a feeling this might be the last time I'd ever see him.

He turned to go, but paused, turned back to face me, thought for a moment, then smiled. For a second he actually looked happy.

"There's something she'd want you to have."

"Great," I said. Whatever it was, I wanted it. Anything. Anything more than a sleeping bag and a stone.

"It's in the car; wait here," he said.

He came back with Tess, on her lead, with her eyes wide, mouth panting and that 'Are we going somewhere?' look on her face.

She wagged her tail and nuzzled into my thigh, hassling me to stroke her.

48

THE VICAR HAD SAID how we mourned 'the loss of one so young'.

He'd talked about 'this terrible tragedy'.

He'd banged on about how 'her star shone bright, but briefly'.

If the whole thing had been designed to make me, Skip and the others feel more guilty, more stupid, more terrible, they'd done a good job. We'd sat through it, and afterwards, we'd taken the sympathy everyone dished out. Only it felt like blame. That's not how it was meant, but was how it felt.

But that wasn't the only reason I felt bad. The service wasn't *enough* somehow. People in black suits and raincoats, mumbling prayers, pretending to sing. Shadows, sucking up the light, listening to some crap out of the Bible. It wasn't proper. Not just because it was grim, but because it wasn't *Jade*. It didn't say anything about her. It didn't *mean* anything.

After Bob left Tess with me, Rag came up.

"We've been talking. We're meeting up at the Old Chapel," he said, "to sort something else out."

"What do you mean something else?" I said.

"Dunno yet. But something for her. And for us too."

So we met there, after we'd gone home and changed out of our jackets and ties. We ordered chips, but no one was hungry. They sat, steaming, going cold. So I fed them to Tess, one at a time.

"We could have a bonfire on the beach," said Skip.

"We could have a party, for everyone that knew her," said Rag.

"We could make a cairn," I said.

"A what?" said Big G.

"Like a monument of rocks, which you build, and put on top of a hill." I was thinking of the tor, looking over the sea.

"Lame. Why don't we go for a surf, somewhere she really liked," said Big G. "Sit in a circle in the water, like they do in Hawaii."

We came up with loads of ideas. But we couldn't get into any of them. We couldn't decide what we should do, where we should go, who we should invite.

When the ideas dried up, we sat in silence.

"Well. Let's think about it," said Big G, sighing. "Everyone puts in their vote tomorrow. If we get a clear fave, we do that. Yeah?"

"Okay," I said. Rag shrugged, as if to say, *Why not?* Big G stood. It was time to go.

"Coming, Skip?" said Rag, standing.

"I know what we should do," said Skip, still sitting, staring into the empty mug in his hands.

"What?" we all said.

"Go back."

Big G froze with one arm in his jacket. Rag sat back down. Almost fell into his chair, like he'd been punched. Me and G sat back down too.

"Back?" said Rag.

Skip didn't need to explain what he meant, or why we should do it. And once he'd said it, there was no other choice. It was a heavy idea. Going back to the Horns felt as big a deal then as the day we'd first decided to go.

"I don't believe in ghosts," said Skip, "or life after death or anything but... but..."

"But what?" said Big G.

"We need closure, don't we?" said Skip.

"What the fuck does that mean?" said G, scowling.

"It means saying goodbye, I guess."

★

That old sea dog Pete took us in his boat, *Sunrise*.

Just us. Me, Big G, Rag, Skip. And Tess.

I offered Pete money when we got on board.

"Thass all right," he said, putting his hands in his pockets. "Wouldn't be right." He walked off to the wheel cabin.

The first time, when me and Jade went, the sea had been

green oil. When we'd gone in the storm, it had been dark and heavy.

This time – the last time – it was different again. The day was torched with a light so strong it hurt my eyes. The wind was fast and sharp, blowing the water into peaks and salt spray I could taste.

Gulls followed, reckoning we were on a fishing trip and waiting for scraps. But struggling, blown about like kites on a beach.

We stood at the bow, watching the sea, feeling the chop and swell, and looking to the horizon. Not talking.

I thought it'd be a trauma. I thought as soon as we saw the islands, it'd all come rushing back. Not just because of what had happened to Jade, but what I'd been through too, in the storm. But this was a different time, and it looked like a different place. I was heavy in the heart, sure. But this was better, *so* much better, than being crammed in some church, listening to stories about a god who couldn't save you.

Sunrise chugged around the Horns till we were just off the lighthouse island. We got into the boat Pete had towed behind, and me and Big G rowed us to shore.

There was no way of getting in dry. We got soaked to the knees with the freezing spring water. Tess loved it. Barking and running and dipping in and out of the shore break.

We checked the lighthouse first. There was the base, just as it had been before. The sea hadn't done it any more damage. It had done its worst. But all our stuff had been washed away.

All of it. There wasn't even a black mark where we'd had the fire.

Back outside, we stood blinking in the light. Was someone going to say something? Were we going to perform some ritual?

"I'd like to say…" Rag started, but he couldn't go on.

"It's all right, mate," said Big G. He put a hand on Rag's shoulder.

Rag shook his head. "No, it isn't."

Big G wasn't the emotional type, but he hugged Rag then. He held his mate, and he comforted him.

Me and Skip wandered off, Skip down to the shore, me climbing up to the highest point on the island, looking down on the reefs. But I couldn't see under the surface. The water was too messed up by wind. I tried to remember what it was like down there. But like I say, it felt like a different place.

I zipped up my jacket, pulled my beanie down and buried my hands in my pockets.

It felt strange, being there, but good. It was where Jade had died, but it was the last place I'd seen her too. I got a sharp tingle on the back of my neck thinking about her. I felt close to her, almost like I could feel her presence. It wasn't a smell, or anything I could see, or hear. But it felt as real as something I *could* sense. Something of her, close by. Like she was *there*.

I had the idea she would just come up out of the water, like that day we'd gone went tombstoning.

"Fooled ya!" she'd say.

I smiled at that. I looked down at the water, really feeling it; that she was there, that she'd just appear. I looked around me, as if to stop her before she sneaked up behind me, put her hands over my eyes and said, "Guess who?"

It was overwhelming, this feeling. Like a tide.

Then I told myself not to be stupid. That it was just emotion messing with my head. That this was all because I was where I'd last seen her. But still, I felt…

"All right?" It was Skip. He came up beside me.

"I guess. It's weird being here. How's Rag?"

"Bawling like a girl. G's looking after him. How are you, Sam? Really?"

"I'm okay. It's good to be here. It's good to say…" I stopped myself from saying "goodbye". Anger flooded up in me. From nowhere. I kicked a stone, sending it clattering down to the sea.

"It's mental, Skip. It's bullshit. There's no one to say goodbye to, is there? She's not fucking here!" I felt angry, really angry, I didn't know why. "And I don't believe in ghosts. Nor God neither, Skip. Okay?"

"Whatever, mate."

I grabbed the collar of his coat, put my face up to his.

"I told you. There's no one to say goodbye to. IS there?" He stood there, open-mouthed. A bit shocked by how pissed off I was. "I said, is there?"

"I don't know, Sam!" He took my hand and yanked it off him.

I turned away, trying to stop the tears. Tess bounded up, licked my hand.

Skip turned, walked off a few feet, keeping some distance, but watching me.

"Stop it, you pussy," I said to myself. I felt for the jade stone in my pocket. I squeezed it so hard it hurt. I looked out to the reef, to the point where that wave had broken.

"You wouldn't listen, Jade. I told you, and you wouldn't bloody listen."

I remembered seeing her standing, naked, right where I was now. I'd been half blind, half crazy. But I had seen her.

And I remembered her right in front of me, out there, in the water, going for that wave, fighting me off, so she could go.

"You wouldn't listen. I warned you. And now you're gone… You stupid bitch. Why? For fuck's sake, why…?"

I looked at the sea. Looked into it, like I was looking into Jade's sea-coloured eyes. I looked so hard I felt dizzy, staring into the depths, trying to see beyond the chop of the waves. The light refracting, sparkling. Thousands and thousands of shapes of light and dark, sun and sea.

She was in there somewhere. If all someone is is energy and matter then that energy was in there, gone from her body and mind like a wave that's made its journey through the ocean and finally broken on the beach.

The geek in me thought about that.

The universe is chaos. But there are patterns in that

367

chaos. Stars, waves. Energy and matter. And that's all that we are.

I was crying then. Feeling her, really feeling her, but knowing that 'she' was no longer here. And I couldn't put those two things together. I turned to Skip, still standing, watching me, wary, like I was a nutter.

"I can't make sense of it, Skip. I can't…"

He came up, looked me square in the eyes. "I reckon no one can, Sam. No matter what they say."

I nodded, still fighting back the tears. Skip walked off, giving me some space.

I looked to the sea.

She was there. Somewhere. Nowhere too. In my memories. In the sea.

With Dad.

And all those thousands of sailors, surfers, divers, fishermen.

★

I stood there a long time. Not thinking any more. Exhausted by thinking. Strung out with it. But getting calmer by the second. Hypnotised by the water.

Hypnotised. And feeling okay.

Because understanding things didn't matter any more. Skip was right. Trying to make sense of it was a waste of time.

I had known her. For that brief time. I had known her. Maybe better than anyone. And she'd known me better than anyone ever had too. That was what mattered. That was all that mattered. Jade didn't understand things. She didn't need to. She didn't try to make sense of things. She just did them.

We're here for a while, to ride a wave. And we're lucky. The chances of any one of us even existing is billions and gazillions to one. Like winning the lottery thousands of times in a row. Impossible, but here we are. And we just get to be that wave, to burn our energy for a bit. And maybe there's no God to look after us. And maybe when we're gone, we're gone. But we still lived, didn't we? In what we did and in the memories of people. Eventually all those memories go too. Stars turned to sand and washed away. That's all. And that's enough.

I was there a long time. Holding on to that stone in my pocket, staring at the sea.

I walked down to the cliff edge. I saw Tess nosing at something down in the rocks below. Whatever it was, it sparkled in the sun.

I climbed down. And I knew. I don't know how. I just did. The camera.

It was wedged in a crevice, among limpets and seaweed. I got a hold, it was held tight, but with a strong tug I pulled it out.

I pushed the buttons. The battery was dead. The casing was scratched. But apart from that, it was okay.

"Hey," I shouted. I clambered back up, waved and shouted to the others. "Hey! Look what I found." They all came running.

"What the fuck?" said Big G, taking it off me, holding it

up to the light, examining it. We passed it round, like a piece of treasure we'd found. Which, I guess, it was.

"Do you reckon…?" I started.

"Yeah, I don't see why not," said Skip. "The footage will be in there."

My heart started hammering. Did I want to see it? Jade getting that wave. Jade *dying*.

"I don't know about this," said Rag, grabbing the camera off Big G, shaking his head. "Maybe we should just chuck it in the sea."

"What would Jade want?" said Skip.

I knew. Like she was there, like she'd whispered it in my ear.

I took the camera off Rag and put it in my pocket. "She'd want it on every website and mag cover we can get it on."

The others nodded. Smiled. Laughed.

"She'll haunt us pretty bad if we don't," said Big G.

"Right," said Rag. He pulled a bottle of rum from his bag. Of course he did. Rag. Powders, herbs and potions for every occasion. Medicine man. He had little tin cups too. He handed them out, and poured some for each of us.

"I wanted to say… well what did that vicar say about Jade?" he said. "Said she was a star, that burned quick and bright."

"Like a shooting star…" said Skip. "What is a shooting star, Sam?"

"It's not a star at all," I said. "It's something no bigger than a grain of sand, burning through the atmosphere. All its matter is used up as it burns into energy."

"But it burns hard and quick," said Skip. "I've seen them. Bright as anything. And that's what Jade was."

I looked into the deep blue and green, and smiled. There were no more words to say. Not to the others anyway.

"Libations," said G. He poured a drop on the rocks and held his tin cup to the sky.

"Libations," I said. The others too. We poured some of our drinks on the ground, clinked, and drank. Rag poured some more.

I walked off, nearer the cliff.

"And yeah, Jade," I said, eventually, surprised by my own words, "In case you didn't know... I loved you."

And I felt calm.

I imagined her there, stood beside me, so close, like I could feel her breath in my ears as she spoke, like I could feel her hair brushing against my cheek.

"Talking to yourself, Sam?" said Rag, walking up and pouring me another.

"Jade," I said, holding my cup up, for us to clink.

"Jade," he said.

Then we got drunk.

Really, really drunk.

49

WE MET IN THE Old Chapel cafe the next day. Skip had a laptop and leads.

My heart punched in my chest while we waited for the camera to wake up and start downloading.

The footage wasn't great. It was shot a long way off; there were drops of sea spray on the lens. But you could see, just…

A black figure, against a grey-blue sea.

Jade, tiny, *tiny*, against the wall of darkness behind her.

She got the wave. She carved a line. A V of white trailing behind her. Down the face, into the pit, back up.

The wave walled up. An avalanche of white, churning water. Sea horses galloping. Hundreds of them. Chasing her down the wave. She couldn't outrun them.

The wave caught her. She disappeared.

They'd reckoned at the inquest she probably would have

been knocked unconscious immediately, just from the force. She wouldn't have known anything.

I hope so. I hope her last thought was, *I did it*.

After that, I thought we'd talk about the Devil's Horns. But we didn't. We remembered Jade instead. All the surfing, the laughs. Singing MGMT's 'Kids' in the back of the bus.

Stuffing our faces with after-surf chips.

A time when we'd gone in, when it had been so stormy we'd paddled for half an hour, then looked back at the shore and seen we hadn't even gone twenty yards.

Jade dancing like a loon at the rave.

Jade at school, staring out of the window.

The others talked about when they learned, when they were younger. How Jade was fierce and determined. How she was always first in and last out of the water. How she stole their waves and gave them the finger mid-ride. A lot of stuff I didn't know too. Stuff I hope Skip will tell me more about.

It was good to talk it through. They were the only ones who knew what it was like. No one else understood, no one else had a clue.

*

We did give the footage to a surf mag.

They put it on their website and cover. They put that ancient pic of the Horns on too, and a frame of Jade, riding the wave, and next to it:

OMFG.
UK'S BIGGEST WAVE.
RIDDEN.

It was as big a wave as someone her size could paddle into. Bigger. They reckoned it was technically *impossible* for her to catch that wave. But she had.

It was the biggest wave ever ridden by a female surfer in the UK.

I didn't know how I felt about all of it. I still don't. I couldn't connect the footage with Jade, or being out there when it happened. It didn't feel like a film of that moment, even though it was.

Still, once it was up online I must have watched it a thousand times, and each time rewinding all the events leading up to that point in my head.

How dumb were we? How stupid had we been? There was no point saying that to myself over and over. But I did.

I *do* know giving the footage to the mag was exactly what Jade would have wanted though. We did the right thing.

Lots of the mags and websites wanted to interview us too. We said no to all of them. We didn't want to make it about us, only about her, and the fact that she'd ridden the wave.

50

I HAD GOOD reason to be afraid of the sea. Good reason to be afraid of the wolf. It had killed my dad. It had killed Jade. It had almost killed me.

That's the sea.

So you wouldn't blame me if I never went near it again.

And you'd think I'd never surf again.

But you'd be wrong.

Fear makes the wolf look bigger. And I knew if I didn't face up to it, that wolf would follow me everywhere. It'd howl outside my window in the middle of the night. It'd sit under my desk at school. If I didn't get back in the water, I'd be afraid of it my whole life.

And what would Jade think about that, stood in her wetsuit, arms folded, eyebrow cocked, with a twisted smile?

"Pussy," she'd say. Sly, quiet, smiling.

★

Winter days passed. Then weeks.

When I was 'better', I went back to school.

I saw the others, and sometimes we talked about Jade, and sometimes about the Devil's Horns. They were the only people I could talk to. The only people I could relate to in any way.

But I knew, somewhere deep inside, that it wasn't good to just talk it over and over, so mostly I kept to myself.

It was the same at home. I needed to be alone. I had to get away from Mum and Grandma and their kindness. I was drowning in it.

I couldn't get back in the water right then, not even if I'd wanted. It wasn't an option, because of my ribs. So on weekends I just got on the bike, or put my boots on and went wandering.

★

There's this place I found. No one told me about it. I just went off cycling one cold, sunny day and came across it. Tess was with me. She loved running, following the bike. Something she'd done with Jade a thousand times.

The coast road had this little lane off it that ended by an old church. I dumped the bike by the graves and followed a path cut through brush trees like an avenue. Then along the cliff, and then down some rocks. I climbed and jumped till I got to the end, expecting a drop straight into the water. I had been doing that a lot – climbing as far as I could over rocks, then sitting, looking down at the sea.

But down at the end of these rocks there was a beach. Mostly it was rocks and boulders, but it was low tide, and beyond the rocks there was a large bank of sand.

I didn't think there'd been a beach there before, else I'd have known about the place. The storm must have stripped rocks and sand off the high tide, making a beach at low.

There were waves too. Shore dumpers that thumped on the sand. No good for surfing. But good for watching, good for just sitting and staring. I'd sit on this one boulder, close as I could to the sea, for as long as I could before the tide came up, staring into the blue, feeling the spray wash over me.

It wasn't just me that liked the place. There was a seal that was always there too. A cheeky young thing that'd come right in close, pop his head up and stare at Tess. Tess'd bark at it like crazy. But she'd never have the nerve to get in the water. And the seal knew it.

Gulls dived in the shallows, getting fish.

Twice I saw the grey arching backs of dolphins, making their steady way across the bay.

There was a rhythm to the place. The waves, the birds, the seal. The tide coming and going. And over the years, the beach coming, disappearing, showing again. Appearing, disappearing.

One day I was at this place, some weeks after I found it, watching the sea at low tide. I saw this wave break, far out. A proper wave, out of nowhere. Wrapping round the headland

and sweeping towards the beach. It looked surfable. I guess the tides had done something to the sand since I'd first found the place. Levelled it out maybe, then created sand bars.

Then another wave broke, a right-hander, about shoulder-high, peeling smoothly round the headland and into the bay.

I got a real itch. Right there, right then. Because I could picture me on that wave, ripping it up.

A new, secret spot. Virgin. Unsurfed.

And what would Jade say?

"I can't surf, can I, Sammy boy? But you can. If you spend your whole life out of the water, if you use me as an excuse not to surf… well that's just a waste. That's taking the piss."

I watched the waves for five minutes more, just to make sure they weren't freak happenings; to make sure they'd be good for a while. Then I went and got the bike and cycled home fast as I could without losing Tess.

I grabbed the knackered old wetsuit Rag had given me – Mum hadn't chucked my surf gear after all – a thermal rash vest, boots, Old Faithful and a towel. I went straight back to the secret beach. Mum, Grandma and Teg never even saw me.

It was a sunny spring day. Summer in the sky, winter in the water. The sea was bone-chilling. When I half duck dived, my head sang with pain for a few seconds after. But I didn't mind it. It just made me paddle that bit faster.

My arms were weak, my body was stiff. I messed up a few, but got one eventually, bumbling unsteadily to my feet then cruising down the line.

I got more after that, and all the time I could imagine Jade on the shore, laughing when I fell, and shouting, "Kook!" and punching the air and whooping when I got a good one.

★

I got to surf the place a lot. It got better every time. I was like a beginner all over again, I was so mad for it. There was no dissing small waves, no being pissed off when it was wind blown. I just rode every wave I could, whenever I could.

Of course, having it all to myself couldn't last. One day I was cycling, Tess behind me, board under my arm, just like Jade had showed me. A car went by, and Rag was in the back, his nose pressed up to the glass, staring at me. Confusion was written all over his face, because I was nowhere *near* Whitesands or Tin-mines or any of the usual spots.

He texted me, "Where were you off to?"

I didn't reply.

On the weekend, a good size swell came in. The place was going to be cranking.

I cycled down there early Saturday morning. As I was getting changed, three surfers turned up, in wetties, boards under their arms.

Rag, Skip, Big G.

"Kook," said Rag, "great to see you, mate. Thanks for telling us about this break."

I felt like a dog caught with its nose in the biscuit tin.

"I needed to get a few myself... I was going to tell you..." I started saying, trying not to smile.

"Bollocks," said Big G.

We all cracked up.

"Well, I was... honest... I just needed a bit of time. D'you know what I mean?"

Big G nodded. So did the others. We stood, quiet for a bit, not knowing what to say. We'd done talking about the Horns by then.

"This is a really fun chat," said G, looking out to sea, "but I'm wasting time standing around with yous lot when I could be out there." He ran to the water.

We all did.

★

After a few weeks, a big spring storm kicked off in the Atlantic, sending a powerful, long-range swell. Big waves, brushed to perfection by light easterlies.

I was game for that. I was casual about it. Compared to the Devil's Horns, it'd be nothing.

It was easy at first. I had no fear. I got into every wave, even ones that looked like they might close out. I just went for it. And every time I got one, it was a super-fast, powerful, rush.

About an hour into the session, I was paddling back out after a mind-meltingly good wave when I saw a real mother of a set sweeping round the headland.

I paddled right out and round the break point, into the deep, over the waves and just in time, span around, and went for the last wave of the set.

I got up, turned…

…too fast. It caught me. My fins snagged. The wave turned me sideways.

I got thumped.

I was churned bad and I went deep. I thought, *Just hold on. Count. You know what to do.*

One.

Two.

Three.

Panic got a grip. It rose up from nowhere. Overwhelmed me. Because right there, right then, I was back in that place. Smack bang down deep, in the silence, like I'd never been away. Like everything between then and now had just been a dream. I was *there.*

I did everything wrong. Everything I *knew* not to do. I spun my arms round, trying to find space, trying to swim up. I tried to tell myself to ride it out, but my body didn't listen. I tried to breathe. I got a lung full of water. When I hit the surface, I was breathing hard, gasping and spluttering. I thought I was going to die. I got on the board and paddled like crazy for the shore.

I sat on the beach, shaking. The others came in, looked after me. I couldn't speak for ages. I sat there a long, long time, clinging to Tess.

So that's that.

No more big wave surfing. Not till I'm ready, anyhow. That might be a few months off. It might be years. Or never. I don't give a shit. I don't have anything to prove. Not any more.

I got back in the next day though, when it was smaller. The wolf wasn't going to get the better of me.

Then we kept going. Every week, and some mornings too. We never told anyone about the place.

We'll surf it as long as it lasts. Till the next big storm comes and changes the layout. It might ruin the break, or it might make it better. No one knows.

Of course, with it being a *new* break, we had to give it a name.

We called it Jade's Point.

51

THE WEEKS WENT BY.

At home we fell into a routine. Grandma's hospital appointments. School for me and Teg. Me surfing. Mum working at the pub.

It may sound odd, but in spite of Jade's death, life began to be better. In some ways, at least.

We were with Grandma and we were out of that tiny cottage. There was space, and light. There was time to think. There was no arguing. Or almost none. No one worried about the small stuff. Maybe that's because of what happened, or maybe it just happened by itself. I don't know.

We didn't talk about the Devil's Horns at home. Mum and Grandma knew there was no point in it. They didn't need to tell me how stupid I'd been. Even if they had, nothing they'd say could make me hurt more. And nothing could make me feel better either.

Mum was just kind to me. She didn't even try and stop me surfing. Like she knew I'd know the limits now, and that I'd never do anything so stupid again. That I'd work all that out myself.

She kept up with her job at the pub. And with Brian too.

A month or two after the Horns, we went to the pub for a meal. He didn't join us at the table, but he served our food and drinks. It was just an excuse to meet him. Mum was really nervous about it.

He was middle-aged, beer-bellied and a rugby fan. Local through and through. I didn't especially like him. I didn't *not* like him either; I just wasn't interested in him. He came round after that, to Grandma's, once in a while. He was nice to Tegan, he brought her books and cakes, and told her stupid jokes. At first I was suspicious. I thought it was a way to worm his way into Mum's heart. But when I'd met him a few times, I sussed he was just a nice guy. Warm-hearted. And I could see how Mum liked him. All round, she was brighter and nicer and less moody.

Sometimes I'd come downstairs and she'd be singing, doing her hair in the mirror. She'd stop when she saw me, and give me a weak smile, like she was guilty about being happy. But you can't hide that kind of happiness. And I didn't want her to.

★

384

It's been months now. More time has gone by than the amount of time I knew Jade.

I have to get an early bus to Penzeal today. Then get the coach up to Truro, to the sixth form, where I have an interview.

I've missed a lot of school. And it's not like I was a model student before Jade died. But if I do a good interview, they'll make 'allowances' on whatever grades I scrape. I'm lucky they're even giving me a chance.

I stood in front of the mirror, first thing. I looked at how I'd changed. The bruises and scars are long gone. And that dead shadow of grief is gone from my eyes too. So is the guilt, the accusation. Now there's a still, blue-green light in them. They're not so different to Jade's. Though not as bright, not as intense.

My face is browner than it was before I came to Cornwall. I've got the muscles from surfing. I'm not that lily-skinned geek from London any more. He's as dead as Jade.

But what, then? Who? A surfer now? One of the gang? Jade's boyfriend? It might have gone that way.

But now? I don't know. I've got to start again I guess. But I feel okay about that; I feel ready.

And maybe I'm not such a kook any more. I guess I'll find out. In time.

But today I put on a jacket and a tie. And brush my hair.

I stand now, leaning against the bus shelter, feeling awkward in the cheap jacket and tie Mum bought me, missing the smell of Jade smoking a pre-bus roll-up.

It's cold. No clouds in the sky. Late spring, promising summer, but with a chill on everything before the sun comes out proper.

A fresh wind is coming off the hill, smelling of cows and straw.

Offshore.

I wonder what the surf's like.

I hear the low rumble of the bus, still with its lights on, coming from Lanust. Coming to get me.

Then I hear a 'boom'. The low, solid sound of a wave hitting the cliffs.

"Reckon the surf's good today, Kook." I hear her voice in my head. Clear. I imagine her standing there, rolling a fag. And what she'd make of me, in my jacket and tie.

"Where you off to then?" she'd say, looking me up and down.

"Interview. Sixth form."

"Fancy that, do you?"

"It's a change. What Mum says I need. A change of scene. A new start."

"A new life. Without me."

I don't have an answer to that.

"What's it gonna be like now, Sam? How's things gonna go? You gonna surf much now I'm gone?"

I don't have an answer for that either. I've spent all my time remembering. I haven't thought about the future much. But I do now, almost like she's forcing me.

I see my life ahead, clear as the morning sun coming over the hill.

All the days. Without Jade. GCSEs. A levels. Then there'll be a degree, somewhere up country. Then a job. And girlfriends. When I'm thirty or so, I'll find one that isn't too much trouble, one that wants kids. We'll get married. We'll take holidays by the sea.

"Yeah," I say. "I reckon I'll surf. When I can."

She shakes her head. Smiling, sarky as ever.

"Not good enough, Sammy boy."

"What then?" I say.

"All those breaks we talked about. Thumping beach barrels in France. Long Moroccan rights, on the desert coast. Barbados. The crooked coast of north Spain…" She makes it sound like choice dishes on the world's best menu. "I'll never see them, Sam… but you can. So you have to promise. You have to."

I have to.

"I promise," I say, thinking… *I'll surf those breaks. All of them.* And when I'm done, when I'm older, I'll get a longboard. I'll ride two-foot waves, out with the kids, the groms and surf schools. And when I haven't got it in me any more, I'll stand knee-deep in the shore break, dipping my grandkids in the water, thrilling the shit out of the little monkeys.

I'll be in the water till my muscles waste, my skin sags and my bones snap.

"I promise," I say, again.

The bus stops. The door opens. The driver waits.

I think about those places. I think about getting on the bus too. But I don't.

"That's good news, Sam. Right fucking choice. Let's start today. There's a fresh swell. Let's go to Jade's Point. We'll have the place to ourselves. Just you and me out there."

"What about the interview?" I say, laughing.

"You all right, son?" says the bus driver. "You getting on or not?"

"Come *on*. It's a good day to go surfing," Jade says. She folds her arms. Raised eyebrow, lopsided smile. It puts a hook in me. "The sun's up; it's offshore. Five-foot walls. Sweet rides. It's a good day to go surfing, Sam. A good day."

Her image fades. Her voice melts in the breeze.

"There'll be other days," I say, looking at the steps on to the bus, then looking back, across the fields, to the sea.

"Not like this one, Sam. Not like this one..."

ACKNOWLEDGEMENTS

Love and thanks to my family for putting up with me, all of those hours and days I spent with my head in a notebook or laptop.

Major thanks to HarperCollins Children's Books and especially Nick Lake for his support, belief and for 'getting it'.

Thanks to my agent, Catherine Clarke, who never puts a foot wrong and whose advice is always spot on.

Thanks to all at the Bath Spa MA: Lucy, Sarah and the whole workshop gang, Julia Green and all the tutors.

Thanks also to G-PL, Tom, Rallsy, Jag, Jim and Rob for all the 'research' trips.

Finally, a big hug and enormous thanks to the fireball of talent that is Lucy Christopher; for inspiring writing, superb mentoring and without whom this book would not exist.

As a footnote: Books come from a writer's own experience

(or at least mine does). But the telling of the story is also influenced by great writing. I owe a debt to the following: Kevin Brooks (*Lucas*, plus everything else he's ever written), Julia Green (*Breathing Underwater*, *Hunter's Heart*), Lucy Christopher (*Stolen*, *The Killing Woods*) and Tim Winton (*Breath*).